BACK

CHRIS SCULLY

TO YOU

RIPTIDE
PUBLISHING

Riptide Publishing
PO Box 1537
Burnsville, NC 28714
www.riptidepublishing.com

Back to You

Cover art: L.C. Chase, lcchase.com/design.htm
Editors: Sarah Lyons; Carole-ann Galloway
Layout: L.C. Chase, lcchase.com/design.htm

ISBN: 978-1-62649-575-3

First edition
June, 2017

Also available in ebook:
ISBN: 978-1-62649-574-6

BACK

CHRIS SCULLY

TO YOU

RIPTIDE
PUBLISHING

To my parents and sister. You are the best family and support system anyone could ask for.

TABLE OF
CONTENTS

CHAPTER ONE

Like any good writer, I've gone over my childhood in my mind so many times, searching for what went wrong, why Dad hadn't fought harder to keep us all together instead of letting Mom bundle us off to Seattle. It was like he'd wanted us to go, couldn't wait to be rid of us. Had he been depressed? Was it the alcohol? Was it me?

After a while, I forced myself not to care. It was better not to dwell on everything we'd left behind.

—From "My Father's Son" by Alex Buchanan

There are people in your life who stick with you forever.

You might forget them for a while or push them to the back of your mind, but they are written on your skin like a tattoo, etched in your bones, in your blood, your very breath. They hold on and never let go. So much a part of you that you don't even know they're there.

Indelible.

Benji Morning was that person for me. It was why, twenty years after I'd last seen him, I was driving east along Highway 16, awash in recollections of that long, hot, bucolic summer of 1996 that had ended in such turmoil, instead of heading for the hospital. It was the summer I first felt those then-uncomfortable feelings that would define the rest of my life, the summer Benji's sister ran away, the summer my once-happy family finally fell apart for good.

Twenty years apart is a long time. I don't mean to give the impression that those years have been shit, or that I've been pining for the awkward, redheaded boy I once knew. There's nothing shorter than a thirteen-year-old boy's attention span, and by the beginning of ninety-seven, I was settled in a new school in Seattle, with a new group of friends to entertain me, girls to chase, and memories of our life in the wilds of British Columbia, of Benji in particular, fading faster than a pair of newly purchased blue jeans in the washer.

Life goes on, whether we want it to or not.

These were the thoughts flitting through my mind as I headed further into the Bulkley Valley in my rented Ford Explorer, the majestic Hudson Bay Mountain in my rearview mirror. It was only the first week of November, but the peaks were snowcapped and ready for ski season to begin. I wished I could blame my strange mood on the jet lag, on the altitude, on the fact it had taken me eighteen hours and four planes—each one successively smaller—to get here from New York, but I couldn't. I'd been on edge since my sister, Janet, had called four days ago to say Dad was in the hospital, dying, and could I please come because he wanted to see me.

I'd like to say I booked the first flight to BC, but I didn't. Dad certainly hadn't wanted to see me at any point in the intervening years. We talked once or twice a year on the phone—brief, impersonal conversations—but I hadn't seen him since shortly before I'd started grad school more than a decade ago. As far as I was concerned, he'd abdicated all parental responsibility the moment he let us go without a fight, and to be honest I was happy with that arrangement.

No, it wasn't Dad, or even Janet, who'd brought me here. The truth was a little less flattering. In the end, it had been Brad, my editor, who had convinced me that it would be good for my career to chronicle my reunion for the *Journal*, the magazine that employed me.

But the minute I landed in Smithers this morning and got behind the wheel of my rental, it was my childhood friend Benji Morning who'd consumed my thoughts. Rather than calling Janet and going immediately to the hospital to see my dad, I turned in the other direction. Toward the place I'd once called home.

It was a compulsion I couldn't ignore.

Truthfully, I hadn't thought of Benji in years. I hadn't let myself. I'd been far too busy growing up, having fun, working my ass off to build a name for myself as a journalist. And being away from him, from the intense connection we'd shared as kids, was easier.

Now everything was coming back, as if it all had happened only yesterday, and spawning this jittery, gaping hole in the pit of my stomach. The sensation only grew stronger the closer I got to Alton. I couldn't explain it.

I *needed* to know where Benji was. What he'd done with his life. And if he was still in the area, I wanted to see my old friend again. If he would still speak to me, that was.

I should have stayed in touch. I should have swallowed my pride, reached out, and begged forgiveness for ignoring him so long.

Shoulda, woulda, coulda, as my ex-wife was fond of saying, usually with an exasperated roll of her eyes.

In hindsight, I suppose I could have Googled him, or found him on Facebook like any other long-lost friend, but I was already in motion, driving the extra hour east purely by instinct, as if Benji were my true north and I the needle on a compass.

Finding him was a long shot—it had been twenty years since Mom, Janet, and I had left BC, and the Mornings could have moved away—but folks in these parts never tended to go far, and my gut instincts, the ones that had served me well in my career, were too strong to ignore.

An early-winter mist hung low in the sky, stretching across the valley and only emphasizing my feeling of isolation as I drove. The Trans-Canada Highway unwound before me, not really a highway at all, but a two-lane, lonely blacktop carved out of the endless forests that pressed in on both sides. Most of the old growth is gone now, and what remains is tall and spindly, but make no mistake—this is pure wilderness; as dangerous as it is breathtaking. There are stretches, like this one, where it's possible to drive for hours with no sign of civilization, and the vast emptiness was a little unnerving to my suburban senses. As a kid, the woods, the lakes, the abandoned logging camps and mines that dotted the region had been the best sort of amusement park, but I'd been gone a long time—replaced the towering lodgepole pines and Engelmann spruce with skyscrapers.

The rhythmic swoosh of the windshield wipers as they battled the falling mist was a comforting balm to my nerves. On my right, a weather-beaten billboard, nestled against the encroaching forest, made my skin crawl with gooseflesh as I passed: *Hitchhiking—Is it worth the risk?*

I shivered and turned the heater up another notch, mentally cataloguing my impressions for later. Brad would appreciate the local color when I filed my story.

With each passing mile, the memories grew thicker, swarming around me like gnats I couldn't swat away. The burning sensation in my chest increased, and I reached for the roll of antacids I'd bought at the airport—definitely shouldn't have had that last glass of airport wine at the stopover in Vancouver.

Finally, another sign leapt into view: *Welcome to Alton. Pop. 3,200*

Unlike the larger, regional center of Smithers, with its quaint chalet-style architecture and overpriced gastropubs for the ski crowd, Alton was a blue-collar resource town. It was nestled squarely between the two princes—Prince Rupert to the west, and Prince George to the east—in the midst of a bounty of natural resources. In its heyday, residents had flocked to work at the Hummingbird or Europa Mines, or at one of the many sawmills in the area.

My heart kicked as I saw the low, green slope of Mount Roddick to the north and the needle of its familiar radio transmission tower. I was close. That rocky terrain and thick woods had been my backyard, my playground, and Benji my fellow explorer.

A few minutes later, on the outskirts of town, I turned off the highway and onto a rural side road, surprising myself by remembering the way. A quarter mile after that, I made another left onto North Star Lane, and the pavement became oiled gravel that crunched beneath the tires. Back in 1996, there had been only two houses on this short, dead-end street—ours and the Mornings'. Benji and I had had the run of the place, zipping back and forth to each other's house, playing one-on-one shinny in the street without having to worry about cars interrupting our game. The story was that some long-ago developer had bought the whole parcel, intending to build an exclusive enclave, only he'd gone bust after the first two slipshod houses.

Now as I slowed to avoid kicking up gravel, I saw someone had built an ugly chalet-style A-frame on the once empty lot at the end. My haze of nostalgia evaporated at the unwelcome reminder that not everything would be the same as I'd left it.

Fortunately, there was no need to wonder if the Mornings were still around. Their name was on the mailbox, spelled out in those black and gold, peel-and-stick letters you could buy for $1.99 in any hardware store. With a hitch in my chest, I turned into the long gravel drive.

The yellow clapboard ranch was just as I remembered. Sure, the siding was faded, the paint peeling in places, and the sloping front lawn more overgrown than I recalled, but considering it had been twenty years, surprisingly little had changed.

There were two vehicles in the driveway. I parked the Explorer behind a well-used silver GMC Jimmy 4X4 and a newer blue Jeep, and walked the rest of the way up the drive to the house. The crisp air was heavy with the scent of snow. I zipped up my jacket and wished I had brought warmer clothing. Then again, I wouldn't be here long.

The large two-car garage nestled behind the low house snagged my attention. Benji's dad had built it as his workshop in the year before he'd died, back before we had moved to the street. At some point since I'd been gone, windows and a door had been added to the second story, as well as a deck that was accessed by an exterior staircase. A neatly stacked cord of chopped wood wrapped one side of the garage, and the sweet smell of smoke in the air brought a lump of homesickness to my throat.

Reaching the front door of the house, I rang the doorbell and waited, my palms sweaty enough that despite the chill, I had to wipe them on my jeans.

Before too long, the inner door opened, and a suspicious face peered out. The stale odor of cigarette smoke wafted through the screen door.

I tried to hide my surprise. Angela Morning was about the same age as my mother, but she looked a decade older now. I might never have recognized her if it weren't for the button she wore pinned to her cardigan. The button was printed with a photo, and it was the familiar young woman's face smiling back at me that made my breath catch.

"Yes?" Mrs. Morning prompted.

I started out of my trance. "Mrs. Morning? Hi, I doubt you remember me but—"

"Oh, finally. I knew you'd come," she growled with the gravelly voice of a long-time smoker.

"You did?"

"Come in." She unlocked the screen door and stepped back so I could enter. "Are you from *Dateline*?"

"Huh?"

"*48 Hours*?"

"No, *The New York Journal* actually, but—"

"I haven't heard of that one."

"We're small, but reputable." Out of habit, I produced one of the business cards I always kept handy. "But Mrs. Morning..." The words crumbled to dust in my mouth as I trailed after her into the front room. It was like walking into the past. Same low-pile beige carpet, same blue velveteen overstuffed sofa. I almost expected twelve-year-old Benji to run out and greet me. But rather than instilling a sense of nostalgia, the hair on the back of my neck rose in unease.

My attention flew to the long wall between living and dining room, which was filled with photographs—more than I remembered. Two or three were of Benji as a kid, and my eyes lingered on them for a moment, and there hung Mr. and Mrs. Morning's old wedding portrait, the only photo I'd ever seen of the late Samson Morning. But most of them were of Ben's sister, Misty. Misty as a smiling child. Misty as a teenager, posing for the camera in that sweet yet sultry way I remembered—her nubile body beckoning you in, while her eyes, those cold, hard eyes, said you could look but never touch. Misty in her graduation cap and gown ready to take on the world.

"She's beautiful, isn't she?" Mrs. Morning murmured at my shoulder.

"She is." And so young. Far younger looking than I remembered. It was a shock to recall that she'd only been seventeen when I last saw her. I'd known that of course, as she'd been Janet's best friend, but she'd always seemed so much older, more mature. Misty Morning had lived up to every bit of her attention-grabbing name. In life—at least to my thirteen-year-old self—she'd been the pinnacle of femininity; an object of both lust and terror. Long legs, sweet tits. Big strawberry-blonde hair. And here she was, preserved in her youth forever.

There was no other way to describe it: this was a shrine.

"Everyone said I was being overconcerned back then. That I was wasting their time. But I knew. A mother always knows."

"I'm sorry, what—" As I turned, my eyes landed on the stack of "Missing" flyers on the coffee table—similar to the ones I'd helped hand out in town in the weeks after Misty ran away—and put it all together. "She never came home," I croaked, aghast. Twenty years later, Mrs. Morning was still looking for her runaway daughter.

Now things made sense. As a writer, I'd encountered my fair share of tragedies, but I'd never felt anything as strong as what I felt now in Mrs. Morning's living room. The sadness was as thick and palpable as the cigarette smoke that hung in the air. I was afraid to breathe it in.

"We're holding a rally this weekend. Hoping to generate new tips and pressure the police into action," Angela said. "Let me give you a button." She rummaged in a box next to the flyers and then thrust a button similar to the one she wore into my hands. "Your timing is great. Maybe you can work the rally into your piece."

Piece? "Mrs. Morning, I think there's been—"

"Please, call me Angela. Let me put the kettle on for some tea."

"No, Mrs. M—" But she was gone before I could tell her that I'd only come in search of Benji. I strode toward the kitchen, intending to correct the misunderstanding, but halted when I saw the newspapers scattered across the dining room table. They were in the process of being clipped and carefully glued into a scrapbook, and the headline of the nearest one read, *Missing girl's case reopened.*

"All this time you never heard from her?" I exclaimed. "How is that possible?"

"You didn't know?" Mrs. Morning asked from the archway. She had lit a cigarette and now blew a trail of smoke from the corner of her mouth. "Didn't they fill you in? I always said Misty was no runaway. Two fishermen found her car near MacFarlane Lake a little over a week ago."

MacFarlane Lake? That was only fifty miles east of here, in the center of the valley. The whole area was a maze of lakes and swampland.

The memory of Misty's white Oldsmobile Cutlass Supreme seeped into my brain, coalescing like a slow-developing Polaroid. Calling it a shit-bucket would have been generous. I'd lost count of the number of times my dad had been over here, replacing parts and mending hoses just to keep it running. But Misty had driven it like it was a Jag and she a princess too good for the rest of us. I guess in this neck of the woods she had been.

"I bought that car for her so she wouldn't have to hitchhike. So she'd be safe, not like those other girls." Her voice cracked. Immediately I thought of the billboard along the highway, and a shiver raced up my spine. "Twenty years and all this time, she's been so close."

My heart broke at the pain in her voice. "Mrs. Morning, I'm so sorry. I had no idea." A thunderous guilt wrenched my gut. If I'd stayed in touch, I would have known.

"My baby's still out there somewhere. She needs me. But ever since they found her car, the police won't tell us a thing."

The journalist in me kicked in. "So there was no sign of her?"

"They sent divers into the lake, brought out the dogs to search the swamp, but nothing turned up." She stubbed her cigarette into an already overflowing ashtray on the table. "When will you start?"

"I'm sorry?"

"The interview. Will your crew be arriving soon? The rally's on Saturday. It would make a good opener to your segment, wouldn't it? We're going to start here at the RCMP detachment and then form a convoy along 16 to Prince George. I've got at least a dozen cars signed up."

For the first time since I'd arrived, fire had leapt into her eyes. Shit. She thought I was here for the story. She had no clue who I was. "Mrs. Morning—Angela—I'm not with a network . . ."

"Oh, right. A New York paper, wasn't it?"

It's me. Alex Colville. I used to sit at this very pine table and do homework with Benji. But the words didn't make it past my lips.

The name on my card was Alex Buchanan, Buchanan being my stepfather's surname. If she hadn't already recognized me, there was little chance she'd tie me to Alex Colville, her son's best friend. I'd worked hard to shed my nerdy fat-boy image. Plus, she'd put in twelve-hour shifts at the mill and hadn't been home much. When she had been, she'd always seemed too preoccupied to notice us.

Angela Morning shrugged. "I was hoping for television, but I guess you'll have to do." She withdrew a crumpled pack of cigarettes from the pocket of her cardigan, saw it was empty, and sighed.

"No, I'm not really here to—"

The kettle's shriek cut me off, and Mrs. Morning left me in the dining room with a promise to be right back.

Now what? All I wanted was to know how I could reach Benji, but the longer I stayed without revealing myself, the more awkward this became. Unless . . . unless I could somehow find out about him without tipping her off. A new worry arced through my mind. What if Benji hated me? I'd promised to write and never had. What if he never wanted to see me again? I'd come here on instinct, without thinking this meeting through.

"I won't forget about you, I promise," I'd said. Had I known then it was a lie? The first of many I'd told over the years. And right now, the one I regretted the most.

Somewhere in the recesses of the house, a door slammed.

"Angela? Whose car is that in the driveway?" demanded an angry voice. "It's blocking me in."

My stomach hollowed. Surely it couldn't be.

"It's a reporter," Mrs. Morning boasted. "You said they wouldn't come, but they did. He's going to do a story on Misty."

"The hell he is." The voice was closer.

I spun around just as the man behind the voice stormed in from the kitchen.

That mop of auburn curls. The scar bisecting the left eyebrow from where I'd caught him with my hockey stick. Those arresting blue eyes.

Benji.

Like I said—indelible.

CHAPTER TWO

It's the second-to-last week of August, and Benji and I are tired and sunburned from a day breaking trails down Mount Raw-dick. My bike is caked with mud, the backs of my legs are covered in mosquito bites, and Benji's arms are scratched from the brush. But we're happy. Soon we'll be back at school and enduring another year of torment, but for a little while longer we're free. We stop to catch our breath and share the last of our water from his canteen.

Benji's eyes sparkle with excitement as they meet mine, and there's that pinch in my chest again. The one that's been popping up a lot this summer.

He tugs the brim of his straw hat lower, and another piece tears away in his hand. It's falling apart, and never sits right on his head, but it used to belong to his dad, so he wears it all the time even though he gets made fun of. Sometimes I think he's brave. Other times I think he wouldn't get picked on so much if he didn't act so weird.

Up ahead through the tall grass, we can see the highway, which means we're not far from home. I can't wait to duck under the hose and cool off, but I also dread going back. With any luck, Dad'll be passed out on the lounger in the backyard when Mom gets home, otherwise the fighting will start. Her and Dad. Her and Janet. It seems like everybody's mad at someone lately. Janet's been grounded all summer—she had to miss the Spring Formal—and it's turned her into a real super-bitch.

"Want to stop at the river for a swim before we go home?" Benji asks. It's like he's read my mind and knows what's waiting for me, knows that I'll do just about anything to stay away a bit longer.

"Hell, yeah."

We're almost to the highway when we hear the throaty rumble of a motor and then the sunlight flashes on the windshield as the white car streaks past us.

"Hey, isn't that Misty's car?" I ask.

"I'd like for you to leave."

Benji's voice, soft but firm, slammed me back to the present. My heart was racing. My mind a jumble of half-formed thoughts:

He hasn't changed—

He's beautiful—

Oh God, I still feel it.

"Please," he added politely, regarding me with a wary tilt to his head and suspicion in those once-trusting eyes. His wild red hair had been tamed a bit and darkened to a rich auburn over the years, but hints of ginger still shot through his close beard. I would have known him anywhere. "We have nothing to say to you."

"I do," Angela insisted.

He swung around to face her. "Angela. You know it's not going to make a difference."

My temporary paralysis lifted, and the bubble of happiness that had been rising in my chest collapsed. Benji hadn't recognized me either. And why should he? It had been a long time. The glasses were gone thanks to laser vision correction in my twenties, and long hours in the gym kept my sturdy build in check. Even my hair had darkened from its youthful blond to an ordinary brown that I kept cut short.

It's me, I wanted to cry.

Had he forgotten me?

Heat surged into my face and neck. I needed to say something, but there was a huge lump in my throat. Now that I was here, that *he* was here, the past and the present were colliding, overlapping like a superimposed photograph, and I was totally unbalanced.

I'd left it too long. They were both watching me. Panic thundered in my chest—I had to get out of here. "You're right," I said. "I should go."

Benji's narrow shoulders relaxed. He never had liked conflict. "Thank you."

A little cry escaped Angela. "But you came all this way . . ."

I was already moving toward the door. "I'm sorry, Mrs. Morning. I can't help you."

Without looking back, I fled the house and practically ran back to my car.

"Shit. Shit. Shit." I punctuated each curse with the slap of my palm on the steering wheel. Well, that had blown up in my face spectacularly. What had happened in there? One minute with Benji and I'd literally fallen to pieces. I held my hands out in front of me and stared at them incredulously. They were trembling.

For a second, I'd felt thirteen again: running out of that house, mouth dry, heart hammering, because my best friend had just kissed me and spun my life into chaos. With time, I'd convinced myself it hadn't been that big a deal, but clearly I'd been wrong, based on my reaction now. Benji. He still felt like home to me, in a way no one ever had. It was a feeling that had scared me twenty years ago, scared me so much I'd cut him out of my life. Now it was back.

Acid surged in my esophagus, and I popped the last of my antacids, which barely dampened the flames clawing their way up from my gut.

A door slammed, and I looked up. Benji had emerged from the house, clad in a khaki anorak jacket. He moved gracefully, long legs eating up the ground as he headed toward the Jimmy parked in front of me, and my heart sped up. He scowled when he saw my Explorer.

I wanted to go to him. To walk into his arms, hug him, to put the past behind us and feel once again that connection we'd had. That warm satisfaction of knowing that there was someone in this world who got me. I'd never felt that with anybody but Benji: not with my ex-wife, not with any of my lovers over the years, male or female.

I got out of my car, gripping the doorframe for support.

"Was there something you wanted?" he asked. His tone was mostly curious, but there was a hint of trepidation underneath.

"I—I'm sorry about Misty."

"Are you? Why?"

"Why?" I repeated, taken aback by his callousness.

"She's nothing to you. I get that you're doing your job here, but dredging this up is a waste of time."

"But doesn't your mom deserve to have some closure? To know the truth about what happened to her daughter?"

Beneath his beard, his jaw tensed. I could see it even from where I stood. He narrowed the gap between us, and I took an involuntary step back. "What she deserves, what we *all* deserve, is to move on with our lives. It's been twenty years. Misty is gone."

It was his tone—flat, dull, lifeless—that made me flinch. Coming from the sensitive boy I remembered, the effect was chilling. "That's an awfully cold thing to say about your sister."

Ben had always had this intense way of staring at people. As a kid his eyes had been too large and deep for his face, making him seem goggle-eyed, like he was constantly surprised. It could be disconcerting at times. More than once it had made me think he could see into my soul.

Now his mature features fit perfectly, but oddly, he wouldn't hold my gaze. "Look around you," he said, nodding toward Mount Roddick. "It took this long for her car to be found. We're surrounded by wilderness. By lakes and swamps and rivers. If she's out there, do you really believe there's anything left to find?"

"So you think she's dead. Not that she just ditched the car and doesn't want to be found."

"You don't know my sister. She wouldn't quietly fade away. Of course she's dead. If not here, then in some random city. Angela knows that too, so how is indulging this . . . this obsession going to help? You're not the first reporter to come here, you know. You stir things up, get your back-page story, and leave. And I'm left holding it all together." His eyes flicked to me, then away again, and I had the sense he was on the verge of tears.

"Ben—"

"Now, do you mind?" he snapped. "I'm going to be late for my class." He whirled around and stalked back to his car. The engine roared to life, and the taillights glowered like angry eyes as he put the car in reverse.

I backed down the driveway, the Jimmy riding my front bumper so closely that I was afraid to stop and check out my old house across the street. As I swung around, I glimpsed brown siding through the foliage screening the property and noted the mailbox at the end of the drive, but then Benji was there, impatient, leaving me no choice but to continue back the way I'd come. He followed me down North Star Lane, to Highway 16, where we turned in opposite directions.

With a heavy heart, I watched him disappear over the horizon in my rearview mirror, the same way as I had once before.

I drove back to Smithers in a daze.

When I came upon another hand-painted billboard, this one with big black letters warning, *Girls, don't hitchhike* and beneath it, three photographs and the word *Missing*, I sucked in a breath and accelerated as if I could outrun the malevolent presence that had suddenly gripped me. What the hell? Had those signs always been there? I couldn't recall. Then again, teenaged boys feel invincible, don't they? And they're notoriously self-absorbed.

By the time I checked myself into the efficiency unit I'd booked at the Summit View Motor Inn on the outskirts of town, jet lag was catching up to me. Janet hadn't offered up her place, and I hadn't asked even though it sure would have been cheaper. Never close, we were essentially strangers these days, and I had no desire to spend more time together than we needed to. Besides, this way if things got too overwhelming, I could escape.

With fishing and hunting seasons winding down, and the ski season yet to begin, I had lucked out and was able to book the cheapest place within easy distance to the hospital. Still, it was costing me $89 a night. For a room that looked as though it hadn't been updated since before I was born. At least it was clean, with free internet and a kitchenette with a small fridge and a microwave. Attached to the motel office was a Chinese restaurant and a liquor store. What else could a man want?

I texted Janet to let her know I'd arrived, and she told me she'd meet me at the hospital as soon as her shift at the Toyota dealership in town ended. I could have gone without her, but frankly, I needed the buffer. I wouldn't be here if it weren't for her.

So with a few hours to kill, I took a long shower and lay down for a short nap. My mind whirled with flashes of Ben and Misty, and my dad as I'd last seen him, and I didn't think I'd be able to sleep, but the hum of cars buzzing along the highway outside my room lulled me, and I was out almost as soon as my head hit the pillow.

When I opened my eyes again, the room was getting dark. I'd slept nearly the whole afternoon, and now I had to scramble to meet Janet on time.

The Bulkley Valley District Hospital in Smithers was the only hospital for the region. It was small, and compared to the overcrowded, noisy hospitals of New York, eerily quiet. At only three stories tall, I doubted I could have gotten lost in it if I tried, but the smiling senior citizen volunteering at the Information Desk gave me directions to Dad's room before I finished saying his name. "You must be Janet's brother," she clucked. "I'm so glad you could make it."

And this was exactly what I disliked about small towns.

My stomach tightened as I navigated the warren of hallways. What would I say? What would *he*? We hadn't seen each other in over a decade, since the summer before I started my journalism degree at UBC. That had been a tense weekend, both of us drowning in silence, not knowing how to talk to each other.

Nothing had really changed.

The door to room 204 stood open. I took a deep breath and entered before I chickened out.

Jesusfuckingchrist. I clapped a hand over my mouth.

There had to be a mistake. The receptionist had sent me to the wrong room. I wasn't even sure this yellow-skinned thing in the bed was a *man*, let alone my dad. Still, as my initial shock wore off, I ventured a step closer.

The man in front of me was a husk, dried out and emptied. I'd never seen a person so hollowed, and yet his belly swelled beneath the blanket—like one of those famine victims in the Save the Children commercials. Bile rose in the back of my throat.

His closed eyes were sunken in their sockets, the eyeballs rolling beneath translucent skin as though he were battling nightmarish creatures in his sleep. His fingers tugged restlessly at the bed linens, and every few seconds, his lips, cracked and shrunken, would twitch.

I held my breath.

Suddenly I couldn't bear the thought of those eyes flying open. I fled. And collided with Janet in the hallway. My hands instinctively flew to her shoulders. "Janet!" I quickly released her.

"Sandy. You're here."

I gritted my teeth at the old nickname. It was a diminutive of Alexander and a holdover from Dad's Scottish heritage, but no one ever knew that. I'd been ribbed mercilessly as a kid. Janet was the only one who still persisted in using it, probably because she knew it irked me.

We didn't hug but stood there awkwardly as she glanced over my shoulder. "Not a pretty sight, is he? I wanted to be here to warn you."

"That's not— That can't be him."

Janet's cheeks and nose were pink—from the cold, I assumed. Then I smelled mouthwash on her breath and knew she'd been drinking. She always hid it well, but when you've grown up with an alcoholic, the tricks become easy to spot. I hadn't seen her since Christmas in Seattle four years ago with Mom and Dan. Rockwellian it had not been, and the day after Christmas, we'd scattered without looking back, like cockroaches scuttling for darkness.

She fidgeted now under my scrutiny. "It's him. No surprise you don't recognize him. When's the last time you bothered to visit? Oh, right, never."

"It's a two-way street, Janet."

"Yeah, 'cause he could afford to fly to New York. Sandy, you're the one who cut us out of your life."

I winced. This had to be a record for us. Five minutes in each other's company and we were already fighting over who the bad guy was. This was an old pattern. Janet defending Dad, me defending Mom. We rehashed it anytime we got together—hence the miserable Christmas in Seattle. "Do we have to do this? I didn't come all this way to bicker."

She thrust her hands into the pockets of a fleecy jacket with the Toyota logo embroidered on the left breast and pursed her lips. Janet was almost five years older than me, and the age gap was big enough that we'd had very little to do with each other growing up. For a woman not yet forty, she hadn't aged well. Silver streaked her straight brown hair, which she had pulled back into an unflattering ponytail.

Next to Misty, Janet had always seemed homely, and that wasn't just a brother talking. She'd inherited Dad's strong features, and while on him they worked—my mother claimed she had fallen for his rakish good looks—on poor Janet they didn't.

"Jesus." I scrubbed a hand across my face and turned back toward Dad's room. "How did this happen?"

She scowled. "How do you think it happened? It's cirrhosis of the liver."

"Cirrhosis." I winced, feeling shitty for not even asking about Dad's illness when she'd called. That was an alcoholic's disease I knew, but never had I imagined it looked like this. It was almost enough to put me off drinking for the rest of my life. "I didn't know it was *this* bad . . ."

Jerry Colville had always been what people politely referred to as a social drinker, but about the time he got laid off, his pattern changed, got serious, and he crossed the threshold into full-blown alcoholic. I never knew if the booze killed my parents' marriage, or if their troubles had fed the booze. Either way, his problem appeared to only have gotten worse. "The last time we spoke, he sounded good. He was talking about a part-time job delivering the weekly flyers."

Janet curled her lip. "He lost that job months ago, along with his driver's license." She shook her head. "God, it must have been at least seven months now."

I frowned. I thought I'd talked to him on Father's Day, as usual, but maybe my memory was playing tricks. "Why is he . . . like that?" I waved my hand in Dad's direction.

"Bloated? It's fluid buildup in his abdomen. His liver is failing," she murmured. We were both speaking in hushed tones, as though he might hear us.

"Can't they do something? A transplant?"

She shook her head. "It's too late. He was diagnosed three years ago. They told him he needed to get sober. He kept drinking."

"And you let him?"

"I didn't know about it, Sandy." She wiped at her eyes with the back of her sleeve and then rummaged in her pocket for a ratty tissue to blow her nose.

I wished I could be more like Janet. All I felt was a detached sort of sympathy. He was, in a sense, a stranger to me.

I remembered us as being a happy, normal family for much of my childhood—of course I'd been only a kid, and everything had seemed simpler then, but we'd had good times. There had been Christmases and birthdays, and the occasional family fishing or camping trips. Benji would often accompany us, as my mom had felt sorry for him being on his own so much.

I was a little hazy on when things changed. I supposed it all started around ninety-two when the mine closed. Dad had worked at the Europa Silver Mine, southwest of Alton, servicing equipment, which meant that he'd board the company bus and be gone for a week at a time.

After the layoffs, the drinking had gone from one can of beer with dinner, to three. Plus the ones during the day when we were at school. Dad had caught some occasional handyman jobs, but they hadn't been enough, and Mom had had to start working as a secretary for the township. She'd become the sole breadwinner. The camping trips had stopped, replaced by tense silences and then shouting behind closed doors. Then came our expulsion to my grandmother's in Seattle and the divorce.

Daniel Buchanan, the guy my mom married a year after we landed in Seattle, was the one who'd been a true father to me. It was Dan who'd been there for those tumultuous teenaged years, who'd called me on my shit when I'd acted out, who'd taught me to drive a stick shift, and bought me my first pack of condoms, who'd beamed with pride at my graduations. It was his name I'd proudly taken.

"Have you talked to Mom lately?" Janet asked.

"Yeah. I let her know I was coming here."

"She didn't want to come."

"I know. You can't really blame her though. They've been divorced for nearly twenty years."

Dad mumbled something in his sleep, too low to make out. His head tossed on the pillow, long, greasy gray strands splaying out like tentacles. I took a cautious step back into the room, leaving Janet lingering in the doorway. "How long has he been like this?" I asked.

"He collapsed a week ago. The doctors said there was nothing more they could do." She gestured to the equipment surrounding the bed. "This is just palliative."

"You said he wanted to see me. Is he even conscious?"

"Sometimes he's lucid. Sometimes he rambles nonsense. His liver can't filter toxins anymore, and they're slowly making their way into his brain. Most of the time he sleeps. They keep him sedated a lot. For the pain." She hugged herself.

A female nurse in purple scrubs stopped outside the door and greeted Janet. I pegged her for early thirties, the youngest person I'd seen in the hospital so far, and pretty in a girl-next-door way. "Thought you'd be here," she said with an easy smile. "Jerry was very agitated today. We had to up his dose of morphine. I don't think he'll be up to talking anytime soon."

"That's fine. This is my brother, Sandy."

"Alex," I corrected.

The nurse—*Katy*, her name tag read—gave me an assessing stare that made me wonder what Janet had told her about me. "Nice to meet you," she finally said. "I'm sorry about the circumstances."

"Do we know how much longer he has?" I asked.

Janet snorted. "Why? You got someplace better to be? I'm so sorry we're inconveniencing you. I forgot how self-centered you are. All you ever think about is yourself."

"I'm trying to be practical, Jan." I'd left my return flight open-ended, but I didn't want to drag this out if I didn't have to.

Katy glanced back and forth between us. "A week? Maybe less," she informed me. "Dr. Pleasanton was by this morning. We can't drain any more fluid—his liver's expanded so much we can't get to it. I'm afraid there's not much else that can be done at this point but make him comfortable." She laid a gentle hand on my arm and gave it a squeeze. Her eyes searched mine, and a pleasant tingle rocketed to my groin. "I'll be around if you need me."

I watched her leave the room and when I turned back, Janet shot me a withering glare.

"What?" I asked innocently.

A whimper from the bed drew my attention. "Can't . . ." Dad's voice was too weak to make out what he was saying. More mumbling. ". . .find her."

"What is it, Dad?" Janet called. "Do you want some ice chips?"

"That's not what he's saying." I leaned down to hear him better.

"Didn't mean to . . ." Dad whispered, his stale breath blowing in my face. "Misty."

The temperature in the room must have plummeted a dozen degrees because gooseflesh prickled my arms. I shivered. *Misty*. "Did you hear that?"

"Hear what?" Janet appeared at my elbow.

"He said 'Misty.'"

"What's misty?"

"No. Her name. Misty Morning."

Janet paled. "Are you sure? You must have heard wrong. Why would he say that?"

"I don't know." Dad had grown quiet again, falling back into his restless sleep. Had I really heard the name? Or were the Mornings just on my mind today? "You remember her, don't you?"

Beside me, Janet stiffened. "Of course. She was my best friend."

"Did you know they found her car? Out near MacFarlane Lake. Isn't that near where we used to camp?"

"I heard." A section of limp hair had escaped its ponytail, and when Janet tucked it behind her ear, I saw that her nails were short and ragged; the cuticles scabbed from repeated biting.

"I always thought she'd run away," I said. "I mean Benji and I *saw* her that day." We'd been the *last* to see her, in fact. "But now . . ."

"Maybe Dad knows about the car too." Janet's forehead creased. "Or overheard it somewhere."

"Yeah, I guess."

"More than likely he was rambling. He doesn't know what he's saying half the time. I wouldn't dwell on it." She straightened the sheets Dad had knocked loose and tucked them tightly under his arms. "You got a place to stay?"

"I'm at the Summit View."

She nodded, clearly relieved. "Good. Good. I've only got a one-bedroom, otherwise I would have . . ."

"It's okay, Janet. I wouldn't want to impose on you and Bruce anyway."

Her breath hitched. "Bruce and I got divorced. Last spring."

"Oh. Sorry. I didn't know." There was a lot I didn't know, apparently.

Janet shrugged.

I lowered my voice and turned my back to the bed. "Should we be making arrangements or something?"

"It's already taken care of. He'll be cremated. There won't be a service."

I sent up a silent prayer of relief. Being here was one thing, but I hadn't looked forward to arranging the details of *after*. Janet would know better than me what his final wishes were.

"But can I . . . can I ask you to do something?" Janet asked, worrying her lower lip.

What else was there? "What is it?"

"Could you start packing up his place? Phil's been a doll about letting me run over here on my breaks, but I can't get any more time off. And I'm not—" Her voice broke. "I don't think I can do it."

Thanks a lot, Janet. I swallowed hard. At least it would keep me busy. "Yeah. Sure."

I gave Dad one final, uncertain look.

What had I got myself into?

CHAPTER THREE

I dreamed of Benji that night.

It's late October and the early-morning sun, such as it is this time of year, is only beginning to rise. I'm watching my out-of-breath thirteen-year-old self huffing across the street to the Morning house while my mom and Janet climb into the U-Haul truck.

There's no pumpkin on the Mornings' front stoop this year, just like there's no pumpkin on mine. Sure, we're the only two houses on the street, and no one comes trick-or-treating, but Benji and I have always carved pumpkins and competed to see whose was best. He always wins.

No one answers my knock, even though I can see Mrs. Morning sitting in the front window. The door is unlocked, so I go ahead and enter as I have so many times. Usually Mrs. Morning is all made up for the camera, but today she's in her bathrobe.

Mrs. Morning's been on TV three times since Misty ran away. She's a regular celebrity, Mom says, but I don't think it's a compliment. They tease Benji about it at school. And about Misty. About how she's probably giving blowjobs in Prince George for drugs.

"Hey, Mrs. Morning. Is Ben up?" It's been over two months now, and I still don't know what to say to her.

"What?" Her eyes look at me but don't seem to see me. It gives me the creeps. "Go on." She waves me in, and I zip down the hall, past Misty's empty bedroom to Benji's. His door is closed but I push it open and boldly walk inside, a little pissed off that he made me come all the way over here.

He's lying facedown on his bed, but on top of the covers, and he bolts up when I enter, wiping his face. It's no use. I can tell he's been crying—his buggy eyes are puffy and ringed with red.

He stares at me without speaking, and I don't know what to say. Even though there's so much to be said. Tell him, my older self, my sleeping self, urges. Tell him how you feel.

But of course I say nothing. Instead, I'm thinking of one of the last things Misty ever said to me: "What do you two do up there anyway? Flog each other's log?"

My anger evaporates. "You didn't come to say good-bye," *I burst out, and, oh no, a sob rises in my chest.*

He shakes his head, and his wild orange curls bob like a clown wig. "I don't want to."

"Mom says it's only for a few months, until Dad gets his act together. We'll probably be back after Christmas. Spring at the latest. So start making those plans for our fort like we talked about."

"Do you really think so?" *He scrambles off the bed, blue eyes lighting up. We'd planned to build a teepee next summer, so we could hang out in our spot even in the rain, and Ben had already been drawing up plans for how it should look. He'd done research at the library and everything to get it right.*

"Yeah," *I say, although we've packed all our stuff so I'm not a hundred percent sure. I'm trying to be grown-up about this, but when Benji hugs me, hard, it's like being wrapped in a warm blanket I don't ever want to leave.* "I'll write to you. Hey, if the school gets a computer, we might be able to email. But stay away from Amy," *I warn him.* "She's mine."

Benji smiles sadly. We don't talk about it, but he doesn't need to be told to keep away from girls. "You didn't get to kiss her like you planned," *he says.*

I shrug like it's no big deal. "There'll be other girls to kiss in Seattle. City girls," *I add. Everyone knows city girls are easy.*

The horn blares. I step away from Benji and lift the curtain to see the U-Haul sitting in the middle of our dead-end street. There's a hole in my chest, and it's getting bigger by the minute.

"Gotta go."

"Don't forget me, okay?" *he whispers.*

"I won't."

"Say it."

"I won't forget about you, I promise."

Before I realize what he's about to do, he leans forward and kisses me. His lips are soft, as soft as a girl's, although I don't really know that for sure—I haven't kissed any girls yet. For my first kiss it's not bad. Not bad at all. In fact, it feels kind of perfect. My lips tingle, and I'm tempted to open my mouth a little, the way people kiss in the movies.

It's over too fast. The impatient horn breaks us apart.

Then my face is burning, and I have to get out of here before I start crying. But it's too late. As I run out the front door and down the drive, I can taste salt on my lips. The lips Benji kissed.

Mom doesn't say anything as I jump in the truck's cab. Janet squeals as I force her to the middle seat. I give one final look back, and there's Benji standing on the lawn with his arms wrapped around himself. And there are bells going off.

No, not bells. A phone. Someone's phone was ringing.

I opened my eyes to find light streaming through the crack in the plaid curtains. It took me a moment to remember where I was and why I was here. Outside my door, a man started talking, like he was on the phone, as he walked past.

My pillow was damp, and when I touched my face, my cheeks were stiff and slightly crusty. Had I been crying in my sleep? Over a silly dream?

But it had felt so real.

Did Ben ever think of that day? How did he remember it? Had it scared him as much as it had scared me? It hadn't been the kiss itself—I'd known for a few months then how Benji thought of me even if I hadn't quite understood what it meant—it had been the unexpected power of it. At thirteen, those sorts of emotions had simply been too overwhelming to handle. So I'd chosen not to.

The dream lingered as I showered and dressed. It didn't fade until after I grabbed a quick bite for breakfast at the drive-thru and was back on the highway again, racking up the miles on my rental as I headed toward Dad's place in Alton.

After we moved to Seattle and it had become clear we weren't coming back, the house on North Star Lane had gone up for sale. Dad had wandered around the province looking for work. About the time the divorce was finalized, he'd settled back in Alton. At least, that was how Mom had told it. Dad never had been big on staying in touch. We hadn't gotten so much as a postcard. To me it had always said something that he'd chosen to stay here, in the middle of nowhere, where he had no steady job or ties to the community. He could have gone anywhere—he could have moved closer to his kids—but he hadn't.

The highway was busier today; I got stuck behind a convoy of logging trucks and had to stay well back to avoid the bits of bark and dirt that flew into my windshield. This time the billboards at the side of the road were less shocking when I passed, although they still made the hair on the back of my neck stand up.

It's funny how your perception changes as you get older. People often talk about their childhood as being a more innocent time, and it's true, or at least that's the way it seems. Back then, we'd had no grasp of danger: of bears and wolves, or hitchhiking, or getting lost. And those were the days before cell phones. When I thought that all Benji and I had had was a pair of walkie-talkies that had occasionally fizzled out if we went out of range, I shuddered. Other than that we were entirely on our own. And loved it. Everything was an adventure.

For his ninth birthday, I gave Benji a compass, and from that point on, he and I had spent every chance we'd gotten exploring forgotten trails or making our own, sometimes on foot, but most of the time on our bikes. We'd made up stories of demented miners who searched the woods for victims, and vied to see who was the best tracker.

Did kids even do that anymore? Run free? Weren't they all locked up in their bedrooms playing video games and sexting each other?

I scanned the side of the highway as I drove, looking for familiar landmarks or evidence of our old adventures. Somewhere out there on the east face of Mount Roddick, buried beneath the hundred-foot spruce next to a secret waterfall, was a metal lunch box that contained all our childish treasures: a penny minted the year I was born, a drawing of Benji's, ticket stubs from *Dumb and Dumber*, the first movie we'd been allowed to see on our own at the rep theater in town. There was probably more, but I couldn't recall what. Silly things. Insignificant things.

Had our box rusted away to nothing? Had Benji ever retrieved it?

I pointedly ignored the turnoff to the Mornings', although the urge to detour was strong, and continued past the volunteer fire station and the conjoined elementary and high schools, and in to Alton proper. Until I could deal with the effect Ben had on me, it would be better to leave the past in the past.

As I drove down the main street, it seemed that every other storefront was soaped or papered over. For Lease signs abounded, and the general air of decay was palpable. Only Taylor's Market—the lone grocery store—had a good crowd.

The Rainbow Mobile Home Park was located on the southeast side of town. I checked the address Janet had given me and parked next to a beat-up brown and beige single-wide. The wooden steps leading to the front door were rotted and on the verge of collapse, the siding dented and caked with decades of grime. I paused to tug a slip of weather-beaten paper out from where it had been tucked into the frame of the aluminum storm door. It was a business card with the logo of the Royal Canadian Mounted Police.

Sergeant Blake McNamara
North District Major Crime Unit

An address in Prince George and a phone number followed. On the back someone had written: *Please call.*

My mouth went dry. What had Dad done now? Had he caused trouble? As far as I knew, he was a harmless drunk—belligerent yes, but not violent. Then again, it had been a long time since I'd seen him.

Pocketing the card, I let myself in using the key Janet had given me, and immediately recoiled at the stench: a mix of booze, stale cigarettes, rotting food, and damp.

The curtains, remnants of the seventies judging by the pattern, were all pulled, enveloping the house in gloom. I felt for a light switch, and a fluorescent overhead light in the kitchen flickered to life, pinging and popping as it bathed the space in a sickly green cast. The plastic cover was speckled with the shadowy remains of dead insects.

Ugh.

The screen door slammed shut with a bang behind me as I stepped farther into the kitchen, cautiously, as though I were venturing into a stranger's home. The floor plan was simple: to my right was a small living room; to the left, a short hallway leading to the bathroom and sole bedroom. I could see the bed from where I stood. The whole house couldn't have been bigger than my six-hundred-square-foot walk-up in Brooklyn.

Newspapers littered the floor, some of them neatly bundled, others scattered across the grungy brown carpet. In the living room, a green leather recliner had pride of place in front of the ancient television set. The TV was a relic from another age, with dials and rabbit ears poking up from the back. The recliner was falling apart; stuffing protruded from a ragged tear along the backrest, like intestines from a gut wound. Crumpled cans and assorted bottles lay in a mound next to the chair, and an ashtray on the battered side table was heaped with butts.

How had this happened? It sickened me to think of him living like this. A pang of guilt I didn't want to feel sliced through my stomach. Here I complained when my super wouldn't fix my running toilet, and Dad was basically a hoarder.

Something crunched under my foot as I ventured farther, and I tried not to think of what it might be. The walls were bare, except for a single framed family photograph—taken at Sears, posed in front of a wood-paneled library backdrop. We looked happy. Janet's smile was a grillwork of metal, which meant I must have been eight or nine at the time, cursed with a horrible bowl haircut that made me cringe. *Poor kid.* I'd have to remember to take this with me—it would make a great addition to my article.

Turning away from the troublesome photo, I stepped back over bundles of newspapers and flattened cardboard boxes, and picked my way through the clutter to the small kitchen. More empty wine bottles lined the battle-scarred countertops. I turned on the faucet, silently praying the water hadn't been turned off. After a deep gurgle and a worrying thump from under the sink, a trickle began to flow from the tap. I let out my breath. Then I made the mistake of opening the fridge and immediately gagged at the stench.

I did not sign up for this, Janet.

Still, I'd rather be here than sitting vigil in that hospital.

First I had to deal with the smell. I hadn't come prepared for a situation of this magnitude, so after I managed to open the window above the kitchen sink to let the place air out, I hopped back in the car and drove to the hardware store, where I picked up cleaning supplies and garbage bags—noting with worry that things here cost twice as much as at home.

No sooner had I returned to the RV park and donned my rubber gloves than someone was banging on the aluminum door. "I know you're in there, Jerry," barked a male voice.

I opened the door to find a short, bearded man in a red plaid bush coat on the rickety steps. He blinked in surprise. "Hey. Where's Jerry?"

"He's over in Smithers. In the hospital. I'm his . . . son." The word felt odd on my lips.

"Ah, thought the cops might have caught up to him. They were here the other day."

The business card burned a hole in my pocket. "Yeah?"

"Wonder what they were after." The guy peered over my shoulder into the house. "They wouldn't say."

"Who knows with cops?"

"I don't put up with no funny stuff around here. Jerry knows that."

"I'm sure it was nothing," I assured him.

"You moving in?"

"Cleaning."

"The bastard's three months late on the rent for this pad again. Tell him I'm going to have him evicted if he doesn't pay up this time."

Shit, Dad. "I thought he owned the home."

"He owns the trailer, but not the land it sits on."

I rubbed the pounding spot between my eyes. "How much does he owe you?"

"It's $300 a month. Let's call it an even thousand."

"That's more than $300 a month," I pointed out.

He shrugged. "Interest."

Even way out here in the middle of nowhere, everyone wanted to make a buck. "Look, let me talk to my sister and see what she wants to do. I'm sure we can work something out. Can you give me some more time? Maybe next week?" I didn't tell him Jerry wouldn't be coming back.

The little man squinted. "If you make it cash."

"Cash?" I doubted that was legal, but I wasn't in a position to argue. Hopefully there would be enough in my account to cover it. "Not a problem."

"Next week, then. You can find me up in the office. Name's Darnell."

Darnell didn't bother to ask my name, and I didn't offer it.

Before I closed the door, I noticed a woman's face peering out at me from behind the window blinds of the neighboring trailer. I gave her a nod, and the slats immediately closed. *Just like home.* With a little smirk, I went back to my cleaning.

What did the Mounties want with Dad? I was almost afraid to find out. I plucked the card from my pocket and reread it. Major Crime Unit in Prince George.

Misty.

The thought leapt into my head.

Taking a deep breath, I dialed the number on the card. Sergeant McNamara wasn't in, or at least wasn't answering, so I left a short message on his voice mail explaining who I was and why I was calling. Then I went back to work.

Since only one local channel came through on the television—currently airing daytime talk shows—for company I found an oldies station on the radio and sang along while I worked.

I elected to tackle the refrigerator first, as that would be the worst part of the job. Considering there wasn't much in it, it sure stank.

By the time afternoon rolled around, the house was freezing from having the windows open, but it smelled a hell of a lot better than it had when I got here. I had hauled eight bags of trash to the big dumpster near the park entrance and poured whatever liquor I found down the sink. In the end, I counted four dozen empty bottles—mostly cheap wines. Those I put aside, intending to return them and collect the deposit later. I hadn't gone into journalism for the money, and every little bit counted.

Now that I'd cleaned out the worst of the trash, the age and neglect of the place was even more evident. The linoleum was peeling, the carpet was loose and embedded with god only knew what. There was no way we'd be able to sell it for much in this condition, assuming that was the plan.

I'd have to talk it over with Janet and see what she wanted to do. Maybe she'd be better off handing it over to Darnell.

My stomach grumbled in hunger, making me realize how long I'd been at it, so I decided to grab a bite to eat before putting in another couple of hours.

There weren't many dining options in Alton, and after driving through town and seeing nothing tempting, I finally settled on the Valley Restaurant, which was located right on the highway and had been around since before I was born. We'd come here for my thirteenth birthday, and a warm glow settled in my chest as I pulled into the parking lot. My Explorer seemed out of place among the extended cab trucks and SUVs, like a child's plaything next to the big boy toys.

The joint was as I remembered. Dated and decidedly not fancy, but clean—folding tables covered with tablecloths, plastic-covered menus boasting homemade pies, and a lone waitress bustling between tables while another manned the counter. It was nearing the end of lunch hour, and most of the seats were still filled with an eclectic mix of ball-cap-wearing workmen and travel-weary tourists in chinos and sweaters taking a break from the long drive along the Trans-Canada Highway.

I took a table for two near the window.

"Hi there." My server greeted me cheerfully, looking as though she'd come directly from central casting. She fit the part of small-town waitress to a tee, right down to the polyester uniform and name tag: Arlene. She slapped a menu in front of me with a smile. "Passing through?"

Used to the anonymity of New York, I'd forgotten how easily strangers were singled out around here. "That obvious?"

"No offense, but you don't look like much of a hunter or a fisherman. And the skiers won't start showing up until the end of the month."

"Yeah, plaid's not really my color." I chuckled. "You got me. I'm visiting family. In Smithers."

"Lucky you. I'll be right back to take your order."

Arlene left me to peruse the menu while she serviced another table. She seemed a bit familiar. Did I know her? Had we gone to school together? She appeared to be about Janet's age, so maybe I had seen her around town.

It had never occurred to me I might run into old acquaintances other than Benji. We'd both been on the low rung of the high school social ladder, and neither one of us particularly great at making friends. For the most part, we'd flown under the radar and kept to ourselves. Less chance of getting beat up that way.

I scanned the menu, and when Arlene returned, ordered the Logger Burger.

"Anything to drink?" she asked without glancing up from her pad.

The sight of Dad's swollen limbs and jaundiced skin still haunted me, making me doubt I'd be able to tackle anything stronger than a light beer ever again. Instead, I settled on a club soda and cranberry juice.

"Is something wrong?" I asked when she didn't immediately leave.

"Sorry." She laughed. "You remind me of someone. But for the life of me I can't think who. Don't worry, it'll come to me. I have a good memory."

I forced a smile. The last thing I wanted was to chat about old times with people who'd never acknowledged me in school except to offer up the occasional snide put-down or toss my backpack out the bus window.

With nothing else to do while I waited, I occupied myself by making a list on the back of a napkin of all the things that would need to be done at Dad's place: painting, putting up new blinds, fitting new carpet . . .

"—the Morning girl." A snippet of conversation from the two older ladies at the table behind me made me stop writing. I angled my head to listen in better.

One of the women clearly hadn't been around very long, because she said, "Morning. Is she the one who's always posting those signs around town?"

"That's her mother," said the other one. "Didn't you see her on the news last week? Anyway, Cathy Gagnon called me terrified they were going to arrest Derek. That cop spent *two* hours interviewing him."

"But why?"

"Because he was the girl's boyfriend," her companion whispered in a knowing tone. "And don't the police always suspect the boyfriend?"

Derek Gagnon had been dating Misty? I hadn't heard that before. Then again, I'd never paid much attention to gossip, especially senior gossip. But Derek? The guy was a high school dropout who had worked in his dad's garage. If memory served, he had a prison record and a reputation as a pothead. He would have already been in his twenties at the time. Knowing Misty, it wasn't so surprising she would have gravitated to the town bad boy.

The arrival of my burger interrupted my eavesdropping, and by the time Arlene departed again, the two women had risen and were paying their bill at the cash register near the front door. As much as I wanted to run after them and hear the end of the story—just what had the police asked Derek anyway?—the fragrant scent of beef and bacon was making my mouth water, and besides, it was none of my business.

I polished off my burger in record time and was halfway through my coconut cream pie when Benji Morning strode into the restaurant, and my day got a whole lot more complicated.

CHAPTER FOUR

The pie stuck in my throat.

Benji approached the woman at the counter with a familiar greeting. She came out from behind the cash register and gave him a quick one-armed hug, then beamed at the boy who accompanied him. The kid was about eleven or twelve, I guessed, and carried a sketch pad under his arm. He sported a head of wild, curly hair—more on the brown side than Benji's auburn, but there was still enough of a resemblance to make me take notice.

Did Benji have a kid?

From the way he placed his hand on the back of the boy's neck to urge him forward, it seemed possible.

The coconut cream curdled in my stomach.

Benji withdrew a handful of folded paper—they looked like brochures—from the canvas satchel on his shoulder and set them on the counter beside the register while the boy ran to the bulletin board near the door and pinned a poster with exacting concentration.

Benji married? A father?

I supposed it wasn't so farfetched. I mean, I'd been married too, briefly. Why not Benji? It didn't feel right, though. In the back of my mind, I'd always imagined him still pining for me.

"Say thank you to Randi," Benji told the boy with a gentle nudge. The boy repeated this carefully, with a dull intonation.

Then, just as Benji turned to go, he caught sight of me. There was a split second when I thought, *This is it, he's recognized me,* because his eyes seemed to glow brighter and his cheeks flushed. But then his smile faded, and his face grew tight.

How could he not know me? Yes, I'd physically changed, but he'd been my best friend. We might have only known each other for seven short years, yet even now, all these years later, I could say with impunity that no relationship in my life had ever come close to the bond I'd shared with Benji. Not my friendships in Seattle, nor my many romantic entanglements. Hell, not even my marriage.

He was supposed to know me. Had I changed that much?

The day after we'd moved into the house on North Star Lane, this squeaky-voiced six-year-old, with big, buggy eyes and wild orange hair, had come running across the street. He'd worn a red bath towel pinned to his shoulders, and it'd hung down to the backs of his knees. "Nice bike," he'd exclaimed, picking up the BMX bike I'd left carelessly on the lawn. "Can I ride it?"

"It's a bribe," I'd told him with all the superiority of an almost-seven-year-old. "For moving out here. Who are you supposed to be?"

"D'uh, Superman."

From that day on, we'd been inseparable.

My face heated as he came toward me now, the reaction uncontrollable. Worse was the curl of attraction unfurling in my stomach and seeping down into my groin. That hadn't been there twenty years ago—not *this* strong. For a split second, I indulged it and let my dick do the thinking, as I would if he were any other guy. By the time he stopped at my table, clutching the strap of his satchel and holding it in front of him like a shield, I was aware of him in a decidedly adult, definitely more-than-friends way. And I really had to stop calling him Benji; he was a man now, over six feet tall, and the boyish name no longer fit.

"You're still here," he said.

Once again I was lost for words, which wasn't like me at all. *Get a grip, Buchanan.* "Uh, yeah."

"I Googled you," he said haughtily. "You're a Pulitzer finalist. Not just once, but twice."

Was he impressed? God, I wanted him to be impressed, even though those successes were several years behind me and only served to remind me of how quickly my career had stalled.

"You know what they say: always the bridesmaid, never the bride."

His eyes narrowed. "Why is someone with your credentials here in the first place? One missing girl is hardly worth the trip."

"I, ah, have other business in the area," I mumbled vaguely. The words were coming from my mouth, but I had no control over them.

"Mm-hmm," he said.

I flushed deeper. "Is that your son?" While we'd been talking, the boy had snuck up behind Benji—Ben—and now he whirled around at my question.

"My . . .?" Ben's eyebrows rose, and a startled giggle burst from his lips. "Sebastian? No, he's in my Saturday morning class." He put a hand on the boy's shoulder and drew him closer. "He's being my helper today. Aren't you, Seb?"

"Mom said I could. Ima good helper," the boy mumbled, barely moving his lips. He wouldn't make eye contact, but stared fixedly at a point to my left.

"Yes, you are." Ben stood there, a notch between his eyebrows as he stared at me. The napkin wilted in my sweaty palms under that scrutiny. It seemed like he was waiting for me to say something more, but I couldn't imagine what.

Then, with a final, hurt look at me, he turned away. "Well, come on, let's go, Sebastian. We've got more places to hit."

Sebastian waved. "Bye."

I watched them leave and disappear around the front of the building. For several minutes after, I pushed around the remainder of my pie on my plate, unable to finish though it was the best thing I'd eaten in a long time. Finally, I waved Arlene down and asked for the bill, then threw down a tip and went up to the cash register to pay.

At the counter, the stack of flyers Benji had left drew my attention. The glossy paper advertised an art show and sale at the Community Hall for next week. In support of an organization called the Alton Art Program.

"Do you know anything about this?" I asked the woman who worked the register. Randi, Ben had called her.

"Sure. That's Ben Morning's group. He puts on that show every year. Even donates some of his own pieces—not that I'm into that modern stuff—all those strange trees he paints. They give me the willies. But it helps raise money for the program, and it gets the kids excited."

Ben was an artist? That made sense. He'd always been doodling when I'd known him—little sketches of superheroes and animals when the rest of us had been drawing big dicks and hairy balls. "Kids?"

"Ben teaches art at the high school, but he also runs a free all-ages drop-in program at the Hall. Art therapy, he calls it. The students seem to get a kick out of showing off their stuff. Some of it's not half bad either. My daughter was in his program last year. At first I thought it was a load of nonsense. But it really helped her work through some stuff, you know."

How noble.

"If you're still in the area then, you should check it out," she advised. "They do it up big. It's catered and everything."

With any luck I'd be back in civilization by next week. Still I said, "I'll keep it in mind. Thanks."

Moving to one side so the customer behind me could pay his bill, I folded the flyer and tucked it inside my coat.

"Hey, wait, I know who you are," Arlene burst out, suddenly at my elbow. "We went to school together. You were on my bus route home. I remember because you hung around with Ben all the time. That's what did it—seeing you two together again." She snapped her fingers together.

"Alex Colville," I supplied, figuring she was trying to recall my name, or rather the name I'd gone by then. The elementary and high schools were located beside each other and shared school buses to save money, so it hadn't been uncommon for the grades to mix. But even on the bus there had been a strict clique system, and those seniors without cars, or friends with cars, had swarmed to the back, while losers like Ben and me had stayed up front, close to the driver for protection. I was surprised that she remembered us.

"That's it!" Arlene said. "Janet's little brother. Sandy, wasn't it? Sandra Dee—like in *Grease*." She laughed, and I wanted to retrieve the tip I'd left her. "Wow, I'd never have recognized you without Ben. It's Arlene, Arlene Aspinall. Jerkovic is my maiden name."

It didn't sound familiar. "You know my sister?"

"Oh, not very well. I didn't run in those circles then. But everyone knew Misty. She always scored the best Mary Jane, you know." Her eyes widened. "Isn't it such a shame? It's all anyone's been talking about lately. You should have been here a couple of weeks ago when they found that car. They had out the dogs, divers, even a helicopter. It was a real circus. Folks are saying she must have been another one."

"Another what?"

"Another missing girl on the Highway of Tears. You know about that, right?"

Those ominous billboards loomed in the back of my mind. "I've seen the signs."

"Dozens of girls, maybe more, have gone missing along this highway, for decades."

My skin prickled with unease. "How is this not bigger news?" the journalist in me asked.

"Oh, it makes the news cycle every so often. Sometimes tourists will have seen that *Dateline* episode and bring it up. I never thought that could have happened to Misty, though. I feel kind of guilty now," Arlene said.

"Why?"

"I always assumed Misty ran away. We all did. Except for her mom. Randall Kennedy even said he saw her in PG a couple of years ago." Here she lowered her voice. "I figured after the things her and Janet got up to . . . you know. And she was always on about getting out of here. But if someone killed her, well, that's different."

"What do you mean, 'the things they got up to'?"

"Oh nothing, really. I shouldn't have said anything—just me and my big mouth. My husband says I'm such a gossip. There was that whole scandal with the Spring Formal, you know. But they were only rumors."

"Table five up," someone called from the kitchen, and Arlene groaned, already moving away, back to her tables.

"Hey, stop by again some time. We can reminisce. And if you see Janet, tell her I said hi."

I promised to do that and made my escape before I ran into someone else from my past. It wasn't until a few hours later, as I prepared to meet Janet at the hospital, Arlene's comment came back to me.

Our high school had been too small to hold a prom only for seniors, so the all-ages Spring Formal had been the social event of the year. But I didn't recall anything odd happening, not that I'd ever gone. Neither had Janet. And what was that bit about her and Misty getting into trouble? As far as I knew, Janet had been a good student. Up until that last semester anyway. She'd barely talked back, let alone been in any sort of trouble. Except—

Except there was that time, just before our last Christmas here— that would have been December of 1995—when the cops brought her home in a squad car. I was in my room when the flashing lights and the angry murmur of voices made me look out the window. Benji had even radioed over on our walkie-talkies, wanting to know what was going on. At first I'd thought it must be about Dad, but when I'd ventured out of my room and peeked down the hall, it had been Janet and Mom arguing in low, hushed tones.

I searched my memories for more details. Mom had been pissed. Something about bad influences and Janet not getting into college. Then Janet screaming, "I'm not going to college anyway," and storming off into her room.

When I'd asked Mom about it the next morning, she'd said it was none of my business. But Janet had been grounded for a long time after that night. Come to think of it, she and Mom had fought a lot more too.

I was so absorbed in my thoughts that I didn't notice Katy, Dad's nurse, in the hallway on my way to Dad's room until she greeted me. "Oh, hey there. I thought it was you. It's Alex, right?" She wore emerald-green scrubs today, and the hue brought out the green in her eyes. "Janet's in with him now."

"Thanks."

She fixed me with a smile. "How are you making out?"

"Still getting re-acclimated."

"Janet says you're from New York."

"That's where I'm based at the moment, yes."

"It's nice that you came all this way. I'm sure Jerry's grateful."

I snorted. "You think?"

"Well, Janet is at least. I know she was hoping you'd come."

That seemed odd. It wasn't like we'd ever been very close, and so far, she'd given me no sign she was thrilled with my presence. "You two are good friends, then?"

"Oh, no, not really. I only know her through your dad. This is a small place. You become close to the patients and their families." She smiled sadly. "She's taking this pretty hard."

"Yeah. She's always been Daddy's girl."

"But not you?"

"Definitely not a daddy's girl," I quipped. She blushed, but her eyes glinted with a wicked humor as she gave me a closer inspection. Absurdly flattered by the attention, I chuckled. "You might say we have a contentious relationship."

"Ah, got it. I have three other siblings." Katy peered at me from beneath her bangs. "You must be going stir-crazy though, away from the big city. I, um, don't normally do this, but are you interested in getting a drink one night?"

I automatically glanced at her left hand, which was happily bare. She caught me at it and smirked. "Divorced."

"Look at that. We already have something in common. Yes, I'd love to grab a drink."

Someone called to her from the far end of the corridor. "Oops, I better go. How's tomorrow?"

I blinked. Assertive. I liked that. "Tomorrow is great."

"Good. I'll meet you at Hannigan's—know where that is?"

"I'm sure I'll find it."

She was already backing down the hall. "Eight?"

"Eight it is." I watched her go, checking out the sway of her hips as she marched away. It took a certain kind of woman to make hospital scrubs sexy. She glanced over her shoulder, gifting me with a wry smile. Yes, my day was definitely improving.

I was still smiling to myself as I entered Dad's room.

"I'm so sorry, Dad."

Janet's words, softly spoken, made my heart seize. My first thought as I saw her, back to me, standing by the bed, was that it was—mercifully—over.

"Is he . . . ?"

Janet whirled around, wiping at her cheeks, giving me a glimpse of Dad laying there with his eyes open. And yellow. "Jesus," I gasped. "His eyes."

"Jaundice." If possible Janet looked worse than the day before, like she'd aged a decade overnight.

"You okay?" I asked.

She smiled weakly. "Hey, Dad. Sandy's here. Just like you wanted. We're all together now."

I quirked an eyebrow but held my tongue.

Dad didn't so much as blink. It was disconcerting.

"Is it a coma?" I asked.

"No, not yet. Sometimes he gets like this." She turned pleading eyes to me. "Why don't you talk to him? He can hear you."

Talk to him? What the hell did I say to a man I hadn't seen in ten years? Nice to see you after all this time? Sorry you never cared enough about us to visit? Why'd you let Mom take us so far away?

Did you really say Misty's name, or was I imagining things?

Janet nudged me.

"Uh, hi, Dad." I might have imagined it, but I thought I saw a flicker of life in his eyes. "Sorry it took me so long to get here." My lips were suddenly as dry and rough as sandpaper. "Um, I've been out at your place." *Throwing your sad, pitiful life into the dumpster.* I looked at Janet for help.

"Sandy's going to stick around awhile," she said with false cheer.

A definite blink that time. A spasm of pain cut across his face. His eyes—those freakish yellow eyes—struggled to focus on me as he came back from wherever he'd been. "Who are you?" he whispered.

"It's Alex—Sandy, Dad."

"Sandy?" Moisture leaked from the corner of his eyes. "I had a boy named Sandy. I don't see him much."

I tamped down on my anger. "That's me. I'm your . . . I'm your son."

"My son?" The papery folds of his sallow skin trembled. A trickle of pity I didn't want to feel stirred in my gut. "You don't look like my Sandy."

"It's been a long time."

"A long time," he repeated. "I wish . . ."

What did he wish? I leaned closer.

"I don't suppose you brought a drink for your old man?"

I jerked away. "Are you serious?"

"This place is as dry as a nun's pussy."

"Dad," Janet admonished.

"What? A little tipple's not going to hurt me now. Might as well enjoy my last days. So, did you?"

"No, Dad, I didn't bring you booze." Furious, I stalked to the other side of the room and then back. Was this what I'd flown three thousand miles for? We hadn't seen each other in years, and the first thing he asked for was a drink? I was a fool to think he'd changed. That he *could* change. This whole trip was a waste of time.

"She was here. Did you see her?" A look of fear crossed over his face. "Her eyes, her eyes . . . I think she's waiting for me." He didn't seem to be talking to us anymore.

I had a sudden thought. "Do you remember Misty Morning, Dad?"

Janet grabbed my shoulder and pulled me aside. "What are you doing?"

"I swear I heard him say her name yesterday."

"So—"

"So, I want to know why."

"What else could I do?" Dad said clearly, and we both spun around.

"Do?" I asked.

"My Janie deserves better. A father's got to do what's best for his family."

Janet sagged. "He's talking about mom. About us."

I sneered. As usual it was all about Janet. *Janet* deserved better. "And what about Mom? Didn't she deserve better too?"

"Did she send you?" Now he fixed those yellow eyes on me. "She did this to me. She ruined my life." His thin face contorted, and suddenly he became a yellow-eyed demon, spewing venom. "Fucking bitch. Cunt. I'm glad she's gone."

My entire body flinched. "Shut the fuck up!" I shouted. "Don't you dare talk about Mom like that."

Janet bodily pushed me to the far corner of the room before I could get too close. She was a big girl and had no trouble.

"What the hell was that?" I demanded, breathing hard.

"He doesn't know what he's saying anymore, Sandy. It's lies and gibberish half the time. The other day he told me he didn't have a daughter." She blew out a breath. "Don't listen to it."

"Fuck! This is crazy." I grabbed my hair, struggling to calm down. "I don't know why I bothered to come."

"Because he's our father," she said tiredly.

"No, maybe he's *your* father. But he's not mine." The old anger rose in my chest before I could stop it. After all this time I thought I'd buried my resentment, but no, it was still there, and being here was bringing it up again.

I glanced over her shoulder at the figure in the bed. While we'd been talking, Dad had fallen asleep.

There were too many emotions roiling in my chest. They pulled in a dozen directions at once, leaving me on the verge of splintering. One thing was for sure, I couldn't spend another minute here.

"Where are you going?" Janet called after me as I raced out of the room.

I didn't answer her, although I knew exactly where I was headed. Back to the place I'd always run to when things got tough at home. The only place where I'd ever felt wanted.

CHAPTER FIVE

My memories of Dad are different from Janet's; whether that's because she had longer with him, or was older when we left, or simply because mine are tinged with decades of animosity, I don't know. She sees him as misunderstood, worn down by the pressure to be the main provider and breadwinner, whereas the image I always fall back on is a man with dead eyes in a stained wifebeater . . .
—From "My Father's Son" by Alex Buchanan

The frantic barking began as soon as I slammed the car door shut. It was only five in the afternoon, but already nearly dark. A sensor light on the side of the garage burst on, and I froze in fear as the dog—a wolf I thought at first—surged toward me. It stopped only a few feet away, pulled up short by the limits of its long leash. The chain stretched taut, and I was relieved to see that it seemed securely looped around the bottom post of the garage staircase.

The dog blew clouds of spittle in the cold air as it snapped and snarled.

The door at the top of the stairs opened, and Ben stepped out from the second floor of the garage. He whistled, and the dog, now clearly a beautiful white, gray, and black husky, instantly loped in his direction, tail wagging. I remained where I was.

"Luna's harmless," Ben called, unsnapping the chain from around the dog's neck. "I have to keep her tied up if she's not in the pen though, so she doesn't run loose and aggravate the bears."

Or unsuspecting visitors. No longer fearing a mauling, I took a tentative step closer, the frozen grass crunching beneath my boots.

Ben wrapped his sweater tighter around his body. "I wondered if you'd ever show up. Come on up, Sandy. Or is it Alexander now?"

I stopped on the third step from the bottom. "You know?"

"A guy never forgets his first kiss."

"Yeah," I mumbled as I climbed the stairs and followed him inside.

The garage loft, which had once only been used for storage, had been converted into one spacious finished room. The dog, Luna, gave a yawn and hunkered down in front of a pot-bellied woodstove that centered the space, head resting on her paws but pale-blue eyes still fixed on me.

"This is nice. I remember when there was nothing up here but mouse droppings and Christmas decorations. Do you live up here?" I asked, noticing the small kitchen and seating area tucked at one end of the loft, and in the corner there was a double bed. With its warm white walls and pine-planked vaulted ceiling, the whole space was rustic and cozy, and I began to relax for the first time since I'd been back.

"I do." Ben stood patiently, watching me as I examined his place. The east-facing end was clearly his studio. There was an easel in front of the large windows and a long work table on one wall littered with brushes, bottles and all sorts of tools I didn't recognize. The tang of paint thinner hung in the air.

"Have you known about me this whole time?" I asked when I was done with my survey and couldn't avoid facing him any longer.

"Only since I looked you up. There was this photo with one of your articles—well, it reminded me of you." He laughed nervously. "Well, the boy I used to know."

"Why didn't you say anything earlier at the restaurant?"

"Why didn't *you*?" He cocked his head and folded his arms across his chest. The sleeves of his long gray cardigan were bunched to his elbows, and a thick leather cuff decorated his left wrist. The fine golden hair dusting his forearms drew my attention and sent a whisper of heat to my groin. "Why all the pretense?"

Time to fess up. I tore my gaze away from his arms. "Would you believe me if I said 'I don't know'? That it just happened?"

Ben made a sound, halfway between a snort and a scoff.

I sighed. "I guess I was afraid of how you'd react to seeing me again. After so long. Your mom assumed I was there about Misty and I . . . just went with it. It was stupid."

"Yeah, it was. Why would you think I wouldn't want to see you?"

"Um, because of how things ended? Because I promised to write to you and I didn't."

"We're not kids anymore, Sandy. Sorry. I mean Alex."

Ben crossed to his workspace and began rearranging items on the table. I caught a glimpse of several faint silvery lines running horizontally across the pale underside of his right forearm. Jesus. What were they?

"Ben?"

He quickly tugged down his sleeves, brushing off my query. "So, you're really not here for a story?"

"Not yours."

"I don't get it."

"Dad's dying."

His face softened. "I'm sorry."

"He's in the hospital in Smithers with end-stage cirrhosis, but he doesn't have long."

"God, I had no idea. I run into your dad in town now and then. Sometimes he recognizes me and says hi. Other times . . ."

"Yeah." It felt like I had glass in my throat. "He didn't know me either."

I fought back the image of yellowed eyes and joined Ben in his studio space. Several smaller canvases in various stages of completion were stacked against the walls, but it was the large one on the easel that drew me in. Art had never really been my thing, but something about this called to me. It was a mountain landscape, but not like any I'd seen before. The brush strokes were bold and chaotic, the colors deep, evoking a sense of danger, of darkness. The skeletal branches of the spruce trees seemed both lifeless and menacing at the same time. I was reminded of the woman in the restaurant who had called them "creepy trees." Now I understood why.

"So, you're an artist," I observed—a dumb thing to say, but my usual conversation skills had deserted me the moment I entered Ben's presence. "These are all yours?"

He shrugged. "It pays the bills."

"Yeah?"

"My clientele are mostly local hotels and restaurants. The tourists love this stuff."

"You're good. I mean, I'm no expert, but I have some friends in the art scene and you're as talented, if not more."

"Thanks." Ben came to stand beside me, and once again I felt that same intense pull that I had in the restaurant. The air turned electric. If I'd met him in New York and the connection was this strong, we'd be in bed by now.

"Is Janet here with you too?" he asked.

"She lives in Smithers. She moved back a couple of years ago."

"Oh, are you staying with her?"

"God no. I've got a room at the Summit View." An awkward silence fell. Now that I was here, I had no clue what to say. "Have there been any further developments on Misty?"

Ben's bearded jaw tightened as he turned away from me. "I'd rather not talk about Misty."

"O-kay." Our conversation stalled. I ached to erase the last twenty years, to knock down these walls that had suddenly appeared. We were like strangers. We hadn't even shaken hands. "How did things turn out so shitty, Benji? Everything was good until that summer."

"You were thirteen. Of course you'd say that," Ben replied quietly. "Everything seems great at that age."

Didn't it though? "How have you been? You look good."

"Do I?"

He was making this difficult, and I had no one to blame but myself. An idea leapt into my head. "Let's go."

"Where?"

"You'll see."

I considered it a good sign that Ben only hesitated a fraction of a second before grabbing a jacket from the hook next to the door and following me out. With a little prodding, he'd always done what I asked.

I'd boxed him in the driveway, so we took my car. Besides, only I knew where we were headed.

"Where *are* we going?" Ben asked as I pulled out of the driveway and turned east.

"Patience."

Several miles down 16, on the other side of the Alton town limits, I turned onto the unmarked service road that led up the mountain to the radio tower. I slowed to a crawl, squinting into the darkness as I searched for the dirt road I remembered. There were hundreds of abandoned and unused roads scattered over this region, but one in particular that Ben and I had traveled many times over the years.

Ben swung around in his seat to face me. "You're not . . . Alex, I don't know if it's even passable."

"There it is!" The tracks were faint, but not totally obscured. The road must still be used by someone, likely teens looking for a private place to make out or get high. I turned off the gravel and onto the hard-packed dirt. Trees enveloped us immediately, and what little light we had from the moon was blotted out. Long-fingered branches screeched menacingly across the windows and made strange shadows in the headlights.

"You're crazy, you know that?" Ben said. "They built a new road up the mountain a couple of years ago. I can't believe I let you talk me into this."

That made me laugh with relief. Not everything had changed after all. "Can't you?" I asked with a knowing grin.

Benji narrowed his eyes and glared back. "We're not thirteen anymore."

We bounced over the lumpy terrain, hard enough for Benji to hit his head on the roof. "Oof." He rubbed the top of his head and braced himself on the dashboard. "Isn't this a rental? You're going to destroy the undercarriage. Not to mention scratch the paint."

He was probably right. I'd lose my deposit, but at the moment I couldn't care less. There was a rush of familiar excitement in my stomach, and Benji was talking to me. That's all that mattered.

"It's getting dark," he warned. "And the bears have been active lately."

"We used to come out here all the time and nothing ever happened."

"In the daylight," Ben pointed out. "And we were stupid then."

"Were we? I'm not so sure. Sometimes I think that kids have it right. Things seem so much clearer when you're young. We knew what we wanted. But when we get older, we start overthinking things and complicating our lives."

"So you'd rather be like Peter Pan and stay a boy forever?"

"I didn't say that." Before my thoughts got too deep, there was a break in the trees and we emerged into a clearing. The Explorer suddenly lost traction and lurched to the left. I quickly spun the wheel and managed to right us before we went off the dirt road.

Ben gripped the door handle. "We're never going to make it in this. If I'd known you wanted to go off-roading, we could have taken my Jimmy—it has four-wheel drive."

We fishtailed again. The road was muddier in this section, and I was losing traction fast.

"You'll get . . . stuck," Ben finished as we came to a shuddering halt. I switched gears and reversed but the wheels only spun.

I tried this a couple of times before giving up and turning off the motor. We sat in silence with only the tick of the cooling engine for company.

"This brings back memories," Benji finally said.

"How so?"

"Here I am, once again blindly following you into peril. Like that time you convinced me we *weren't* tramping through a patch of poison ivy."

I bit the inside of my mouth to hold back a laugh. "That was something, wasn't it?"

"At least *you* were wearing long pants. I had shorts on."

We looked at each other. Ben's lips twitched, a sure sign we were *both* recalling the image of him painted pink with calamine lotion. I grinned, and before long we were both laughing,

And it was good.

"Thank you," I said with a huff of relief.

"For what?

"For not saying 'I told you so.' You always were good about that."

Ben folded his arms across his chest. "Now what, fearless leader? I suppose you expect me to get out and push too."

"Nope." I opened my door.

"*Now* what are you doing?" he asked.

I bent down and gave him my patented persuasive smile—the one I used on difficult subjects—before shutting the door and walking around to sit on the hood. Between the trees, the inky sky was thick with stars so bright it seemed I could reach out and touch them.

A few minutes later, Ben joined me, although he stayed on the ground and merely leaned against the hood. "Are you nuts? It's cold, Alex."

"Wuss. All we need is a six-pack and a good joint so we can have ourselves a proper bush party. Isn't that what the cool kids did?"

"Wouldn't know."

I turned my head away so he wouldn't see my smile. The engine was warm beneath my ass, keeping some of the chill at bay. "I'd forgotten what the open sky looked like."

"Where do you live now?"

"New York. Well, Brooklyn, but New York sounds better."

"What were you trying to prove, Alex?" Ben demanded. A very good question—one I'd asked myself dozens of times. But I gathered Ben was referring to us being here and not the state of my life in general.

"I don't know. I wanted to see it all of a sudden. The spot we used to go to." I sat back up. It hadn't been much of a hideout, really. Just a sheltered spot in the forest halfway up the mountain, beside a cold, clear stream. The drooping lower branches of that giant spruce had seemed to form a shield around us. "Did you ever go back?" It was selfish of me, I know, but it suddenly seemed very important that Benji hadn't taken anyone else there. It was *our* place.

"A couple of times after you left. But there wasn't much point in being there without you."

I had to peek at him then, secretly pleased by his response. He had his head down, hair falling across his face, and his hands jammed in the pockets of his jacket. The position was so familiar, so ... dear to me that a swirl of emotion rose in my chest. I couldn't imagine any other place I'd rather be right now.

Benji cleared his throat and straightened. "Your mom? How's she doing?"

"She's good. She got remarried not long after we left. She's in Seattle."

"So you're on the East Coast, your mom's on the West, and Janet's up here? Geez, you guys couldn't get farther away from each other if you tried, could you?"

There was more truth to that statement than I wanted to admit. Mom might have taken us both to Seattle, but as soon as we could, Janet and I had gone our own ways. Janet had flunked out of junior college in her first year and then high-tailed it back to BC, while I eventually went off to Vancouver and the University of British Columbia. I'm sure a psychologist would have had a lot to say about our family dynamic.

I tried to change the subject. "How long have you lived above the garage?"

"Oh wow, a long time. I went to UVic for college. But that didn't work out . . ." Ben jabbed his hands deeper into his pockets and hunched forward. I had the sense there was more to the story, but he clearly didn't want to tell it. Which frustrated the hell out of me, because I was desperate to know every little thing about him and all that had happened in the last two decades.

"You've been in Alton this whole time, then? Why would you stay? It's only taken me two days and already I can see this town is dying."

"I like it here. Besides, Angela needs someone to keep an eye on her. I can't really leave her on her own."

"That bad?"

"She's obsessed, Alex. Or hadn't you noticed?" His breath blew steam in the air. Still he wouldn't look at me. "You weren't around—after. You've seen what she's like now; you should have seen her then. She was fired from the mill for taking too much time off. She's blown through most of her savings and Dad's insurance hiring private investigators. And psychics. Then there are the people who call and say they have information but want money in return."

"No wonder you didn't want me around."

"Just when things finally start to die down, there'll be another tip, another sighting, another fraudster dangling the bait. And she always takes it."

"Why stay, then? She's not your responsibility."

"She's my mother," he said with a furrowed brow. "Besides, I feel . . . like I'm tied to this place. Like it's part of me."

I had a hard time determining if he was happy or sad about that. "I'm sorry, Ben."

"It's not your fault." He shrugged and, finally, sent me a small smile. The wall between us began to crumble, and I reached for something, anything, to keep it going.

"I saw your flyer in the restaurant. The one for the art show next week. The ladies there sure think highly of you."

Ben's smile was bashful. "I do what I can. There aren't a lot of resources around here . . ."

"For kids like Sebastian? What's wrong with him anyway?" I winced. "That sounded douche-y, didn't it?"

"Little bit, yeah. There's nothing *wrong* with him. He's on the spectrum. But my classes aren't only for those with special needs. They're for anyone who's struggling—adults, teens. Art helped me get through a lot of things, so I want to give that to others." He frowned. "Why are you smiling?"

"Because I knew you'd turn out like this."

"Like what?"

"Altruistic. Helping others. It's who you are." If I had been the bolder, take-charge one, Benji had always been the thoughtful heart of our friendship. He had been the one to calm me down when I got angry, or make me laugh when my parents' fighting got to be too much. He'd always been the one I'd turned to when things got dark, even though he'd had enough problems of his own. "You haven't changed."

"We all change." Benji fell silent after that cryptic remark.

"So. Anyone special in your life?" I ventured.

In the deepening shadows, I glimpsed a flirty smile. "Are you fishing?"

Was I? Maybe. I couldn't deny there was a spark there. It wouldn't take much to turn it into something bigger. "No. Just making conversation."

Ben shrugged. "No one special. I can count on one hand the number of gay men within a hundred-mile radius." The easy confirmation of his sexuality made my heart rate spike. *That's not why I'm here.*

"Not much of a dating pool."

Ben continued, oblivious. "During ski season, I can sometimes get lucky, but that's really not my scene. Otherwise I'll take a few days and go over to Prince George. I have a friend there."

"That's almost two hundred miles," I exclaimed. "No serious relationships, then?"

"I haven't been pining for you, if that's what you're getting at."

It wasn't, but the fact he'd brought it up pleased me. "But you're out?"

He laughed. "Yes, I'm out. I don't think it was much of a surprise to anyone."

"And no problems with that up here in the great white north?"

"Well, I'm not exactly parading lovers through town, but no, no problems. At least none that get said to my face." He turned his head to me. "What about you? I mean relationship-wise. You're not wearing a ring."

Coward. "One divorce. One failed long-term relationship," I enumerated. My ten-month marriage to Tanya right after college didn't bear repeating. She'd long ago remarried—a guy more "emotionally available"—and moved on with her life. And my treatment of Will during our years together wasn't something I was proud of or wanted to discuss. Ben likely already thought I was an ass for lying to his mom. He didn't need me to confirm it. "No kids, thank God. Us Colvilles have a hard enough time with relationships, I can't imagine adding kids to the mix. Did I mention Janet divorced her third husband?"

"But things worked out for your mom," Ben pointed out. "She's happy, right?"

"Yeah, the second time around."

The memory of our first and last kiss still lingered in my mind. I waited for Ben to bring it up, to ask *the* question. The one I knew he wanted to. Hell, the one *I* wanted him to. But he didn't. And then the opportunity to come fully clean passed.

"Tell me about your career," he said. "Apparently you're a hot-shot writer."

I scoffed. "Not anymore, I'm not."

"Are you serious? You have a whole Wikipedia page. That makes you famous in my book. I had no idea you were so successful. A finalist for your first Pulitzer at twenty-seven, winner of a Sigma Delta Chi Award. And now a writer for the *New York Journal*. That's impressive, Alex."

"Is it? Did you happen to check those dates? It's been three years since I wrote anything of note. I'm stuck in a rut and going nowhere fast. It's frustrating as hell." Now it sounded like I was moaning. Which I was.

"What happened?" Ben asked.

"No idea. I freelanced for a while, and then did a brief stint with the Associated Press, but about the time I hit thirty, my 'rising' career hit a wall. The ideas dried up. I couldn't pitch a story to save my life. Now, everything I produce is mediocre, and there's nothing worse than mediocrity

for a writer. Oh, it's fine for doctors' waiting rooms, but the *Journal* was supposed to be my stepping stone to something better—maybe the *Times* or the *New Yorker*—and that hasn't panned out the way I'd hoped."

"You can't expect to produce a work of literature every time. If it's any consolation, I thought you should have won that last Pulitzer. Your account of that family in Las Vegas fighting to save their home from foreclosure was heartbreaking."

"You read it?"

Ben ducked his head. "It was there—online. You have a real way with words, Alex. I could feel their desperation. I don't know how many times I teared up. It was far more interesting than the piece on municipal corruption that won. Not that my opinion counts for anything."

"It means a lot, actually. Thanks." I cleared my throat. "That's probably as close as I'll ever get. I don't even have my own column; I'm only a floater."

"What's that?"

"I fill in with sections when someone's sick or on vacation."

"That sounds interesting. You must get to cover a variety of subjects."

"That's one way to look at it."

"Self-pity much?"

I laughed. "Okay, yes, you're right. I'm whining. Who needs a Pulitzer when I can write fluff pieces like 'How I survived my absentee father'?"

"What?"

"It's something my editor talked me in to—he promised me a feature spot to write about coming home and my feelings at reuniting with Dad. He thinks it has a human-interest angle that readers will love."

"Let me get this straight—you're planning to exploit your father's death? *That's* the story you're working on?"

The judgment lacing his tone made me stiffen. "You make it sound so . . . cold."

"It *is* cold. After twenty years, the only thing that's got you back here is the promise of a headline?"

"It's a solid concept," I insisted. Fuck him, I didn't need to justify my actions to Ben, or anyone. "Plenty of great writers use their own experiences as material, and it's coming together nicely—I've already started writing. In fact, it could be a good piece; maybe not Pulitzer good, but still respectable."

Ben snorted. "I could tell you were driven, but is there anything you won't do for a story?"

"There's nothing wrong with wanting to be the best," I snapped. "And don't talk to me about cold."

"What's that supposed to mean?"

"Nothing." I jumped off the hood and headed for the driver's seat. It was time to see what I could do to get us out of here. An ominous rustling in the underbrush transformed the woods into an eerie, dangerous place, and the temperature was dropping steadily.

"No, seriously. What are you getting at?" Ben asked as he dogged my footsteps.

I lashed out without thinking. "Your sister has been missing for twenty goddamn years, and you don't seem overly concerned about finding out what happened. *That's* cold."

"You don't have any right to say those things to me, Alexander Colville. Not anymore. You have no idea what things were like."

Dropping back into the driver's seat, I put the Explorer in drive and gave it just a bit of gas to rock the wheels.

The front wheels continued to spin.

Without a word, Ben stalked into the trees.

"What are you doing?" I shouted. Was he going to walk away and leave me there, in the middle of the woods?

"What does it look like?" he said. "Getting us out of here."

I heard the rustle of leaves and the crack of wood, and then he stepped back into the glare of the headlights, dragging a long branch behind him. He disappeared for a second as he crouched in front of the vehicle, then popped up again and moved to the side. "Now reverse slowly."

I did as he instructed. There was a slight resistance at first, and then the Explorer broke free. I kept going until I was sure I was on solid ground.

"Holy cow, MacGyver," I said in admiration when Ben joined me.

He grunted. "Just basic skills. Wedging a branch behind the tires usually does the trick."

"I'll remember that next time I'm stuck in the woods," I joked, but he sat stiffly beside me and didn't take the bait.

We drove back to Ben's much the same way as we'd left it—in silence.

Gravel crunched beneath the wheels as I pulled into his driveway. I was relieved when he didn't immediately jump out. Only now did it hit me how much I was dreading the lonely drive back to the motel, how much I wanted to hold on to this, to him, a little while longer.

"I'm sorry, about earlier," I said. "You're right. I shouldn't have said it."

"Twenty years is a long time, Alex. We're not the same people anymore. We can't pick up where we left off."

The odd thing was, to me it felt like we were doing exactly that. Yes, he was different. I was different. But at the same time, being together felt unbelievably familiar. I didn't say that to him though.

Finally, Ben spoke. "How long are you going to be around?"

"I don't know. I guess until Dad . . ." I winced. I'd almost forgotten about him tonight and wished Ben hadn't reminded me. "That sounds awful, doesn't it?"

"Why are you even here with me instead of spending whatever time you have left with him? You won't get your story that way."

I couldn't get Dad's words, those blazing yellow eyes, out of my head. "It's complicated."

"He's your dad, Alex. I know you probably have a lot of hard feelings, but don't do something you'll regret later." He opened the car door.

I grasped his wrist to halt him. "Ben, it was really good seeing you. Maybe we could get together again? Have dinner or something? I promise I won't be such a dick next time."

He searched my face. "I learned something else about you online."

"Oh?" My lungs seized.

"You're bisexual."

"Did you get that from Google too?"

"Wikipedia actually. It said you're dating a foreign correspondent. A *male* correspondent. Is that true?"

"Wikipedia is a little out of date. That was the long-term relationship I mentioned earlier. It's been over for a while."

Ben's arm tensed beneath my hand. "When did you figure it out?" His voice had become tight, and I thought I understood why.

"College," I hedged. *Liar. You knew much earlier. You just didn't have a name for it.* My head urged me to tell him more, tell him what he'd meant to me. Damn it, what he still apparently meant to me, judging by the fierce hold I had on his arm.

"Well, congratulations on coming out I guess. Were you planning to keep that a secret too?"

"It's clearly not a secret if it's on the internet. I didn't know how to bring it up with you."

Ben snorted, swinging around to fully face me. "Anything else you forgot to mention?"

"No, I think that's it."

"I'm not sleeping with you."

"I don't recall asking. Besides, that's not why I'm here."

"Isn't it?" he challenged.

I wouldn't say it hadn't been on my mind. In some ways we had unfinished business. But I also knew that if I had to choose, I didn't want to ruin the memory of our friendship with sex. So I tried to make light of it. "Well, Prince George *is* a long way to go just to get laid."

Ben sighed and mumbled something under his breath. Then, "Give me your phone."

I unlocked it and handed it over, watching as he sent a text to himself.

"There. Now you've got my number. I teach Tuesday, Wednesday, and Thursday afternoons, and Saturday mornings I've got my class. Other than that, I'm free if you're sticking around for a while."

He climbed out of my car, paused for a second, and then leaned back in. "But I'm not sleeping with you. You're about twenty years too late for that."

CHAPTER SIX

I thought a lot about what Ben had said. About avoiding my dad. I was a grown man. I should be the bigger person for once and put my hard feelings aside. Ben made it sound so simple though.

He'd always been my conscience, I realized with a start. My better half. When I'd wanted to join the Barry brothers and throw water balloons from the roof of the school, he'd talked me out of it, and saved me a month of detention. When I'd decided I was going to be a BMX daredevil and tried a jump down Mount Roddick, he'd convinced me to wear a helmet, so all I'd wound up with was a broken arm instead of a split skull. I guess I could say he'd saved my life.

Too bad he hadn't been around for the last twenty years.

And whose fault is that?

"Oh, shut up," I snapped as I pulled into the plaza where the hardware store was located the next day. The discovery of mouse droppings in Dad's kitchen cupboard had prompted my second trip in as many days. I should have simply turned the trailer over to Darnell and walked away instead of wasting my time cleaning, but if there was still a chance of selling it and making a small profit, then it could be worth it.

I parked the car, but as I headed toward the store, I was distracted by a man and a woman arguing a couple of rows away. Was that Angela Morning?

"For fuck's sake, leave me alone," the guy shouted, visibly tensing with anger. He wore a red polo shirt with the hardware store emblem on his bulky chest.

I hurried across the parking lot without thinking. "Mrs. Morning, are you all right?"

"Is *she* all right?" His thick mustache twitched with irritation as he splayed his hands wide. "She's the one harassing *me*."

"Just tell me where she is. Please," Angela begged. "That's all I want to know."

The man's face flushed darkly, all the way up to his receding hairline, until he was almost as red as his polo shirt. "For the last time, I don't know where she's at. I had nothing to do with it. If you don't stay away from me, from my family . . ." He left the threat hanging, whirled, and stomped off toward the hardware store.

"Who was that?" I asked.

"Misty's boyfriend."

"Derek Gagnon?" A million questions were running through my brain, but I wasn't certain I wanted to ask them. I'd promised myself to not get involved.

"Will you be okay?" I asked instead.

"I'll never be okay. Not as long as she's still out there."

"And you think Derek knows where she is?"

"I'm sure of it. He killed her."

The steel in her voice surprised me.

Walk away, Alex. Just walk away.

"Can I ask you something? Why are you so certain she didn't run away?" I'd recently read about the case of a man who went missing and was presumed dead by his family, only to turn up in Toronto thirty years later under another name. It did happen.

"Misty wouldn't do that to me," Angela asserted. "Besides, They found some scraps of clothes and her purse in her car. The purse was vinyl—it hardly looked touched. She wouldn't go anywhere without her purse."

"Was there anything else?"

"A necklace. One she used to always wear. The pendant was half—"

"A heart," I finished weakly. "I remember. Janet had the other half. When you put the two halves together it read, *Best Friends*."

No wonder Ben had been so certain.

"So you see? Something bad happened to my baby. I *feel* it."

I shook myself out of the daze that had claimed me. "But what makes you think Derek's involved?"

"Don't you watch *Dateline*? It's almost always the boyfriend."

I bit back a smile. "You'll need a bit more than television formulas to go on."

"He has a history."

Did she know that the police had paid Derek a visit too? I opened my mouth to ask but then shut it. I was here for mousetraps. I needed to remember that. But the siren song of a good story was beckoning.

Angela turned to me. "You're still here. Does that mean you've changed your mind?"

Crap. I hung my head. "I misled you, Mrs. Morning. I'm Alex Colville, Ben's—"

"Colville? Benji's friend. The chubby one? With the glasses? You lived across the street."

"Yeah, that's me."

"I'd never have recognized you." She narrowed her eyes. "So you're not a reporter then?"

I hesitated. What to tell her? "I am, but I'm not here for a story. My dad's dying."

"Oh, I'm sorry." Angela frowned. "But you could still investigate. I mean that's what you do, isn't it?"

"You seem to be doing well on your own."

"No one talks to me." She snorted. "No one cares anymore. Even the police have stopped taking my calls."

"I'm sorry, Angela, but—"

"I know I wasn't the best mother. I made mistakes. But . . . I need to do this. I need to bring my baby home." She clutched my arm. "Please. Can't you just ask around a bit? Someone has to know something. People don't just vanish."

"I'm not a private investigator—"

"I've hired private investigators. They weren't any help. Not when there's no trace to investigate. But you, you're from here. You knew Misty. You knew her friends."

I groaned inwardly. There was likely nothing I could do, but how was I supposed to ignore a request like that? I *wanted* to help.

And the truth was, I was interested. There was something worth exploring here. Maybe not Misty's story, but I couldn't deny the buzz of excitement running through me. The pitch was already crystalizing in my head. "How about this? I'll keep my ears open, and if I hear anything that might be important, I'll let you know."

"Thank you," she gushed. "Thank you."

"I'm not promising anything," I warned.

"I understand."

Did she? I worried that she might be expecting too much.

There was a sinking feeling in my stomach.

Ben would kill me when he learned about this.

Inside the hardware store, I grabbed what I needed. I was headed toward the checkout with my purchases when I saw Derek Gagnon there in aisle five doing inventory, and Angela Morning's anxious face swam in front of my eyes. Was it really possible that he'd killed Misty?

Before I knew it, I was backtracking, grabbing a box of rat poison off the shelf and then approaching the former bad boy.

"Excuse me." With a sheepish smile, I held up the traps in one hand and the poison in the other. "Could you tell me which one is better?"

He stiffened when he saw me. Suspicion streaked across his face, but he stopped short of outright hostility. Likely he didn't want to risk losing a customer. "That depends. The traps are generally faster but you gotta empty 'em. The poison now, problem is those critters can crawl off and die in the walls, and then you're stuck with the stink."

I gave an exaggerated shudder. "Thanks. Guess I'll go for the traps." I turned away, then back as if I'd forgotten something. "Hey, it's Derek, right?"

"Do I know you?"

"Alex Colville. I lived across the street from the Mornings."

His face turned crimson. "Fuck. I got the cops hounding me, that bitch, and now I got to worry about you messing up my life too?"

I held up my hands. "No, no. I'm only visiting. I just wanted to apologize for earlier—for Angela. She's under a lot of stress, as you can imagine."

He snorted. "You want to talk about stress? That bitch has been stirring up trouble for the last decade. But she's gone completely off her rocker since they found that car. She sits outside my house, accosts my wife—it's gotten to the point my son is afraid to leave home."

I grimaced. Maybe Angela *was* a bit unstable.

"Wait. Are you . . . Janet's brother?" he asked.

"That's me." It wasn't surprising Derek remembered my sister. He would have hung out with Misty's friends.

"I'm sick and tired of being treated like a suspect." He pointed his finger in my face. "I didn't touch her."

"I agree Angela's gone a bit overboard, but you have to admit that you do have a bit of a reputation." I searched my memories for more substantial rumors to see how he'd react. "You have a record, don't you?"

"I sold pot. I sure as hell didn't kill anybody. And I've cleaned up my act since then. I haven't been in trouble since—you can ask my wife."

The passion in his voice convinced me. "My mistake. Sorry. You know how small-town gossip is."

"If you heard shit about me from Janet, it's bullshit. She was always jealous, hated anybody Misty spent time with. 'Course that didn't stop her from enjoying my stash now and then." Before I could ask why he'd brought up Janet, Derek thrust out an arm to pound the metal shelf next to my head. I jumped.

"I keep telling people Misty and I weren't serious, man," he continued. "I wasn't a jealous boyfriend. We hooked up when one of us was horny, but she made it pretty clear that's all it was. Sometimes I got the feeling I was just for show—to piss her mom off."

"And you were fine with that?"

He gave me an *Are you crazy?* look. "Come on. You remember how hot she was. But trust me, if I'd known how much trouble that chick would cause me and my family, I never would have gotten involved."

I raised an eyebrow, and he snorted. "Who am I kidding? I probably still would have banged her. Never did have good sense back then."

"Let me ask you something, then: what did you think when she went missing?"

"Honestly, I figured she took off. She hated this place. Hated her mom. She talked about going to Banff and working in one of the hotels all the time."

"And you can't think of anyone who'd want to hurt her?" His eyes narrowed. Shit, had I pushed too far? "Hey, man, I'm only trying to help you out. If Angela had another viable suspect, she might leave you alone."

"Trust me, I would have said if I did. Do you think I like living under a cloud? But . . ."

"But?"

"Look, it's not like we were exclusive. But sometimes when we had sex, she'd just lay there, and I'd swear she was thinking of someone else."

"Who?"

He shrugged. "I told the cops all this."

"Any idea of who it might have been?"

"Take your pick. Half the town wanted to get into her pants."

Talking to Derek was leaving a bad taste in my mouth. For all her wayward behavior, Misty had still technically been underage. "Thanks, man. Sorry about earlier."

"Will you tell Angela to leave me alone now?"

"I'll see what I can do." I turned to leave.

"Hey!" Derek called. "Don't forget these." He held up my mousetraps.

I paid for them and left.

So much for staying out of it.

The afternoon passed quickly. I threw myself into cleaning, sorting, and packing. Most of Dad's clothes were too worn or filthy to give away, so they went out with the trash, along with the bedsheets and the grimy towels from the bathroom. A few small personal effects, like the family portrait and a framed picture of Mom and Dad on their wedding day, I packed up for keeping.

It was late in the afternoon, as I was taking a break from cleaning, that my eyes lit on the low walnut television stand that was next on my list to tackle. With a defeated sigh, I tugged one swollen door open and groaned. Inside was a stack of magazines. Great. More junk.

But these weren't just any magazines, as I saw when I hauled them out. My breath caught. These were *mine*. The ones I'd written for over the years. *Mother Jones*, *Forbes*, the *Rolling Stone* edition that marked my first big break—the issue with the chicks from that old show *The Hills* on the cover. Either Dad's reading tastes were incredibly eclectic or he had been following my career.

I leafed through them, stirring up memories, along with the dust. How had he obtained these all the way up here? I doubted the local 7-Eleven stocked *Harper's Bazaar*. Had Mom sent them? These magazines went back a good eight years. They'd been stored away neatly—well, neatly for him—and not left scattered about like the rest of the newspapers. And the edges of the pages were dog-eared, like he'd actually read them.

My knees suddenly weak, I sat down in the recliner. All these years, he'd never shown any interest in my career, in my life for that matter; never called to offer congratulations, never asked what I was up to. I'd assumed he didn't care.

Regret splashed in the back of my throat. I tried to picture him sitting here in this rundown tin can, surrounded by clutter and reading my words. What had he thought? Had I made him proud?

I set the magazines in the box I'd designated for keeping. Why? I didn't know. I had my own copies at home, but I didn't want them going into the garbage.

A slight breeze wafted across the back of my neck, and I shivered. Now that I'd stopped moving around, the trailer felt chilled again, and damn, was it that late? I still had to drive back to the motel, shower, and meet Katy for dinner. It would be good to just go out and have fun. The thought of the night ahead filled me with unexpected anticipation and warmed me up.

I was locking the door when my phone rang. It was the first time since I'd been here, and the sound made me jump.

"Mr. Buchanan?" An unfamiliar man's voice. My first thought was that it was the hospital, and my stomach twisted sharply.

"Yep, that's me," I replied cautiously, steeling myself for the news.

"Jerry Colville's son?"

"Yes."

"It's Blake McNamara. From the RCMP," he said. "Thanks for calling yesterday."

I exhaled a sigh of relief. "No problem." Quickly, I explained about Dad being in the hospital in Smithers and then paused. "What's this about?"

"You must have heard we're taking another look at the Morning case."

"You're twenty years too late, Sergeant. Maybe if you'd been more thorough when she first went missing, you wouldn't be scrambling now."

McNamara coughed. "I'll admit it wasn't handled well back then," he said brusquely. "But Misty was nearly eighteen years old. Her purse and clothes were gone, along with her vehicle—there was no reason to believe she wasn't a runaway."

And runaways didn't warrant major investigations. "So why do you want to talk to my dad?"

"I'm running down some statements from back then, and Jerry was one of the last people to see her."

"He was?" That was news to me. Alton had only a handful of officers, and back in ninety-six, it had taken a week before they finally passed the case to the regional detachment. I vaguely recalled a big, bald man in a suit sitting in our living room interviewing Mom, as well as Dad, Janet, and me. But then we'd never heard from them again. And of course a couple of months later, we were gone.

"Mm-hmm," said Sergeant McNamara. I didn't hear him rifling through papers, which made me think he knew the case well. "She was having car problems that morning, and he had a look. That's the last time anyone saw or spoke to her. Except for you boys of course."

I wasn't sure I liked his implication. "I'm sorry, but Dad can barely talk."

"I know. My colleague stopped by the hospital a couple of days ago after speaking with your sister." That stunned me into silence. The Mounties had interviewed Janet? Why hadn't she mentioned that?

McNamara continued, "I'd like to ask you some questions if you don't mind?"

"I'll help if I can, but it was a long time ago." The next-door neighbor was at her window again. I waved just to spite her and then hurried to the car.

"It says in the file that you saw Miss Morning's vehicle on Highway 16 on the afternoon of August 20."

"That's right. Ben and I had been out on Mount Roddick and were heading back."

"And this was what time?"

"Oh I couldn't tell you. Late afternoon? Maybe three o'clock? I remember being hungry."

"But you didn't go home."

"No, we went to the river instead. To cool off."

"What direction was the car headed?"

The abrupt turn of questioning threw me. He was good; I had to give him that. "East," I said after I'd thought about it a bit.

"Toward Burns Lake? And you're sure she was behind the wheel?" McNamara asked. "That she was alone?"

"I don't know. I couldn't tell. She had those tinted windows . . ."

"What time did you get home then?"

"Five maybe?"

"And your dad? Was he there when you got home?"

A chill slid down my spine, like someone had tipped an ice cube down my back. "Hang on, where are you going with this?"

"Just confirming the timeline," he reassured me. "Was anybody home?"

I searched my memory. Shouting good-bye to Benji, waving to Dad who had finally been fixing the broken front step Mom had constantly complained about, dropping my bike on the front lawn as I ran around the back. "Mom wasn't home from work yet. But, yes, Dad was there. And Janet. She was grounded for the summer."

"Great. Almost done. Tell me, how was Ben's relationship with his sister?"

Jesus. Is Ben a suspect? "Why?"

"I understand they didn't get along."

Irrational fury surged up from my chest. "You want to know about Misty and Ben? Well this ought to sum it up: when Benji and I were eleven, he rescued a bird with an injured wing." *A tree swallow.* Funny how easily that came back to me. Ben had had this *Birds of British Columbia* book and he'd looked it up. "Anyway," I continued, brushing aside the details. "He fixed up a box as a nest, dug up worms to feed her . . . Then one morning, he wakes up and can't find her where he left her. He finds the box outside, empty, and feathers on the ground. Know why? Because Misty put her out there—on purpose— and the coyotes got her.

"That's what Misty and Ben were like. And, for the record, Benji and I were together the day she went missing—the *whole* day. Misty was alive and well that morning, and as bitchy as usual." *"Have fun choking the chicken, you two."* "That's all I've got to say."

Hanging up on the RCMP was probably not the wisest move I'd ever made, but it did make me feel a hell of a lot better.

My anger had only slightly abated by the time I met Katy a few hours later at a restaurant in town called Hannigan's. The place was done up in the chalet-style that seemed so popular in Smithers, with dark wood paneling, muted lighting, and even a stone-clad fireplace.

I didn't recognize her at first, out of her scrubs and with her dark hair loose and softly curled around her face. She was even prettier than I originally thought, and her smile of welcome, not to mention her tight-fitting jeans and semisheer red blouse, made me think it was going to be a good night. After my disturbing conversation with the sergeant, I could use one.

"Have you been waiting long?" I asked.

"No, just arrived."

One hostess took my coat, while another led us through the nearly full dining room to a table near the fireplace. "I didn't think it would be so busy," I observed. "It's the off season."

"We're not all complete hicks up here," Katy teased. "We do like to eat out now and then."

Within seconds a waiter appeared and handed me an overpriced wine list before he lit the votive candle on our table with a seasoned flourish. I took one look at the menu and passed it to Katy.

She didn't bother to open it. "I think I'll have a beer. Whatever local brew is on tap."

"A woman after my own heart. Make that two."

Katy waited until the server departed before saying, "I don't think Janet was very pleased that I asked you out."

"You told her?"

Her beautiful green eyes narrowed. "I didn't know it was a secret."

"It's not. I guess I'm just not used to family members being involved in my business. Janet and I aren't terribly close these days."

"Right, you said you had a tense relationship. Is that why your other sister isn't here?"

I frowned. "Other sister? There's only me and Janet."

"Oh, my mistake. From the way Jerry talks sometimes, I thought he had another daughter."

"What did he say?"

"I don't remember his exact words now. He doesn't always make sense. He talks about Janet, of course, and someone named Diane?"

"Our mom."

"But I could have sworn there was another name." She shrugged. "I must have been mistaken."

There it was again: that tingle of unease along my spine. "Was it 'Misty'?"

"Yes, that's it! That's the name." Katy leaned forward in her chair. "Who is it? Your ex?"

I struggled to contain my expression. "Just someone from the past. What . . . what did he say about her?"

"It wasn't so much about her as *to* her. He seemed upset."

The server arrived with our drinks, and Katy sipped her beer while I pondered what she'd told me. So I hadn't misheard Dad before. But what did it mean? I was so preoccupied with the question that I almost missed the query Katy directed my way. "You're a writer of some kind? Is that right? Janet was vague about what you do for a living."

"I'm a journalist." Apparently Katy hadn't Googled me like Ben had. "I mostly write human-interest pieces for magazines."

"I'm not much of a reader. I've got a six-year-old—who has time? Are you working on something now?"

"I'm writing a story about my dad."

"That's nice."

"You don't think it's . . . exploitive?"

"I suppose that's up to you. But I think it's lovely that you want to eulogize him."

I coughed as my drink went down the wrong way. I definitely wasn't writing a eulogy.

But Katy didn't press me for more details or pretend to be interested, and I was grateful for that. Both of us clearly knew that this wasn't going to amount to anything serious, so there was no point in sharing the minutiae of our lives.

After ordering our meals, and another round of drinks, we fell into an easy conversation. She asked about my life in New York, but I tried to brush aside her questions and put the focus on her: how she got into nursing, how she ended up in northern BC. As it turned out, she had come with her ex who worked in the lumber industry, and stayed because they shared custody of a young son.

As we talked, my eyes kept drifting over Katy's shoulder to the artwork decorating the paneled walls. One in particular—a landscape—seemed familiar. I squinted. The arching trees, limbs outstretched, were unmistakable. I knew if I got close enough it would be Ben's signature scrawled at the bottom.

"Something wrong?" Katy asked. "You're awfully quiet. I feel like I'm hogging the conversation." Her eyes sparkled in the candlelight.

"No, not at all." I smiled and tried to focus back on Katy, but with Ben's painting staring at me, it felt like he was here with us. I couldn't seem to escape the Mornings no matter where I went.

The meal was surprisingly good. The company even better once I eventually stopped worrying about Dad and Misty. And Ben. It had been a long time since I'd done this—actually had a conversation with someone. Since Will, I hadn't put much time or energy into dating. If I wanted to get laid, usually I hit the bars, or if I was feeling lazy, swiped right on my phone. But Katy flirted unabashedly, and I knew I wouldn't have to go back to the motel alone if I didn't want to.

Still, my mind wandered a couple of times during the evening. There had to be something wrong with me, because as smart and sexy as Katy was, it wasn't long before I found myself wishing I was with Ben instead. Last night had left me with a taste for more. It was funny: for years I'd managed not to think of him, and now I couldn't get him out of my head.

We stayed until it became clear the restaurant was getting ready to close. I got the bill, despite Katy's protests to split it, and walked her to her car.

When we got there, she laid her hand on my coat sleeve and leaned in close. "Would you like to come back to my place for a drink? My ex has our son this week, so we'd have it all to ourselves."

It was very tempting. I didn't want to be alone. I reached out and tucked a strand of hair behind her ear. "I'd like to . . ."

"But?"

"I, ah, I'm not really looking for something serious right now."

She laughed. "You're so sweet. Who said I wanted serious? You're single, I'm single . . . Why not have fun while you're here?"

"When you put it that way . . ."

Katy moved first. She stood up on her toes and brushed her lips across mine. Her mouth was soft and warm, and tasted like the chocolate we'd had for dessert.

I won't lie. It was a damn good kiss. My body was ready to take her up on her offer, and yet something held me back. Or rather *someone*. Damn, I'd already decided Ben was off-limits.

Katy must have sensed my indecision, because she drew back with a little frown. "Did I misread some signals here?"

"No. I think you're a very attractive woman."

"Well, that's a good place to start. I think you're a very handsome man."

"I can't do this, though." My words surprised me. Up until a few minutes ago, I'd been planning to sleep with her.

"Are you sure about that? Your lips were saying differently."

"I'm sure."

She studied me closely and then sighed, her breath a puff of smoke in the cool night air. "I get it. There's someone else."

Is there? I wasn't sure.

She gave my arm a final pat. "Just my luck to find a man with scruples."

"I'm sorry. I didn't mean to—"

"Lead me on?" she finished with a laugh. "Relax, I've been turned down before. Not often, mind you, but it does happen."

She dropped a kiss on my cheek and climbed into her car. I closed the door behind her, and she lowered the window. "Last chance. Are you sure I can't change your mind about that drink?"

"You probably could. But then I'd have to deal with the guilt tomorrow." I stepped back. "Good night, Katy."

Why would I have felt guilty for sleeping with Katy? I wondered as I walked to my vehicle. I was single, unattached, and yet there it was, daring me to admit it.

I wanted Ben.

A train whistle blew somewhere in the distance. It sounded lonely and plaintive, not unlike the way I felt. For so many reasons, this journey home was not going as planned.

CHAPTER SEVEN

"I kid you not, Brad, it's like stepping through a wormhole. The only thing that's changed is the number of boarded-up businesses downtown."

After another restless night at the Summit View Motor Inn—alone—listening to the far-off cries of coyotes, I'd risen early Saturday morning, choked back some tasteless brown water from the in-room coffee maker, and was now checking in with my editor at the *Journal*. New York was three hours ahead, and Brad was glued to his phone, even on the weekends, so I had no fear of disturbing him. We'd known each other since the early days of my career when we were both struggling writers. I counted him as a friend, and when he'd offered me the position at the *Journal*, I'd accepted.

"It's hard to go back sometimes," Brad said. "I remember my fifteen-year reunion. It was a total bust."

"This is not a high school reunion."

"I know, but you seemed kind of touchy when I asked about your dad, so . . ."

"Don't worry, you'll get your article," I said.

Writing about my father, or rather my relationship with my father, was easy. Two thousand words should be a breeze—after all, I had years of angst to draw from—but now that I was reaching the current part of my story, the words weren't flowing as freely. My eyes slid over to the magazines I'd found yesterday and that currently sat on the coffee table.

Was it possible I'd misjudged him?

What if you spent your life hating a man who didn't deserve it?

"I'm not worried about the article, Alex." Brad's tone was so serious that I sat up straighter. "If you want to talk—"

"Oh no, don't you dare get mushy on me now. I'm not equipped to handle it. I'm tired and caffeine deprived and ready to sacrifice my left nut for a decent Americano."

"All right, no worries on that account. I am a little disappointed in you though. Here I was picturing you banging some hot former cheerleader and all you're doing is moping around a dreary motel room."

Brad had a vulgar sense of humor, and I'd never appreciated his lack of sentimentality more than I did right now.

"No cheerleaders. There were less than two hundred kids in the high school—we didn't even have a football team."

"Tragic."

"And why are you thinking about my sex life anyway?"

"Because I'm married with two kids under five. I can't remember the last time I had sex and I need to live vicariously."

"You had your shot, Brad," I teased.

"At least tell me you're reconnecting with an old flame. Like a Nicholas Sparks novel. Make an old man happy, please."

"Ah, not exactly. And I never would have pegged you for a Sparks fan."

"Not me," he insisted. "Maddy."

"Whatever you say. I won't judge." I hesitated. "But I do have another story idea I think you'd be interested in."

"Pitch it to me."

"There's a girl I once knew—my best friend's sister—"

"Daaaddyyy, come on," a high-pitched voice cried in the background. "The tea party's ready."

Brad coughed, and I smothered my laugh. "You'd better go. I think your tea's getting cold."

"Yeah, yeah. Email me the details, okay?"

"Will do. And hey, Brad. Thanks for making me come here."

"I didn't make you do anything."

"No, but you pushed me in the right direction. I should have just manned up and come on my own in the first place."

"I hope it works out, Alex."

"Me too. I'll talk to you later." My eyes stung as I hung up. God, I missed New York.

Katy wasn't on duty in Dad's ward when I arrived at the hospital, which was a relief after last night. Surprisingly, Janet wasn't there either, and without her as my buffer with Dad, I lost some of my nerve. I hadn't been alone with him before, and I paced the hallway for a few minutes until I worked up the courage to go in. In the end, I didn't have to worry—Dad was sleeping when I entered.

I sat down in one of the visitor chairs. I'd stick around a bit for appearances' sake, then head back to Dad's trailer and continue the cleanup.

"Why did you want me here, Dad?" I grumbled out loud. "You're the one who gave up on us, remember? If this is your way of making me feel guilty, it's not working." But it was, and that irritated me even more.

To kill time, I began checking work email on my phone, but only a few minutes had passed when a whimper from the bed drew my attention. "Dad?" His eyes were open, but they had that far-off look to them again. "Dad? It's Sandy." I set down my phone and crept closer but still maintained a safe distance. I couldn't bring myself to touch him yet.

His gaze darted about the room before landing on me. "Sandy."

"What is it?" I steeled myself for another outburst.

"Jan . . ." His voice sounded so thin, like he was speaking from miles away.

"Janet? Janet's not here. Do you want me to call her? Do you need a nurse?"

He extended a skeletal hand toward the side table where a plastic cup rested. Some melted ice chips were swimming around in the bottom. I fished out one with the accompanying spoon and held it to his lips. His tongue wriggled like a pale worm as he slurped the ice into his mouth.

"Another?" I asked.

He shook his head weakly. "Where's Diane?"

"Mom's in Seattle."

"Seattle?"

He clearly didn't remember. "Dad, you guys divorced twenty years ago."

"Oh." His lips trembled, and his eyes grew wet. "Oh. Tell . . . tell her I'm sorry."

Sorry for what? For being a shitty husband? For abandoning your kids?

"I shouldn't have . . . shouldn't have done it."

"Done what?"

I almost shrieked when his cold, bony fingers latched on to my wrist. Jesus, he was still surprisingly strong.

"Wanted to do the right thing. Turned out wrong. You hate me," he said. I didn't deny it. "Made too many mistakes."

A lump rose swiftly to my throat. "Why, Dad? Why? Just tell me that much." *Why did you love the booze more than us?*

But already the grip on my wrist was weakening, and his eyelids drooped. "No choice. What else . . . do?" His words came out slurred, and I had to strain to make them out. "Too late now anyway. I deserve this."

Did he? I wasn't so sure anymore. I wasn't sure anyone deserved this.

"Take care of Janet," he whispered. "She needs you."

I bit back a swift retort and tried to remember the magazines I'd found at his place. In his own way, he must have cared about me once, but it didn't stop the pinch of jealousy at how quickly she took precedence. "Janet doesn't need me, Dad," I said tightly. "She can take care of herself."

"Promise . . ."

"I'm not making a deathbed promise to a man who couldn't be bothered to attend his son's graduation."

His smile looked like a grimace. "Knew you were okay . . . You're just like me . . ."

"I am nothing like you."

"Sandy!" Janet's voice made me jump. "I didn't expect to see you here." Was that a touch of defensiveness I heard?

"Why wouldn't I be here? I thought that was the whole point. But I assumed you must be at work."

"My shift doesn't start until noon today." She joined me at Dad's bedside, and I did a double take when I saw her up close. Her eyes were red-rimmed and her hair unwashed. The minty smell of mouthwash was strong, and her cheekbones seemed even sharper than yesterday. Dad's death was clearly taking its toll on her.

Was he right? Did I need to worry about her?

"Has he been awake?" she asked.

"Only for a few minutes."

"How was he? Did he say anything?"

"Nothing that made sense."

Janet bumped me out of the way to sit on the edge of the mattress. She stroked Dad's forehead tenderly. He'd fallen asleep again, and his face twitched beneath her touch.

"I don't know how much longer I can do this." Her voice trembled.

I shifted uncomfortably, searching for an escape. Emotional scenes weren't my thing, and seeing Janet like this was unsettling. But what the hell, I was on a roll. "Have you eaten breakfast yet?"

"I'm not much of a breakfast person."

Obviously. She looked as though she hadn't eaten in a week. "Let me buy you a coffee, then," I urged.

She took so long to respond that I thought she was going to decline, but she surprised me. "Sure. I know a place."

We left the hospital together, and I followed Janet's rusted-out pickup truck. She bypassed the big chain in favor of a small café downtown. The décor was complete mountain-lodge, but the prices were decent and the aroma of freshly brewed coffee was amazing as we entered.

I ordered a full breakfast, but Janet stuck with coffee and a croissant. She picked at it while we sat across from each other, our gazes turned to the television mounted to the wall behind the coffee bar so we wouldn't have to talk to each other. Never had local news seemed so riveting.

"How was your date?" she finally asked. Her tone was laced with judgment.

"It was good. Why? What did you hear?"

"Nothing."

"Then why are you all bent out of shape?"

"I just think it's callous of you to be picking up women while Dad is dying."

"Can you skip the lecture? It's not like I need to be at his side twenty-four hours a day. And *she* picked me up."

"'I don't want to see Katy hurt.'"

"You overestimate my appeal. Trust me, Katy knows what she's doing." I set down my fork. "We need to talk. Does Dad have a will?"

"A will? No, not that I know of. He doesn't own anything to will away."

"Except his trailer. What do you want to do with it?"

"Do?"

"Yeah. Do you want to sell it? I don't know how much you can get for it—the market seems fairly depressed—but it would be something."

She shrugged. "I don't care."

"Or you could try to rent it out. But Dad owes some back rent, so if you want the trailer, you'll have to pay up. It needs a lot of—" The words *A mother's resolve* popped up across the bottom of the television screen. The image jumped from the newsroom to a young male reporter interviewing a woman wearing a familiar pink T-shirt beneath her unbuttoned coat, and who was standing in front of the Alton RCMP detachment.

"Hey, isn't that Angela Morning?" I abandoned my coffee on the table and wandered over closer to the television.

"Hey," Janet cried.

The newscast cut to the requisite photo of Misty, the one Angela had made into buttons. Who wouldn't be moved by such a beautiful young woman? The volume was low, and I strained to hear the reporter's voice-over:

"Misty Morning disappeared along Highway 16 in August 1996. Two weeks ago, her empty car was found submerged in the marsh at the south end of MacFarlane Lake by a pair of fishermen. Police

say last summer's drought likely played a factor in lower than normal
water levels."

Cue the footage of a rusted sedan being winched out of the lake,
then onto a flatbed trailer behind a tow truck. A shiver of disquiet
rose the hair on the back of my neck. After twenty years underwater,
Misty's Olds was still recognizable.

A few curious onlookers stood nearby, watching divers in the
murky water.

Back to the live reporter, and now a tip line number flashing on
the screen.

"Police are refusing to comment, saying only that this is still an
active investigation."

"Active my ass," snorted the barista, who had joined me by the
TV. She was a young Indigenous woman, possibly from one of
the neighboring reservations.

"I'm sorry?"

"My aunt's case is 'active' too, but no one's working very hard on
that one. Those guys couldn't find their own assholes if you gave them
a roadmap."

"Your aunt is missing?" Those billboards along the highway
sprang to my mind.

She lowered her eyes. "Murdered—eight years ago. And not a
single suspect." She gestured to the television. "They don't care. They
show the white girl's picture, but what about the Aboriginal girls?
They deserve some attention too."

The news anchor in the studio had moved on to another story, so
I returned to the table, a niggling thought worrying unformed in the
back of my mind.

Janet's face was pale when I sat down. The tattered croissant
trembled in her hand.

"What's wrong?" I asked.

"Just brings back bad memories, you know."

I nodded. I did know. I might have only been thirteen at the
time, but even I had sensed the seriousness of the situation, the way
everyone suddenly spoke in hushed tones.

"Have the cops talked to you?" I asked. "They left a card at Dad's
trailer. And I spoke to one of them yesterday."

She nodded. "A couple of days ago. Before you arrived. They came by the dealership looking for Dad."

"What did they ask you?"

"Could I think of anyone who would harm Misty? What was she like the last time I saw her? The same questions they asked back then." She tugged on her ponytail. "Why? What did they ask you?"

It was on the tip of my tongue to tell her about McNamara's interest in Dad, but I hesitated. In Janet's eyes, Jerry Colville could do no wrong, and I really didn't feel up to hashing out old arguments. "The same."

Janet's eyes flew back to the TV, where a laxative commercial was now playing. "When she disappeared, we all thought—hoped—she'd just run away. She always talked about it, you know. How she was going to escape this place and make it big as a model. She wanted to be famous." Her laugh was hard. "I guess she sort of is. Maybe some people are better off missing."

The offhand comment made me start. Benji had said something similar too.

"What does that mean? You two were besties." I could remember Janet trotting after Misty the way Benji used to trot after me. Memories of Barbie dolls spread across the back porch, endless giggles and whispers coming from Janet's room next to mine. When Misty disappeared, she'd been broken-hearted, moping and crying for weeks after.

"We were. But it was different when we were kids. Everything changed when we hit high school." Did I detect a note of adolescent jealousy there? "Don't you remember what she was like?"

"Oh, I remember." I'd had my own encounter with Misty, one I'd never told anyone about. And then there was the way she always treated Benji. *"Hey, Loser,"* she'd chime gleefully, often giving him a none-too-gentle knock on the head. She'd made the character of Regina George in *Mean Girls* look like Snow White.

"She could be cruel." Janet cupped both hands around her mug as if trying to get warm. "But she had this other side too. This . . . power, or something, that made you want to be near her, even though you hated her at the same time."

A piece of toast lodged in my throat.

"I feel terrible for Mrs. Morning, but she should let it go," Janet mumbled.

"She won't," I said. "You should see the house. It's like time stopped. Like she's waiting for Misty to come back any minute."

Janet's head jerked up. "You've seen Angela?"

"Yeah. And Benji too. I mean Ben."

"When was this? Why didn't you mention it before?"

I shrugged. "I didn't think it was important. I went to see Ben when I first got here, and Angela mistook me for a reporter—I mean a reporter covering the story. She wanted me to investigate."

"And are you?"

"Of course not." Janet searched my face until I grew uncomfortable. "Oh, I also ran into a friend of yours in town. Arlene . . . Jerkovic I think it was. She says hi."

"Arlene the Jerk?"

"Oh, that's nice. Original too. Did Misty come up with that one?" For the first time I wondered about my sister. Janet had been Misty's shadow, so maybe she'd been a bit of a mean girl too. "Hey, she brought up something about Spring Formal that year—do you know what she's talking about?" Was I grilling my own sister like a suspect?

"No, not at all."

"Weren't you chair of the dance committee?"

"Yes, but if you'll recall, I didn't even go to the Spring Formal. I was grounded, remember?" Her eyes narrowed. "Now you're sounding like the cops. Why all these questions?"

"Habit, I suppose. Sorry. But you were Misty's best friend. You would have known if something were . . . off, wouldn't you?"

"I've already answered the police's questions. I don't need to answer to you too. Besides, I thought you weren't looking into this."

I shoveled the last of my cold eggs into my mouth and chewed. "Jan, do you think Dad's involved?" I asked after swallowing.

Two spots of color burst onto her cheeks. "No, I don't."

"He talks about her. He said her name."

"When? I've been at his side every day, and he's said nothing about her to me."

"Katy said—"

"Oh, well, if Katy said it, it must be true," she snapped. "Why do you want to blame him for everything? You always have."

"Janet," I sighed wearily.

"It's not all his fault, Sandy."

"What's not?"

"The divorce. Mom's leaving."

I set down my fork again. Apparently we were about to hash out the old arguments after all.

"You're probably too young to remember," Janet continued, "but she wasn't exactly sympathetic when he lost his job. She complained to all her friends about it. Made him feel small."

"So you're blaming Mom. Again."

"No, I'm not. Can we stop acting like kids for a minute here? Sometimes it's no one's fault, Sandy. Shit just happens."

Didn't I know that? I shifted in the hard wooden seat. "I don't blame him."

"No?" Her sharp gaze pierced me.

Okay, maybe I did a bit. The rational part of me knew that marriages, and divorces, were complicated—my own divorce had shown me that—but that thirteen-year-old boy was still there, wondering how he could have let us go so easily. "It's not the divorce that bothers me. Plenty of parents get divorced and manage to stick around just fine."

"He made a mistake—I'm agreeing with you here—but you've punished him for it for twenty years. Isn't it time to stop?"

"Me? Punish him?"

"You're both so damned stubborn." Janet pointed the remains of her croissant at me. "You keep saying Dad walked away from us—but haven't you done the same thing?"

"What are you talking about?"

"When's the last time we saw each other?"

"Christmas at Mom and Dan's in Seattle, four years ago."

"And if I remember correctly, you spent the whole time on your phone ignoring us. Like you couldn't wait to get the hell out of there."

"I'm surprised you remember much about it at all after the amount you and Bruce put away," I bit.

Her face crumpled. "That's a low blow, Sandy."

Now I felt like an asshole. "Yeah, I'm sorry. I'm not very good company today."

"When are you good company? I'd really like to know. I've seen you twice in ten years. Mom the same. You hardly ever call—"

"I've been working," I insisted. "You know I travel a lot."

"Your work is an excuse—it's your crutch. The way alcohol is for me and Dad. There's this thing called a cell phone now—you can even send emails from it. Instead, we have to look you up online to see what's going on in your life. You're doing so well, and you didn't bother to tell us." She ducked her head and blotted her eyes with the balled-up napkin. "So, the next time you blame Dad for not being part of your life, maybe you should look at yourself."

Her words seared me, all the more so because I recognized the ring of truth to them. Damn her for bringing this up now, as if I didn't have enough problems to deal with at the moment.

She sniffled and reached for the stack of extra napkins next to my plate.

"Jan?" I caught her wrist, and her eyes flew to mine. It's shameful to admit, but I saw my sister clearly for the first time in my life, not as an adolescent nuisance, or the older sibling I had to compete with for attention, but as a thrice-divorced, middle-aged woman barely holding it together. My irritation faded. "I'm sorry."

Tears tracked down her papery cheek. "Do you believe in karma, Sandy?"

I squinted at the abrupt change of topic. "You mean like past lives?"

"No. That all our deeds have consequences. Like if you do bad things, your life will turn out shitty. Sort of like payback."

Was she talking about Dad? Hell, she could have been talking about me for that matter. "I guess so. To some extent. But not because of any bullshit divine retribution; usually it's because one bad decision leads to another. We do it to ourselves. But it's never too late to make amends."

"Even for Dad?"

She'd caught me. "Yeah, even Dad." I peered at her closely. "Are you okay, Jan?"

"I should get to work." She downed the dregs of her coffee and reached for her purse.

"Don't worry about it. I've got this covered."

Hesitation flickered across her haggard face, but she didn't protest. "Thanks," she said. "See ya later?"

After our conversation, it surprised me that she still wanted me around. "Yeah," I agreed, "maybe I'll see you at the hospital tonight."

She stood. "Sandy. I know I can be a bitch, but I am glad you're here. It's been good to see you again," she said in a rush, then departed, leaving me speechless.

I finished my breakfast, paid the check, and climbed into the Explorer. There was a dusting of snow on the side mirror and I lowered the window to brush it off. That's when it hit me. What had seemed so off on the newscast. On the footage, the camera had done a slow pan over the rusted hulk of Misty's car, and the driver's-side window had been down. Not so unusual for August, but now my mind was telling me that the rotting skeleton of the seat had been pushed back. But had I really seen that? Misty hadn't been a tall girl, not much over five feet. She'd had to drive with the seat up as far as it would go, almost hugging the wheel.

I sat there in the parking lot a minute, fingers tapping on the wheel. But like an itch beneath my skin, it wouldn't go away.

There was a payphone outside the café. Not all the businesses in the valley had joined the internet revolution yet—many still operated old school. So on a hunch, I wedged myself into the narrow cubicle and pulled out the Yellow Pages. I scanned three pages of tow truck and auto body companies, searching for the logo I'd seen on TV. Bingo. Kirby's Towing out of Topley, which was the town on the other side of Alton. I took note of the address.

I had to go that direction anyway. I'd figure out what to do on the way.

CHAPTER EIGHT

F or most of my childhood, Dad worked out of a mining camp and would be gone for weeks at a time. This was a normal way of life for most families in the valley, and I saw nothing unusual in it. Mom always picked up the slack, and I had my best friend Benji to provide all the entertainment I needed. At least I had two parents, I had reasoned then—there were plenty who hadn't, including Benji.

By the time the mine closed, Dad had been absent so much that I barely noticed his inattention at first, even when we were in the same room.

It wasn't until my mom remarried that I understood what a father should be.

—From "My Father's Son" by Alex Buchanan

On the way into town, I made a detour to Ben's house. If anyone could talk me out of chasing shadows, it would be Ben. But when I got there, there were no cars in the driveway. It was Saturday. Had he taken one of his road trips to Prince George? The thought made my stomach flip.

I turned on my phone and sent him a text: *you around?*

He didn't reply straight away. Not a good sign. Either he was still pissed and ignoring me, or he was getting his brains fucked out. Frankly, I didn't like either option, but just as I was about to give up, his reply arrived.

Class until noon.

Right. Ben had said he taught an art class on weekends. Relief loosened the knot in my shoulders. I drove into town, keeping an eye out for his SUV—Alton was small enough that you could do that—and found it easily in the parking lot at the Community Hall. The dark and dirty windows from the empty storefronts across the street seemed to follow me as I locked the car and strode toward the building.

When I was a kid, before the new rec center near the highway had been built, they'd held extracurricular classes in the basement, so I headed around to the side entrance, giving the small group of teens gathered on the front steps with their skateboards a wary glance. They were too busy smoking and watching one of their group doing flip tricks to pay me any attention.

The side door was unlocked, and as I took the stairs, the rising sound of voices told me I'd been correct. I ducked my head through the open door of the first room I came to and blinked in surprise. I'd been imagining three, maybe four kids, but there had to have been more than twenty people jammed into the small room, seated around four tables. Some were painting, others sketched in notepads. One or two were even sprawled on the floor. About half seemed to be in their late teens, but there were a number of adults as well—mostly middle-aged men oddly enough—and one or two younger kids. Sebastian, the boy I'd seen with Benji, was sitting cross-legged on the floor, charcoal pencil flying across the page of a large sketchbook. His entire body moved as he drew. It was fascinating to watch. When I peered over his shoulder, I gasped at the vivid portrait that was taking shape. His subject was the girl who sat across from him, and Sebastian had captured the concentration on her face perfectly as she worked on her own painting.

Ben was talking to a young black woman, pointing to something on her canvas. He hadn't yet seen me. But others had.

"Yo, dude. This is a private space," one of the teenagers, a tough-looking youth with a tattoo on his neck and a bar though his nose, barked. Heads swiveled my way.

"I know. I'm here for—"

"Alex!" Ben rose from his crouch and strode toward me, stopping to murmur a word of encouragement to a silver-haired lady dripping with beaded necklaces.

"Hey," I said when he reached me, wishing my voice sounded more confident. "This is some turnout you've got here. Are they all your students?"

"I don't think of them as students. It's a drop-in program. There's no set curriculum. Mostly I let them work on whatever they want to." He frowned. "What are you doing here?"

"Is this your boyfriend, Mr. M?" asked the girl nearest us, loud enough that several of the others tittered.

Ben choked. "No! This is absolutely not my boyfriend, Stella."

"Too bad, he's kind of cute."

I grinned. Ben's cheeks turned scarlet as he drew me to the side of the room. "Don't even go there," he warned as I opened my mouth to speak.

"Hey, it's not my fault the girl has good taste."

"Again, why are you here?"

"Can we maybe grab a drink when you're done?" I asked. Ben's lips tightened. "Please? Coffee?"

He inclined his head toward a folding table in the corner where a coffee urn sat next to a box of bagels and muffins.

"Oh," I said. "I guess you're probably not interested in lunch either." My mind scrambled for another suggestion.

Ben huffed. "Okay, fine. We can have coffee. That stuff is awful anyway." He glanced over his shoulder at the class, which meant he missed my smile at the small victory. "We wrap up in ten minutes if you want to come back then."

"I'll hang around here if that's all right with you."

It was anything but all right judging by the set of his shoulders. Still he shrugged. "Suit yourself."

I found a spot in the corner and watched Benji in his element, offering up advice, a whispered word of encouragement. And they soaked it up. I remembered what that was like, to bask in that attention, to have those big blue eyes turned on me.

Damned if I didn't want it again.

What was it about Ben that had this effect on me? That brought out this strange mix of tenderness and lust. My fingers itched to slide through those wayward curls of his, to stroke the russet hairs of his beard. I'd always been attracted to bearded men. I loved to feel the scrape against my neck, the insides of my thighs. My nipples tightened as though he had actually teased them into points with his scruff.

Oh God, now that I'd let these thoughts out of the neat little box I'd kept them in for so long, I couldn't seem to put them back in again.

Ben looked up. His eyes locked with mine, widened, clearly aware of my attention, and for a second, I glimpsed a similar need in his gaze, a need strong enough to make me hard. Hard*er*, since I was already halfway there. His cheeks flushed above the line of his beard, and then he scowled and swung back to his student.

Even his scowl made my heart flutter and want to laugh with delight. The rational side of my brain was telling me he wasn't my type—he wasn't typically handsome, he wasn't sophisticated, but he was Ben. *My Ben.* And because of that, to me he was simply perfect.

Ben clapped his hands. "Okay folks. It's time to start cleaning up." A chorus of groans erupted. "Remember, the show is on Tuesday, and there are a few of you who still need to get me your pieces. I need them dropped off here by tomorrow afternoon so we have time to get them framed. And please, take these snacks with you—I don't want to have to carry them home."

It took a long time for the room to empty. There were brushes to wash and supplies to pack up, and no one seemed in a particular hurry to leave. Finally, we were alone. Benji began to stack chairs, and I went to help him. He kept casting sidelong glances at me.

"I didn't expect to see you again so soon," he said.

"Soon? It's been two whole days. I thought I'd at least give you a chance to miss me."

"Like I ever stopped." Ben quickly turned his head away, as if surprised by his own words.

The power in that simple statement caught me off guard. Really? He'd missed me? I tamped down the burst of pleasure rocketing through my veins.

Nothing good can come of this, remember? But my head had stopped listening to reason.

"Do you do this every weekend?" I asked once I'd recovered my voice.

"Most of them. We break for a bit during the summer. There's a lot of people in crisis here—I don't like to leave them alone for long.

All the social services have moved to Smithers, so this is it in terms of programming." Ben loaded two plastic bins onto a wheeled cart and gestured to a third. "Can you get that box for me?"

"Sure."

He turned out the lights, and we headed to his car. "How's your dad? I was wondering if I should go and see him."

"He's in and out. When's he's awake, he doesn't really make a lot of sense." I immediately changed the subject. "You know, I could put you in touch with some of my art contacts in New York if you're interested."

Ben raised the tailgate, and I hefted in the box of supplies I was carrying. "Why would you do that?"

"Because you're good. It seems a shame to see you wasting your talent up here where no one can see it."

"I'm not *wasting* anything. Besides, I'm content with the way things are."

I winced. "Why do I always seem to say the wrong thing around you? I'm usually much better with words. What I meant is that you're talented, and you shouldn't be hiding it."

His eyes narrowed. "I'm not hiding. I just don't have anything to prove." *Like you*, was the unspoken implication.

"Was that a dig?"

"Alex, are you really going to pretend that the reason you push yourself so hard, that your fixation on awards isn't because you're trying to prove you're good enough to your dad? This is me, remember? We're the same. The only difference is I gave up trying to get Angela's approval a long time ago."

"What the f—"

"Hey, Ben." The approach of a man in a torn black coat and a ratty, gray woolen toque killed my outrage and made me pull Ben protectively to my side. Even two feet away, I could smell the stale sweat and booze seeping from his pores.

Ben shot me a strange glance and stepped forward to shake hands with the stranger. "Hi, Garrett. I haven't seen you around lately. How are you?"

"Oh, same ol', same ol'. Hangin' in there." The man was missing an incisor, providing a disturbing glimpse of pink tongue as he smiled.

"Just wondering if you got any work for me. I'm a bit short this month. Damn government's late with the check."

"No, sorry, Garrett," Ben said. "I can't think of anything that needs doing. Oh, but I've got something else for you. Hang on a sec." He darted around to the front of the car, leaving me alone with the shabby-looking man. We stared at each other warily until Ben returned.

"Hey, Gar, you remember Sandy Colville, right?"

His rheumy eyes widened. "Sandra Dee! Yeah, I remember. Good times. How are ya, man?"

I gaped rudely as the name finally resonated. I'd only known one Garrett. My childhood nemesis. *This* was the bully who stole my lunch money on a regular basis throughout seventh grade?

"Here you go, Garrett," Ben said with a frown in my direction. He handed the man a plastic gift card for the coffee shop down the street. "I'm not really a coffee drinker, so I'd rather give it to someone who can use it. Treat yourself to a coffee, maybe a sandwich too."

"Thanks, man." Garrett swallowed hard, his inner struggle streaking across the weathered planes of his face as he accepted the card. "'Preciate it."

"You don't drink coffee?" I asked as we watched him weave through traffic to the other side of the street. Had that been Dad not too long ago?

"No, I do," Ben replied.

"But . . . ah."

"He still has some pride."

"And you just happened to have an unused gift card handy?"

Ben shrugged.

"I can't believe *that's* Garrett Wilde."

"Yeah, I guess he's not so scary now, eh?"

"What happened to him?"

"Laid off from the mill when it closed two years ago. We lost over two hundred jobs. Garrett's been going downhill ever since."

"Jesus."

"I used to pay him to do odd jobs, but most of that went straight into liquor. So now I try to make sure he at least has something to eat."

"The guy bullied you—us—all through school."

"I think he's paid for that ten times over. Besides, you can't hold grudges for things that happened twenty years ago." That barb was clearly aimed straight at me.

"Touché. I admit I have some issues. More than I realized actually."

A shadow crossed Ben's face, making him look like a guilty child. "I, ah, did the same for your dad when I could."

"What do you mean? Dad came to you for handouts?"

"Asking for a helping hand is not a handout," he admonished, shouldering me out of the way to load the last box into the car.

Once again, I'd put my foot in my mouth. "Yes, you're right. So what happened?"

Ben pivoted to face me, a quizzical lift to his left eyebrow—the one with the scar. "A couple of years ago, Jerry showed up at the house and asked if there was anything he could do—he didn't ask for money; I offered. Jerry built most of my deck."

I blinked. "Why didn't you mention this before?"

"Before? Like when you showed up on my doorstep after two decades of silence?" He shook his head. "Besides, I wasn't sure you'd want to hear it."

I sat down on the bumper. "What was he like?"

"Quiet. He did a good job—when he was sober."

"And when he wasn't?"

"Then he wouldn't show up." Ben's lips twitched. "It took about five months to get that deck built. He did some other odd jobs around the house for a while, but eventually he stopped coming around, and I'd only see him occasionally in town."

"Thank you . . . for trying." I dragged a hand over my face. "God, I don't know how I'm supposed to feel anymore."

Ben squeezed my shoulder, and his touch filled me with warmth. "Was there a reason you stopped by, or do you just like disturbing me?" he asked.

"Oh, do I disturb you?"

"I think you know the answer to that." Our eyes met briefly, before his gaze slid away from mine.

"Okay, okay, I wanted to ask you something. It's about Misty's car."

He stiffened. His hand pulled away. "What about it?"

"I was thinking about going over to Kirby's Towing. Thought you might want to come with me."

"Why, did your rental quit?" he asked archly.

"No. They're the ones who towed Misty's car from the lake."

"Yeah, I know. We were there. Angela wouldn't leave until she knew . . . until she knew if Misty was in there."

I replayed our last glimpse of that white Olds growling along 16 in my mind, trying to recall if I'd actually seen Misty behind the wheel. "Do you remember that day, Ben?"

Ben slammed the tailgate shut, narrowly missing my fingers, and whirled on me, his face tight. "What are you doing, Alex? Mom said you're helping her—she thinks you're her goddamn savior—but I didn't believe it. Not after what I told you."

"I only promised to keep my ears open."

"And now you're off to Kirby's? That sounds like more than 'keeping your ears open.'"

"Doesn't it feel . . .? It just feels like we're missing something here." I scrambled to explain, but hell, I couldn't even explain my unease to myself, let alone Ben. "On the news . . . it looked to me like the driver's seat was pushed back. Back far enough that Misty never would have been able to reach the pedals."

"Alex, stop!" Ben stabbed his hands through his hair, almost tearing it out by the roots. His eyes had gone cold. "I told you I don't want to talk about this. I know she's dead. *Everybody* knows she's dead. Let her rest in peace. Let me."

With those parting words, he leapt into his car and roared out of the parking lot.

CHAPTER NINE

The North is a place where time stands still. It is raw, primitive, elemental; unchanged since Mount Roddick was first birthed from the earth's crust eons ago. Beyond the picture-postcard view, there is a crack in the thin veneer of civilization through which something darker can be glimpsed; a darkness the tourists never get to see. Never had I felt as small, as inconsequential, as alone, as I did standing on the bank of MacFarlane Lake, the wind whispering through the trees, the wet bog seeping through my thin hiking boots, sucking me down into its cold, dank embrace. The same way it had claimed Misty Morning's Oldsmobile. That was when I knew—

A burst of raucous laughter from the courtyard cut through the headphones and yanked me from my writing trance. Damn it.

Saturday night at the Summit View Motor Inn was bustling. In the room next to mine, a TV blared an obnoxious laugh track. The walls might as well have been made of cardboard for all the good they did. Across the parking lot, someone had set up a hibachi on the tailgate of a truck and a party was underway.

The Marriott this was not, but I'd stayed in worse places over the years, struggling on a freelance journalist's sporadic salary.

I blinked as the time swam into view—almost ten. No wonder my eyes felt like sandpaper and my shoulders ached. I'd been hunched in front of my laptop for hours writing. I stretched and groaned as my muscles unkinked.

What are you doing, Alex? asked the voice in my head. Janet's words haunted me. Was this sudden itch to delve into a twenty-year-old case simply a diversion? One more excuse to avoid dealing with the reason I was here in the first place? Possibly. Almost certainly. But my instincts told me there was a story here.

I turned up the thermostat, unable to get warm since my sojourn to MacFarlane Lake. I'd been drawn there after my visit to the towing company. Hank Whitefish had been happy to talk once he learned I was a local, and the twenty bucks I offered him hadn't hurt either.

I'd spent a good half an hour listening to him explain the hard time they'd had getting Misty's car hooked up. She'd been wheels down in the mud, and stuck good, to use Hank's expression. The south end of MacFarlane Lake was all marsh, and it had taken the divers a couple of hours to clear enough sediment to use the chains.

Hank had hauled the vehicle to Prince George, where forensic analysts had probably combed through it, although after so long underwater, it was unlikely there'd be much physical evidence.

I shivered again and settled back in front of the laptop, hoping to regain my earlier momentum. I had just donned my headphones, when the flare of headlights burst through the crack in the curtains, blinding me. Jerking back, I blinked the spots from my eyes.

The vehicle didn't move but sat there in the courtyard idling, lighting up my room like a hospital OR. What a dick.

I pulled aside the curtain, made out the familiar shape of an SUV parked next to my Explorer. Mist sparkled on the roof like diamonds.

The flutter in my chest told me who it was.

I went to the door and opened it, stood there in the opening, waiting. The headlights went dark, and a few minutes later Benji was striding toward me across the parking lot, through the gently falling rain.

He shouldered past me into the room.

"Why didn't you answer my text?" Ben began to pace the narrow space between the bed and the kitchenette as he spoke. Anxiety was rolling off him in waves.

"Battery's dead. I'm recharging now." I frowned. "What's wrong?"

"What? Oh." He stopped his pacing and exhaled. I had the feeling he'd come here prepared to do battle and I'd somehow hijacked his plans.

"Why did you have to come here, Alex?" he suddenly burst out. "Why now?"

"I guess you'd have to take that up with my dad. Or God if you're into that."

"That's bullshit. You coming to see *me*, that has nothing to do with your dad."

I looked away from his probing gaze. He wasn't wrong.

He moved, and the next thing I heard was him sucking in a sharp breath. "What is this?" Ben had paused in front of my laptop, reading my words on the screen. "What happened to just keeping your ears open? Are you writing a story?"

My conscience jabbed. I couldn't deny it. I'd already made the pitch to Brad earlier this afternoon.

Ben clicked through the tabs I had open, scanned the notes I'd been taking. "I was right not to trust you. That's all we are to you, isn't it? Subjects? This is my life we're talking about—not some headline to win you the Pulitzer."

I winced. The Pulitzer hadn't even crossed my mind, although Ben wasn't likely to believe that. "Ben, it's not like that."

"I don't get why this matters to you so much."

Hadn't I been wondering the same thing? "I don't have a good answer for you. I don't fully understand it either. There's a good story here, but it's more than that—maybe I feel like I owe you. Like I owe *her*. Maybe because if we hadn't said we saw her driving that day, they would have searched a little harder."

He stopped pacing. "But we *did* see her."

"We saw her car. Did you actually see her behind the wheel? Because I didn't. What if she was already dead and her killer was in that car?" I threw up my arms. "I went out there, to the lake. You've seen the spot. You know how remote it is. It's a good fifty feet from the road. She didn't accidentally go off the road and into that lake. And it would have taken at least two people to push that car into the swamp. *Someone* went to a lot of effort to hide it."

Ben crumpled to the couch as if his knees could no longer support him. I went to the small fridge and pulled two cans from the six-pack I'd purchased earlier. "Here, you look like you could use this."

"I can't drink. It messes with my Xanax."

A million questions surged to the tip of my tongue. Was Ben alright? Why was he on anxiety medication? Did it have something to do with those marks I'd seen on his arm? "It's light beer, and I hate to break it to you, but I don't think your pills are working." I left the can on the side table and popped the tab on my own. "Would you prefer coffee, then? It tastes like shit, but maybe you could use the jolt."

He shook his head, damp curls flinging a fine mist everywhere. "I shouldn't even be here."

The last thing I wanted was for him to bolt. "Hey, let me hang up your coat." I tugged the damp anorak off his shoulders before he could stop me, and draped it over a chair near the heating unit.

Ben gazed up at me with wide, haunted eyes. "What else did you learn today?"

"Maybe we should talk about something else."

"Like the weather? How about the Canucks' chances of making the playoffs?"

"Fine. Hank says all the doors were rusted shut, the seat belts in place—no signs that anyone had tried to escape unless it had been through the driver's-side window which, by the way, was rolled down, not broken. And," I crowed, "the driver's seat was pushed back, like it was last used for a much taller person than Misty. This was done *before* the car went into the water, because it was like that when they towed it out."

Ben nodded.

"The keys were also in the ignition, and the gear was in neutral."

"Oh. That I didn't know." He chewed on a fingernail as he studied his feet.

I fell back onto the sofa with a tired sigh.

"Do you know how many girls have gone missing or had their bodies dumped along this highway? Dozens. Depending on whose account you believe, it goes back decades. Most of them were even younger than Misty. I've been reading about them all afternoon." Their pictures haunted me in a way that few subjects had.

"It's no secret, Alex. It's a hard life up here sometimes. It doesn't always bring out the best in people."

"I don't know what's more disturbing—the thought that Misty might have been killed by someone she knew, or by a random stranger."

"Why do you owe me?" Ben asked abruptly.

"Huh?"

"You said you felt like you owed me."

"For how I left things between us."

"You were a kid, Alex. It's not like you had any say in the matter."

"I could have written. I could have called."

"That's a lot of 'could haves.'" Ben patted my thigh and then leaned forward to cradle his face in his hands. "I hated her, Alex."

His blunt confession seared me. "I know."

"She was such a bitch. You have no idea."

"I remember." It had been bad enough that Ben had eaten dinner at our place at least once a week since no one had thought to buy any groceries, but how many times had I shared my lunch with him too because Misty had taken all the lunch money Angela had left? In revenge, sometimes we'd scrub the toilet with Misty's toothbrush when she wasn't around, or else we'd spit in her drink when she wasn't looking.

Once, when Ben had threatened to complain, Misty had sucked bruises onto her arm right in front of us and then threatened to say he'd hurt her if he went to Angela.

There was probably lots more that went on that he never told me about.

We'd never talked about our respective family dysfunctions in detail—we'd never needed to. We'd both known they were there. I knew about Misty's taunts and cruel teasing. I knew how Angela had always favored her daughter. Just like Benji knew about my dad's drinking and the state of my parents' marriage. We had been each other's escape from all that.

"You don't know how many times I wished she would disappear," Ben said.

He blamed himself. How had I not seen that before?

"It's not your fault, Ben."

"Isn't it? I was glad when she left. I didn't want her to come back. But then nothing changed anyway. It was all still about Misty. I've lived my whole life in her fucking shadow."

I'm not an empathetic person—just ask my ex-wife—but this was Benji, the guy who'd once been the most important person in my life—who maybe, in a strange way, still was. My heart ached to see him like this. He needed me now, like he'd needed me then.

I shifted beside him on the sofa, wincing when an errant spring poked my ass. He let me place my hand on his back, and the bony knots of his spine nudged my palm through the flannel of his shirt.

"Just when everything was almost good again . . . this happens. It's like she won't stay gone." Ben turned those big, pleading eyes on me. "Why won't she stay gone?"

I put a tentative arm around his shoulders. For a brief moment, he leaned into me, and things were almost like they were before. When we were young.

"I'm sorry," I murmured into his hair. The familiar smell of Benji's shampoo, like the woods after the rain, was stirring up memories. "I'll stop. I won't write about this if it bothers you so much." A twinge of regret pinched my chest. I'd have to give Brad some excuse for not following through, but I'd do it for Ben.

With Ben's shirtsleeves rolled sloppily to his elbows, I couldn't help notice the silvery lines on the underside of both his forearms. I brushed my thumb over one of the faint ridges. His entire body stiffened, and he pulled away, tugging his sleeves down as far as they would go. "Listen to me. I sound like I'm ten years old again." He exhaled a shaky breath, visibly collecting himself. "I'm fine now. Sorry to fall apart on you like that. I guess this whole thing has been tougher on me than I thought."

"Don't apologize."

"To hell with it," Ben said and reached for the beer, chugged it like a freshman at his first kegger, and then belched. I bit my cheek to keep from laughing and got up to grab a couple more.

When I returned, Ben was leafing through the magazines I'd brought back from Dad's trailer. "Are these all yours?" he asked without looking up.

"Dad had them. Don't," I warned when his jaw dropped.

"Don't what?"

"Don't say it means something."

"But it does." His lips thinned as I shook my head, but wisely he didn't pursue the topic. Instead, he opened *Mother Jones* to my article and began to read.

"Don't read that." I snatched the magazine from his lap.

"Hey!" he cried. "Why can't I read it?"

"It's weird."

"Weird? You're a writer—people are supposed to read what you write."

"Not you. It's too . . . personal somehow."

I shifted the magazines to the chair, out of reach, and sat down beside him. He seemed to have finally relaxed, and now he tilted his head back and propped his feet up on the coffee table. Either the Xanax had kicked in, or the beer. "Are you afraid I won't like it?"

I blushed.

"I bet your dad liked it. I bet he was proud of you."

"Ben," I growled. His eyes were wide and innocent over the rim of the can as he drank. "Okay, yes, I think you were right—about me trying to be good enough for him. Is that what you want me to say?"

"You don't need to say it. Of course I'm right." He poked me in the arm. "I always was. You just never listened."

"Uh-uh. I always listened to you." When Ben cocked an eyebrow, I laughed. "Eventually."

Not for the first time that night, I caught him looking at me with a secret smile.

"What?" I asked.

A deep flush spread across his cheekbones. "You've changed. A lot."

"It's been twenty years. We've all changed. You said so yourself."

"Not as much as you." His brow wrinkled. It would have been a blow to my ego if I hadn't already read the interest in his eyes.

"That hideous, am I?"

"As if." Ben snorted. "But there was something appealing about the old Sandy. I miss him."

"Ugh, fatty four-eyes." Just one of the many nicknames I'd been called growing up.

"You weren't fat," he insisted. "You were . . . cuddly. You always made me feel safe."

"I did?"

"Why is that so surprising?"

"It's not, I suppose. But I always thought of you as *my* rock, not the other way around." This conversation was getting far too heavy. "I'm still cuddly, you know? Come here and I'll prove it."

"I'm serious. I didn't think you were fat. I thought you were perfect. For the longest time, I used to dream you'd come back and rescue me." His lips twisted ruefully. "But it's not healthy to put that on someone else."

My throat closed up, and I had to look away. "It's a good thing I'm low on beer. You're cut off."

"Why didn't you ever write?" Ben's luminous eyes beseeched me. "It was because of the kiss, wasn't it? I knew I'd freaked you out and I'd probably never hear from you again. That you would think I was disgusting and hate me."

"No! No," I repeated. Firmly. Guilt punched me in the solar plexus. "Never. Please don't tell me you've thought this way for the last twenty years." *Oh God, I'd fucked up so bad.*

"I got over it eventually. I wonder if that's why I kissed you in the first place," he said, frowning as if the idea was only occurring to him now. "So that it would be a clean break when you left."

"I know I can't ever go back and fix things, Ben, but I'm here now."

"Only because your dad's dying."

"Maybe that's why I came back. But it's not why I'm *here* with you right now—drinking godawful light beer from a can and thinking this is the best evening I've had in a long time. From the moment I landed, I . . ."

"You what?"

But I'd already said too much. "Nothing."

He squinted at me. "It's so strange. I keep seeing the you I remember, but also the you that's here now."

"I know. It's the same for me." I reached out and brushed the hair off his forehead because I couldn't resist it. The soft curls tugged at my fingers as if reluctant to let go. God, I wanted to touch him so bad.

"You feel it too, don't you?" Ben asked, his voice barely above a whisper. "This thing between us?"

I nodded. "I do. Do you ever wonder what might have happened if my parents hadn't split?"

"I try not to. The present is hard enough to get through sometimes without dwelling on what-ifs." Ben studied his hands. "I don't think we should sleep together."

I raised an eyebrow. "You keep bringing that up. I'm flattered."

"Flattered I won't sleep with you?"

"Flattered you want to."

That made him laugh. "I'm abstinent, not crazy."

"Abstinent? What about your friend in Prince George?"

"Mmm. It's been seven months. I'd say that officially makes me abstinent."

"Seven months? How have you not spontaneously combusted?"

Ben threw me a dirty look.

"I take it your . . . arrangement is not serious, then."

"No, not serious."

It was wrong of me to be so pleased by his statement. It wasn't like I intended to do anything about it. As much as I might want to jump his bones, a part of me knew that sex with Ben wouldn't be just sex. "It's probably for the best," I agreed. "Us not having sex." Damned conscience. "I bet it would be really hot though."

Ben's eyebrows shot up, but he recovered quickly. "You think? It might be a letdown. All those expectations . . . Could be hard to live up to them."

"Expectations?"

His eyes slid over my body slowly, blatantly, lingering at my groin before rising to meet mine. "Oh yeah. Lots of them."

CHAPTER TEN

"**B**enjamin Andrew Morning," I joked, "I am shocked. You were such a nice boy." By now, my erection was pushing at the fly of my jeans. "You're not making this easy, you know?"

Ben grinned and then chuckled.

"What are you thinking about?" I asked.

"I'm just remembering that time you stole your dad's *Penthouse*."

I laughed too. "I was so sex obsessed."

It had been one of our final summer afternoons together. Both Dad and Janet had been home that day, and sneaking into Dad's secret stash at the back of my parents' closet hadn't been easy. I'd been terrified of getting caught. As Benji and I had made our way up the mountain to our hideout, the magazine had seemed to burn a hole in my backpack.

Benji sat next to me on our rock, his breath fanning my neck as he leaned over my shoulder to gawk at the magazine. I tilted my head to breathe in the smell of his shampoo, the warmth of his chest against my arm, the tickle of the fine red-gold down on his legs as he shifted position.

Both of us gaped at the naked model cupping her breasts and offering them to the camera. Her breasts were even bigger than Misty's, but I didn't mention that in front of Ben. Instead I said something uncool like, "Whoa, look at those jugs. They're almost as big as Mrs. Turner's."

"Ew. She's my teacher," Benji cried.

"So? She's got ginormous tits."

I flipped the pages. Tried to ignore the warmth down in my groin.

"Why do you like looking at naked ladies so much?" Benji asked.

I shrugged. "I'm a man. That's what men do."

"You're not a man," he giggled.

"Am too." I lifted my T-shirt to show him the hair sprouting under my arms. Then I snapped my elastic waistband. "Got more down there too. What's the matter? Don't you like boobs?"

"I guess."

I turned the page. This model had her legs spread wide, revealing what I'd only seen in diagrams in Health class up to that point.

"What do you think it's like?" Benji asked.

"Pussy? I heard some of the seniors talking. Joel says it's warm and wet."

"Wet?" he exclaimed with a grimace. "Why would it be wet?"

"How should I know? But I bet it's good. Kinda like when you use hand lotion to beat off."

Benji made a little squeak. Then, "You've got a boner."

"Yeah, so?" I'd been unable to control it, and there was a part of me that knew it wasn't just the magazine getting me hard. I shoved Benji away. "Quit breathing on me. You smell like peanut butter."

He blew a peanut-scented gust of air in my face to spite me. "This is boring anyway," he said, sliding off the rock and wandering toward the stream. I was happy to see him go.

I looked at him now. "If I recall correctly, you were pretty grossed out by the whole thing."

"I think it was the first, and last, time I saw lady parts up close."

"So you've never . . .?"

"Nope." He flashed a generous smile. "Poor you. You had that whole plan to lose your virginity with Amy Mikelson that fall."

"Oh right, even though she'd barely talked to me." I chuckled. "Talk about cocky. It was another two years before I finally did the deed."

"I hate to tell you, but Amy went on to have the worst reputation in high school. Last I heard, she had five kids and had moved to Prince George. Just think—that could have been you."

"Good God, that sounds horrible."

Ben laughed. "I figured it would."

I became aware of how close we sat to each other. Shoulders, arms, hips, thighs touching. My attention wandered to Ben's long legs, propped up on the coffee table. If I concentrated hard enough, I could almost feel that soft abrasion again. Had that golden down I'd admired as a teenager thickened with age? Did it cling to his chest, his belly, lower?

Great. Now I was imagining him naked.

My jeans were suddenly uncomfortably tight.

"Uh-oh, what are *you* thinking?" Ben asked with a grin.

"Are you sure you want to know?"

"Well, now I am."

I bravely faced him as I said, "I'm thinking about the way the sun would catch the hair on your legs and turn it to gold. I always wanted to touch it and see if it was as soft as it appeared."

He blinked. "You looked at my legs?"

"I looked at a lot of things."

His teasing smile slowly faded. "You did? Why didn't you ever say anything?" he demanded in a voice tremulous with betrayal.

A twinge of regret pinged beneath my breastbone. "Back then—"

"Never mind. It doesn't matter," he said quickly, moving to rise.

"Clearly it does." I grabbed his arm and pulled him back down to the couch. "Back then I didn't really know what was happening, Ben. No, that's not true. I knew you had a crush on me, but I mean, I liked girls. I didn't understand that you could like both. And you..."

"Yeah."

"You made me feel things I didn't want to." *You still do.* I searched the stained ceiling for clues on how to say this without making things worse. "Not for one moment did I believe that it was wrong. That kiss was perfect, Ben. *You* were perfect. It was like in that moment I saw the way everything should be. But we were so young, and I was leaving, and the feelings were so strong. They scared me." *How could you find your soul mate before you'd even started shaving?* "So I tried to forget you—*that's* the real reason I never wrote. Because I was a coward."

I scrubbed a hand over my face. "You have no idea how much I regret that."

"Me too. But maybe things worked out the way they were meant to. What are the chances we would have kept in touch anyway? We were kids—in different countries no less. Out of sight, out of mind."

I knew he was right, but that didn't absolve my guilt.

"Was it difficult for you to come out as bisexual?" he asked. "Because you seem . . . comfortable."

There was no way to respond to that question without it seeming like another betrayal. "I am. Sexual compatibility is easy. I never struggled with that. The relationship part is tougher for me—with men *and* women."

"This boyfriend of yours—"

"*Ex*-boyfriend."

"Is he the only one?"

"The only guy I've been with?"

He nodded and licked his lips. I tracked the movement with a sharp throb in my groin and quickly averted my eyes.

"No, I've dated both sexes since college. But it was the most serious relationship I've had with a man, yes." *Other than you.*

"Is that what ended your marriage?"

"God, no. My marriage ended because I was young and stupid and married the wrong person. It was long before I met Will."

"Will," he repeated. "Why aren't you still together?"

I'd been afraid he'd ask that. "That's a long story, but the condensed version is that neither one of us was willing to put in the effort for it to work. Our careers were too important. In the end, I messed up. I cheated. Thought I could have it all and not have to pay the price." I let out a derisive snort. "Janet had me pegged when she said I push people away."

"How long ago did you break up?"

"A little over a year." Did he think less of me now? I tried to see myself through Ben's eyes—liar, cheater, coward—and I wanted to hide. I was learning a hell of a lot about myself on this trip and most of it wasn't good.

Ben sighed. "I should go." But I hadn't released his arm and he made no attempt to break my hold.

"Stay here tonight," I urged. My heart slammed against my ribs at the thought of letting him out of my sight.

Ben gave a watery laugh.

"Seriously. It's slick out. They were calling for freezing rain earlier. I don't think it's safe for you to drive in this condition."

"Oh, now that's a good line."

"No line. And no sex," I assured him. "The sofa is a pull-out. I'll even let you use my toothbrush."

"Swapping spit with a stranger? That's brave of you."

"You're not a stranger. And I promise not to give you cooties."

He pursed his lips. "You're right. I am a little buzzed. What time is it, anyway?"

A quick glance at the clock on the microwave showed that it was after midnight. We'd been talking for hours. Just like old times.

I shutdown my laptop while Ben used the bathroom. Then we traded places. When I emerged, the room was dark except for the floor lamp in the corner. Benji had claimed the bed, pulling the covers up to his ears, so I resigned myself to the sleeper sofa. But as I grabbed the seat cushions, he stopped me. "You might want to reconsider. That mattress is an inch thick. I already checked. There's room in here."

"Are you sure?"

"We've shared a bed before."

"Yeah, but we were kids then."

"Don't worry, I'll keep my hands to myself."

"That's what I'm afraid of."

Benji's chuckle made my skin prickle with awareness. I undressed in the dark, donning my flannel sleep pants and T-shirt slowly, so that Ben would have ample time to look if he wanted.

A muffled curse erupted from the bed. "You're evil." He had looked, then.

"You didn't have to watch," I teased.

"Didn't I?"

The neighbors had finally turned off the television, but the party was still going across the parking lot as I climbed into bed. It wasn't that much different from an average weekend at my apartment building, but with Benji next to me, there was no way I would be able to sleep. I kept thinking about the marks on his arms.

Please tell me those scars aren't because of me.

"Benji?"

No response came from his side of the bed, although I didn't believe he was asleep, and a part of me was glad. Who knew what I might say if given the chance? "I'm glad you're here, Ben," was as close as I came to uttering the truth.

I rolled to my side and fell into a restless sleep.

I jerked awake with a start, not knowing what had woken me. It took me a second to get my bearings and remember where I was. And that I wasn't alone. Blindly, I reached to my right but encountered only empty mattress. The room was pitch-black, except for the sliver of light that shone between the drapes and silhouetted Ben's form as he sat on the edge of the mattress with his back toward me.

I raised myself up on one elbow. "Ben?"

"I want you to do it."

"What?" I reached for the bedside lamp so I could see his face.

"No. Leave it off," he ordered as he twisted around. "I changed my mind. Go ahead and write your story. Ask questions. See what you can dig up. It's always going to be there, no matter how hard I try to ignore it, so maybe it's time we all knew the truth."

"Are you sure?"

"I trust you to do it right."

Ben's vote of confidence made me suddenly unsure. It was a big responsibility.

"Now you're backing out?" he asked when I didn't immediately respond.

"I don't know if I'll find anything. And after twenty years . . ." Why had I even started down this path? I was probably setting myself up for failure. And Ben was the last person I wanted to disappoint. Except my earlier excitement was back. Vague snippets of phrases were already forming in my head, and if Ben weren't there, I would probably have headed straight for my computer.

"You're thinking about it now, aren't you? I can feel your mind buzzing."

"Ben . . ."

"I get the same way with a new painting. It's like I can't rest until it's out on the canvas."

Ben swung his legs around and crawled back under the blankets. He arranged himself on his side, facing me, his head inches from mine. A distant memory leapt into my head. Another night, Benji lying next to me in the dark. He'd been sleeping over, and as usual, we'd shared my bed—only this time had been different because I'd spent the night trying to talk myself out of a boner. It hadn't worked, and I'd stroked myself to orgasm, biting my lip to keep quiet, with Ben asleep beside me.

As if my body remembered too, my dick began to thicken. Damn, it was going to be a long night.

"What if I do find out something?" I asked. "Have you thought of that?"

"I'll worry about that if it happens. I don't see how it could be any worse than what's already been running through my head, though. Watching folks in town, always wondering who knows more than they're saying."

"And your mom? I should probably talk to her. She already has so much material."

Ben was slow in responding. "I'll tell her. Does that mean you'll do it? Dig a little? Until you have to leave?"

Leave. My throat tightened. New York seemed a long way away at the moment.

"What else have I got to do, right?"

It grew quiet, and I thought Ben might have fallen asleep, so it surprised me when he spoke again.

"Do you remember the last time I slept over? It was just before you left for Seattle." I sucked in a startled breath. How had he read my mind? "I'm pretty sure you were whacking off next to me."

I groaned.

"I'm right, aren't I?" He chuckled softly, his breath blowing hot on my cheek. "At first I thought you were having a nightmare because you were breathing so heavily. And I was going to wake you up, but then I could feel your arm moving under the covers. Up until then I'd never actually masturbated, you know. I mean I'd had a wet dream or two, and I'd got hard before, but that was it. But they talked about it in sex ed, so I figured out what you must be doing."

The next morning, I'd jumped out of bed and made a beeline for the shower so he wouldn't notice my crusty pajamas. I couldn't even look at him for days after, and, oh my god, he'd been awake the whole time.

I cupped my hands over my face. "Could we not talk about this?"

"It made me feel weird, listening to you, but an excited weird." Ben's voice had grown low and husky. "It got me hard. I wanted to touch you so bad. To touch myself." He sounded like he had the whole thing committed to memory. "You made this quiet gasp, and then your body shook. And then after there was this faint scent . . . like pancake batter almost."

I moaned.

"I didn't know what it was until after. The smell of your come. I could never get that smell out of my head."

A warm, rough hand slipped under my T-shirt, flattening on my stomach. All thoughts of sleep flew out the window as my cock lifted eagerly. "Ben," I choked. "I thought you said—"

"Shut up." That hand delved into my flannel pajama bottoms and grasped me roughly, fingers tight enough to make me gasp and thrust upward. Ben, the dark, and the blankets piled around us—it was like every teenaged fantasy I'd never allowed myself come to life. I went rock-hard.

"Twenty years is a long time, Alex," Ben whispered in my ear as he began to stroke. Long and slow, then short and fast. I couldn't help twitching as those questing fingers closed over the head of my cock and deliberately rubbed. Brought me dangerously close to the edge before sliding back down.

Under the covers, I reached for him, fumbling one-handed until I had my fingers inside his boxers. Benji was as hard as me, his skin smooth and hot beneath my palm, and when I slid my hand up, I found the head slick with pre-come. "Ah, Benji."

He jerked me roughly, and I loved it. I matched his rhythm, wishing I could see more, but then there was something so fitting about this, about the whisper of our mingled breaths, the slap of skin on skin.

The covers were abruptly flung back, the cool air a shock against my heated skin. I lost my grip on Ben's dick as he moved, but before I could draw a breath, Benji had dragged my pants down my hips. My body bowed at the first touch of his mouth on my cock. "Fu-uck."

He sucked me greedily, with no finesse, but I was fine with that. Fuck finesse. His thick curls slid like silk between my fingers as I grabbed his hair. When his mouth disappeared, I moaned in disappointment and blindly tried to steer him back. But he'd only shifted to suck on my balls, and now my climax began to mount as his beard tickled my inner thigh and his hand returned to my cock.

"Yesss, come for me," he urged, followed by some gentle suction on my ball sack.

A few more strokes and I was there, the tremors turning me almost inside out with their intensity. Lashes of come landed hot on my chest and belly. I barely registered that Benji was nuzzling my stomach, licking me clean, and when I did, the thought sent me into dry spasms again.

It was over way too fast. I lay there, slightly stunned, willing my heart to slow and my head to clear. My fingers still clutched Ben's hair. I brushed it back off his face. "Your turn."

"Beat you to it," he said with a hoarse chuckle.

"Oh." The disappointment rocked me more than I expected. "Next time, then."

Ben curled against me and rested his head on my shoulder. I wasn't really a cuddler, and I debated extricating myself, but Ben felt absurdly right where he was. "You still smell like pancake batter," he murmured.

I laughed. "You realize I'm never going to be able to eat pancakes again after that."

Against my shoulder, Ben's lips curved. That was the last thing I remembered. Moments later I fell into a dreamless sleep.

In the morning, I woke to find Benji already up and half dressed. I caught a glimpse of bare back as he slipped on his shirt, and immediately wanted to tug him into bed with me. Something more than a quick handjob this time. "Hey, what's the rush?" I teased as I rubbed the sleep from my eyes.

Ben sat down on the chair to lace up his boots. His shoulders were tense, and he wasn't looking at me.

"Ben?" I raised up on one elbow.

He sighed. "I can't do this with you." His gaze was truly regretful as it swept down my body, which was covered only to the waist. "I'm sorry. I thought I could."

I sat up, stomach tight as Ben got to his feet. "What does that mean?"

"It means we can work together until you find something, or until you get bored and go home, but last night can't happen again."

"I don't get it. Why not?"

"Because I'm going to fall in love with you," he replied simply, with one hand on the doorknob. "And you're going to rip out my heart when you leave. I won't be able to handle it this time."

Ben's words were a bittersweet one-two punch to the gut. He didn't wait for a reaction, and all I could do was gape as the door closed firmly behind him.

CHAPTER ELEVEN

"**I**'m going to fall in love with you . . . I won't be able to handle it this time."

Ben's words clung to me long after he walked out. And every time I replayed them, something wrenched in my chest.

I couldn't face Dad, not until I'd straightened out some of the feelings ricocheting around in my head, so I headed to Alton to do some more cleaning at the trailer. In this instance at least, Janet's accusation was most certainly true.

Three hours later, the trailer was finally empty; my mind, however, was not. That was how I found myself once again on Angela Morning's doorstep, only to discover Ben wasn't there. He had prepared her though.

Now that she had an audience to listen, Angela was eager to talk. She ushered me inside, made us tea, and filled me in on the leads that had been chased, which were surprisingly few, and all of them dead-ends. How did you track a girl with no credit cards, no passport, no GPS-enabled cell phone, not even a social insurance number?

Angela had copies of the original police reports and updates from the private investigators she'd hired over the years. She'd kept a log of everything—everyone she'd spoken to, every letter she'd written, every tip, every time she'd called the police for an update. There had been a couple of credible sightings over the years, including one that Misty was working as a prostitute in Victoria, and Angela had followed up herself, gone down there, but the girl had been somebody else's daughter.

While the reports were painfully thin, I was impressed. She would have made a good journalist if it weren't for her total bias against Derek Gagnon. The whole time we talked, I wanted to shake her for being so obsessed, for not seeing that she had another child who needed her attention. The image of Ben last night, distraught and vulnerable, made my heart ache for both of them. Ben had stood by her, supported her all these years, and she didn't once mention his name in conversation.

I didn't know whether to feel sorry for her or hate her.

"Do you want to see her room?" Angela asked, already on her feet and leaving me no choice but to follow.

I didn't see how it would be any help, but I wasn't going to tell Angela that. The police would already have gone through Misty's room twenty years ago, looking for any clue of where she might have gone.

But as Angela opened the door, the air whooshed from my lungs.

If the house was a time capsule, this was the heart of the shrine. The room was exactly as I remembered: pink and girly, as if waiting for Misty to walk back in and curl up in her frilly canopied bed beneath the Backstreet Boys poster tacked to the wall.

It even still smelled like her. Calvin Klein's Obsession. How was that possible after so long?

That was when I noticed the perfume bottles cluttering the dresser. One was full, as though it was a new bottle. Was Angela using these to preserve the smell?

Gooseflesh pimpled my arms. Now I fully understood Ben's agitation. This careful preservation went beyond grief. This wasn't healthy.

"I come in here sometimes," Angela said. "To think, to feel close to her."

If Angela Morning had ever been warm and nurturing to her children, it had been long before I arrived on the scene. Maybe things had been different when her husband was alive, but I never recalled her being home very much. She worked twelve-hour shifts at the mill, and when she did come home, she usually crashed. Misty had been officially left in charge of her younger brother, although once she turned sixteen and got wheels, she was hardly around too. From my perspective, Ben had raised himself.

Was Angela's unhealthy obsession and grief over Misty a case of too little, too late, or was this her idea of penance? To subject herself to the torment of Misty's absence every day?

Did Ben's room look like it had twenty years ago too? Somehow I doubted it.

Angela picked up one of the stuffed animals littering the bed and held it to her nose. The childish remnants seemed so incongruous with the sensual young woman I remembered. Was that how Angela still saw Misty—like her sweet, innocent baby daughter?

I peered at the faded Polaroids of Janet and Misty that were tucked into the frame of the mirror. Janet had bought that used Polaroid camera at a rummage sale in town, and I laughed quietly at the memory of how for weeks afterward, she would pop up unexpectedly, the flash blinding her unsuspecting subjects so that we all ended up with our eyes closed or mouths gaping open.

My fingers trailed lightly over the dresser top—Misty's hairbrush, an ancient hair crimper, and a wooden jewelry box with gilded edges—afraid to actually touch anything. I couldn't shake the feeling Misty would burst in any minute and catch me snooping.

"Have you ever seen a naked girl, Sandy?"

If I closed my eyes, I could still see Misty, the way she'd been that warm spring day. Benji and I had been playing in his backyard after school, his mom at work as usual, and I'd run in to take a leak. But as I'd gone down the hallway to the bathroom, there had been Misty in her bedroom, with the door wide open. She'd been wearing nothing but a towel, her wet hair cascading down her back as she combed it. We'd stared at each other.

"Uh, uh . . . sorry," I'd stammered, heat rushing to my face and other places. "I was . . ." I'd known I should avert my eyes—this was Benji's sister—except I couldn't look away. And Misty hadn't seemed the least bit embarrassed.

She'd taken a step closer. Drew her comb across her chest, teasing it over the knot holding her towel in place. "Have you ever seen a naked girl, Sandy?"

My mouth had gone dry. "Not . . . not in real life."

Her lips had curved. And then the towel had fallen to her feet, revealing full, pale breasts with rosy nipples, and a triangle of strawberry hair between her thighs. She'd continued combing her hair as if this were normal, as if I weren't even there.

"Well, will you look at that?" Misty had cooed. I'd followed the direction of her gaze and had seen that my dick was tenting my pants. "You do like girls after all. And all this time, Janet and I thought you and Benji were jerk buddies." She'd giggled. How had I ever forgotten that sound? A combination of victory and mockery. "Won't he be disappointed when I tell him? He's got a crush on you, you know."

Jesus. I pushed the memory out of my head. I felt dirty just remembering it. I'd never mentioned the encounter to Benji, but Misty's words had stayed with me all that summer. *He's got a crush on you.* Was that what had started it all? Because nothing had been the same for me after that. We had still been best friends, but I hadn't been able to help but see him differently.

I raised the lid on the jewelry box. A plastic ballerina slowly whirled, the tune off-key and unrecognizable. She stopped in mid-pirouette.

"You have to wind it," Angela offered.

I grimaced, thinking of her in here, listening to the tinkle of Misty's music box, spritzing the air with her perfume.

"What does Ben think of all this?" I asked.

"Ben?" She said his name like he was a stranger.

"Yes, Ben. Your son."

She continued to gaze at me like I'd grown two heads. "Ben doesn't come in here. He lives above the garage. They said that was better for him when he left that place."

"That place?" My heart tripped.

"The hospital in Victoria. Well, it wasn't a real hospital." She blanched. "Oh, I shouldn't have said anything. He doesn't like to talk about this."

Talk about what? Ben had been hospitalized? "Angela," I growled, desperate for more information.

She shook her head.

"Are you saying Ben was in a psychiatric facility? Why?"

"He wouldn't want me to say anything." Her tone brooked no argument. *Damn.*

Angela marched to my side and took the jewelry box from my hand. I'd forgotten I was holding it. She gave the tattered ballerina a tender stroke with her finger. "Misty always wanted to be a ballerina," she said fondly.

"Angela, you can't bring up something like that and then expect me to drop it." She was closing the jewelry box lid when something caught my eye. "Wait," I cried.

What the hell?

Nestled amid the rhinestones and beaded bangles was a pair of simple gold drop earrings. They were art deco in style, stamped with an embossed pattern, and studded with a bead of black onyx. I recognized these earrings. They were my mom's. She'd always worn them on special occasions when I was growing up.

What were the chances a teenaged girl would have the same pair? Zero.

They were unique, vintage, once belonging to my great-grandmother. I even remembered the fuss Mom had made when she'd unpacked in Seattle and realized they weren't with her other jewelry. How had Misty gotten them?

"Did you give these to Misty?" I asked.

Angela peered into my hand. "No, not me. But people were always giving things to her."

Not expensive antique jewelry, they weren't. The earrings were classy; not exactly something a guy like Derek Gagnon would give his girlfriend, even if he could afford them.

Suddenly, I couldn't wait to get out of there, away from the oppressive grief that filled the house. Away from the troubling earrings. I put them back in the box, made some vague excuses to Angela, and left, carrying with me a stack of her binders.

That feeling clung to me long after I left. Only once I was back on the road did I finally manage to shake off Misty's presence. Except all I could think about now was Ben and whatever might have happened in Victoria. Then there were those earrings of Mom's. And in the back of my mind, a new worry was building.

The hospital, with its antiseptic smell and pall of death, actually seemed like a reprieve after the Morning house.

I encountered Katy in the hallway. It was the first time I'd seen her since our date on Friday, and I wasn't sure how to act.

She greeted me with a warm smile. "Hey, Alex, you just missed your friend."

"Friend?"

"Guy with curly hair and a beard?"

Ben? Ben had come to visit Dad? I was touched that he'd do that.

"Too bad it's not one of his better days. He's been confused. I'm sorry, but I have to run." Katy hustled down the corridor, then stopped and swung back around. "Hey, Sam's going to be at his dad's tomorrow night. You want to come over for dinner? I make a mean chicken parm."

My gut clenched, and that was when I knew this thing with Ben went deeper than I'd feared. "I, uh . . ."

She sighed. "Never mind. I know when to give up."

I cursed under my breath as she disappeared from view. "Idiot." Who turned down no-strings sex? Especially when Ben had made it clear he was off-limits. But after last night, I knew Katy wasn't the person I wanted right now. Pretending she was would only make things worse.

Dad was lying in bed with his eyes open, staring at the ceiling when I entered his room. Someone had shaved him so he didn't look so rough.

"Hi, Dad—" The words caught in my throat. He hadn't stirred, hadn't blinked at my entry. I was just about to whirl and run for Katy when a soft breath rattled in his chest. His eyelids flickered.

On the heart monitor, the lines were holding steady.

Jesus. Would it be like this from here on in? Always wondering if today would be the last day?

Shaking off the remnants of my panic, I tossed my coat on the guest chair and sat down. "Um, hi, Dad. It's me." Did he even know I was there anymore? I looked at my watch. Where was Janet? She usually stopped by in the late afternoon.

I was anxious to get back to my motel room and comb through the files Angela had given me. Throwing myself into this project was just what I needed. Sure there wasn't much to go on, but I might come across an avenue that hadn't been explored.

But there was something I had to know first.

I jumped to my feet and crossed over to the window. It was four o'clock and the daylight was rapidly fading. The lights in the parking light fluttered on.

"Guess who I saw today, Dad? Angela Morning. Remember the Mornings? You should see their house now. It's like time stopped in August 1996. Mrs. Morning, Angela, hasn't touched Misty's room."

I spun back toward the bed. Dad still hadn't moved and the rattle of his breath was unnerving.

"I'm writing about Misty—about her disappearance. It feels like there's a story here. Angela let me look around, but it was pointless. All it did was creep me out. I didn't find anything useful, not that I was expecting a secret diary under the mattress. Let's be honest, Misty wasn't really the diary kind of girl, was she? But I'm guessing she had lots of secrets."

I stepped closer, searching his face for signs that he heard me, that he understood what I was saying. The nightlight over the bed cast long shadows and made his cheeks seem even gaunter. He was shrinking right before my eyes.

Who are you?

"The more I think about it, while I wouldn't have put it past Misty to run away, she wouldn't have slunk off like that. She would have made a big production of it, like she did for everything else. You remember how she was, don't you? I wish I'd paid more attention back then. To everything. Was it someone else driving her car that day? I close my eyes and try to remember, but we weren't close enough."

No response, of course. Only the slow, steady beeps of the machines and the rasp of his breath.

All the times Misty had been in our house sliced through my mind—flashes of sleepovers, birthday parties, her and Janet lying out on towels in the backyard soaking up the sun in the summer. I hadn't wanted to notice then how he'd look at her. The flush that would rush to his face or the embarrassing way he'd flirt when Mom wasn't around.

Had he had his eye on her then? When she was just a kid?

After he was laid off, he'd been around the house a lot more. With Mom at work and us at school, he'd had the place to himself. My stomach heaved. I pictured Misty as she'd once stood before me, that knowing smirk. The towel dropping. *"Have you ever seen a naked girl?"*

Misty had been a *girl*, not a woman. She'd been a teenager, a minor. *Oh God, please don't tell me you took advantage of her, Dad.*

"Did you do it?" I asked, my throat tight, my mouth filled with disgust. "Did you sleep with her? Did you give her Mom's earrings?" Someone had, or else she'd stolen them herself.

A tiny moan issued from his lips. His fingers scrabbled on the sheets.

"Tell me, you bastard. Was it you? You can't leave it like this."

He turned his head and gazed up at me, eyes alert now, almost pleading. His mouth moved as he struggled to speak. I tried not to flinch when his fetid breath blew in my face. "She . . . she . . ." A tear slid down one withered cheek.

"I swear to god if you did this . . ."

He grabbed my wrist, and this time I managed not to jump at the touch of his skeletal fingers. "Don't have . . . much longer. I'm ready to go. Need you . . . to do something but don't tell Janet."

"God, you're unbelievable," I spat. "Why can't you tell the truth? For once in your life, do the right thing."

"Trying to. Please."

It was the quiet plea that slipped under my guard. I couldn't recall my father ever asking me for anything beyond grabbing him a cold Canadian from the fridge. "What is it?" I asked tightly.

His voice was thin, not much above a whisper. "When I'm gone . . . pictures . . . in my house—"

"What pictures? Do you mean the family portrait in your living room? I've got that one at the motel."

Dad's head rolled frantically on the pillow. "Uh, uh, uh. Not that . . . Others."

"I've been cleaning your place. There *aren't* any other pictures." I ground my teeth. What a waste of time. I should have known Jerry Colville wouldn't have the balls to step up at the end.

"You'll know what to do with them." He patted my hand weakly. His lips curved. "Always knew you could look after yourself. Never needed me."

My throat constricted unexpectedly. "You're wrong, Dad," I choked. "I did need you." My vision blurred, and shit, I was about to cry.

Dad moaned in pain. His hand tightened on mine. "Don't want . . . to die alone. Forgive me?"

"For what?" I wanted to hear him say the words.

"Everything."

Could I? I opened my mouth, but the words wouldn't come, so I closed it again, and held his hand until he fell asleep.

That was how Janet found us.

Janet and I grabbed an uneasy dinner from the Chinese restaurant next to my motel after our visit, and then I spent the rest of the night in my room pouring over Angela's files. It was almost a relief to throw myself into this rather than think about Dad.

"People don't just vanish," Angela had said. But Misty had done exactly that.

I began to map out a strategy, compiling a list of everyone who had provided statements or been questioned by the police. The actual transcripts were missing from Angela's collection, but there was enough in the notes to indicate that nothing of any use had been uncovered. Most of those interviewed had been Misty's friends. Many names jumped out at me—seniors from the high school. There was Janet of course, and Derek, and good old Garrett Wilde.

It was hard to get a sense of guilt or innocence by reading words on the page. I'd have to see who was still around and if they'd be willing to talk. One of them had to know something. Oh, and while I was at it, maybe I could track down some of the cops who had worked the case. I settled in for a long night.

What seemed like hours later, my eyes burning from all the reading, I took a break and stretched out on my lumpy bed. Maybe I was looking at this from the wrong angle, seeing connections where there weren't any. The earrings couldn't be discounted, but maybe Misty had simply had car trouble—hadn't Dad always been tinkering with that crap bucket of hers?—and been in the wrong place at the wrong time.

I wanted desperately to believe that.

Suddenly, I needed to hear Ben's voice, but after last night, I wasn't sure he would even talk to me. *Stop acting like a teenager*, I told myself, and called.

The phone rang for a long time before Ben answered with a grunt.

"Hey," I said all cheery. "I heard you stopped by to visit Dad today. That was nice of you."

"Hmm." He sounded half-asleep.

"Are you in bed?"

"It's after midnight. What do you think?"

"Oh, is it that late?"

"Yes, Alex, it's that late."

"Are you alone?"

"Not really, no."

"No?" I bolted upright.

"Luna's with me." I could practically hear his smirk over the phone.

"Jerk," I said.

"Dumbass."

I wished I was there with him now, snuggled in bed with a fire burning in the woodstove instead of in this dumpy motel room alone. "You know, if you're looking for a bed warmer . . ."

His chuckle was low and sexy. My cock stirred, and I had to resist the urge to slip my hand down the front of my pants. "Don't push," he cautioned. "My willpower is low enough as it is."

"You tell me that, and you want me to stop? I don't get it. You want me. I want you. We could be enjoying this time together instead of dancing around it."

"Please, Alex."

"Fine. Want to take a road trip with me tomorrow?"

"Huh?"

Adorable. I began shutting down my laptop for the night. "I found him."

"Found who?"

"Cleary. One of the cops who originally worked Misty's case. He retired to Prince Rupert."

"How did you find him so quickly?"

He sounded so impressed that I hated to tell him the truth. "Google. He's a real estate agent now. Would you believe he advertises on the RCMP annuitant website? I emailed him asking if he could meet with us tomorrow."

"Meet? That's a four-hour drive. Can't you just use the phone?"

"In my experience, people are more forthcoming when you're in front of them, and it's harder to lie that way."

He sighed.

"Ben?"

"I'm thinking."

"It would be nice to spend some time together. While I'm here."

"All right."

"I can pick you up—"

"No need. I don't want you to have to backtrack. I'll meet you at your motel at eight. Is that okay?"

"Perfect."

Another long silence. I couldn't bring myself to hang up, silly and childish as that was. As long as Ben was there on the other end of the line, I didn't have to deal with reality. Plus his sleep-roughened voice was sexy as hell. It was making me think of last night.

"Are you going to hang up?" he finally asked.

"*You* hang up first."

"You called *me*. How old are you again?"

I laughed. "Hey, do you remember how we used to do this with our walkie-talkies?" How many nights had Benji gotten me through? With his voice on the other end of the radio anchoring me, I had been able to shut out the sound of Mom and Dad arguing. Back in those days, it was all we'd had.

"Yeah," he replied. "Thank goodness for cell phones, so I don't have to keep saying 'over' when I'm done speaking."

"Roger that, Red One."

He groaned at my use of his childhood code name.

I grinned to myself. "Only you didn't have such a sexy voice then."

"Go to bed, Alex."

"Mmm, got to take a shower first. Maybe jerk off. You've got me all horny now."

He sucked in a breath. "You are such a bastard. See you tomorrow."

"Over and out, Red One."

CHAPTER TWELVE

True to his word, Ben was waiting in the parking lot the next morning at eight. I filled a thermos with crap coffee and ran out to hop in his car.

"You don't even come to the door to pick me up? What kind of date are you?"

He blinked at my teasing, but swiftly recovered. "Not a date for one thing."

"Your loss. I put out." When Benji narrowed his eyes, I gave his shoulder a little shove. "Hey, I'm joking. Trying to lighten the mood. You're looking awfully rugged this morning, by the way."

"Rugged?"

I flashed a smirk at his plaid flannel shirt and quilted vest. "Like a tall, thin, gay lumberjack. It's hot."

Ben's lips twitched. "You're—"

"Incorrigible? Charming? Devastatingly handsome?"

"I give up," he sighed, but he was smiling as he said it, and anyway my levity had worked; any tension from our night together was gone.

"Do you still want to do this?" I asked.

"Do you?"

"God, yes."

"Then let's go." We began the ascent into the mountains in silence, with only the radio for company. If we didn't run into any construction, or logging trucks, or accidents, we could make Prince Rupert by noon, and so far, things were looking good. The sun even began to peek through the clouds as we climbed out of the valley.

"So how did you convince this guy we're meeting to talk to you?" Ben asked.

I winced. "We're looking for a house."

"What?"

"I needed to make sure he'd be around. I made us an appointment. You're my partner and we want to buy a house in Prince Rupert."

"And how do you suppose he's going to react when you tell him why you're really there? He's an ex-cop, remember?"

"All part of my plan. I've found it's a lot harder to turn someone down when they're on your doorstep."

"I hope you're right. It's a long way to go only to have a door slammed in our face."

I suppressed a smile. Ben might not have been thrilled to be here, but he was still here. You had to love a guy who had your back, no matter what.

The winding route through the mountains from Smithers to Prince Rupert on the coast was scenic but most of it passed me by. My attention was on the man behind the wheel. Watching him was far more enjoyable than stewing about my dad.

There was green paint beneath his nails and another fleck on the back of one hand. "Were you painting this morning?" I asked about an hour into our journey.

"Yeah, I was up early. Couldn't sleep."

Because of me? I hoped so.

"Are you going to watch me drive the whole trip?" Ben finally asked. Two vertical lines popped between his brows as he navigated a tight turn.

"Maybe. You're awfully cute when you're concentrating."

He rolled his eyes and nodded to my crotch "Keep it zipped, mister. And behave."

I grinned. "And if I don't?"

"Don't you ever get tired of being shot down?"

"Apparently not by you." If I'd sensed any hostility or genuine irritation, I would have reined in the flirting, but the lines crinkling around Ben's eyes told me he was enjoying me pushing his buttons.

"How did you become an artist?" I asked. "Is that what you majored in?"

"No, I didn't make it past the first semester of college at UVic. I'm mostly self-taught. You know I was always into drawing as a kid."

"What made you get into teaching?"

"Are you interviewing me?" he queried with a smirk.

"No, just trying to catch up."

"I started volunteering at the high school about five or six years ago, running an after-school program. It got so popular that they found the funding to add it to the regular curriculum and hired me. These kids out here—there's not a lot for them."

"I remember. It seems to have gotten worse," I added, thinking about the groups of aimless teens I'd seen in town. With most families having one or both parents working shift work, there was a lot of absentee parenting.

"It has. When the mill closed, it put a lot of people out of work. That's when I found a grant and started the weekend all-ages class. It helps keep the younger kids busy and out of trouble, and it gives the adults an escape. In the spring, I've been invited to hold a weekly session for seniors at Pine Point."

"You love it, don't you?"

He smiled. "I do. I don't fool myself that I'm making a huge difference, but it gives me a sense of purpose, makes me feel valued."

Because he never felt valued growing up.

"So I'm not completely selfless you see, I get something out of it too," he added. "Okay, my turn. Why are we really out here?"

"Um, we're going to see Douglas Cleary."

"Misty's been gone for two decades. A few days is hardly going to matter. Why the sudden rush to see this guy when you could—should—be spending the time with your dad?"

I stared out the window at the passing scenery.

"Oh, so now you don't want to talk. You can pry into my life, but yours is off-limits?"

"I just don't understand why I'm supposed to be all upset and falling to pieces over this. He hasn't been part of my life for years. If he wanted us to gather round, maybe he shouldn't have pushed us away."

"Way to be an adult, Alex."

"I can't help it. He was our dad. He was supposed to love us, but once we were gone, we didn't exist anymore. It's like he never looked back."

Ben snorted. The sudden tension in the car matched the hard line of his jaw. "Never looked back, huh? Sounds familiar."

Shit. Hadn't I done the same to him? Forgotten about him the minute we left?

"Why did you come, then?" Ben asked. "If you dislike him so much? Surely you didn't have to come all this way to write your article."

I let my head fall back on the headrest. "I guess . . . I guess I was hoping to finally get an answer to why he pushed us away."

"If he's an alcoholic, you might not ever get that answer. Or at least not one you're satisfied with. It's all about the booze."

"I know that. I've interviewed addicts. It's just . . ."

"Different when it's *your* dad?" I didn't answer. Didn't need to. Ben had always been able to read me. "Alex, this is it. This is the life you have. There's no going back and changing the past. You either accept who he is and try to forge a new relationship while you can, or you hold on to that resentment until it eats you up. And trust me, it will eat you up."

"Is that what you've done with your mom?"

"It's what I try to do." His lips quirked. "Doesn't always work. But seriously, if you don't make peace with him now, you'll regret it later."

"You think I'm selfish, don't you?"

"You said it, not me."

I pressed my forehead to the cool glass of the window. "I'm afraid. I've spent so many years resenting him for the way he hurt us, all of us. It's easier to hate him for being weak and selfish than to focus on the alternative—that he didn't want us, didn't want *me*, that I was the reason he stopped being a father. Now, when it comes down to it, I'm not sure I can handle the truth."

"It's his loss, Alex." Ben took his hand from the wheel to squeeze my thigh. "But I don't believe that you're at fault. As children, we tend to think of our parents only in terms of ourselves—we forget they're people too. People who make mistakes, who do stupid things; people with their own problems."

That sounded like something a shrink would say, and I immediately thought of what Angela had let slip. "That's very profound. Where did you learn that?" I wanted him to tell me about Victoria and whatever had happened there.

Ben stiffened and withdrew his hand, leaving a void behind on my leg. "You're not the only one with family issues, remember?"

After that, we fell into another silence. There was an ease to it that comforted me. Ben and I had always been good with silence; even as kids neither one of us had ever felt compelled to make idle conversation. Often, we'd spent hours in our wilderness hideout just reading side by side, or Ben would doodle while I played my Game Boy.

The radio was set to a local talk radio station, and an hour-long discussion of highway safety upgrades—four new webcams planned—quickly lulled me to sleep. I must have been out for a while when the newscaster's voice cut through my doze.

"—father and son from Prince George are facing charges of attempted murder, aggravated assault, and kidnapping after a young woman was found in distress on the side of Highway 16 on Saturday night."

My eyes flew open, and Ben and I both straightened at the same time. "Jesus," I breathed, swiveling to look at him.

"She is recovering in hospital. The RCMP say the accused and the victim were known to each other and believe the attack was targeted. The investigation is ongoing. Anyone with any information is asked to call—"

Ben turned the dial until he came across a retro seventies, eighties, and nineties station with a strong enough signal. Neither of us spoke. We didn't need to. We were both clearly thinking the same thing.

The news report was an unwelcome reminder that this wasn't just a scenic day trip—that Misty hadn't been as fortunate as that poor girl.

We drove almost a hundred miles before I began to relax again. "How often does that happen up here?" I finally asked. The fact that Ben knew exactly what I was referring to, told me it was still on his mind as well.

"Not often enough to be commonplace, but too often for comfort. I told you—it's a hard life for many people."

"I don't ever recall things like that when we were kids, but it must have happened. Some of those Highway of Tears cases go back decades."

"We were in our own little world. Real life didn't penetrate. I bet there was a lot we didn't see."

I shot Ben a startled glance, searching for a hidden meaning in his words. What had he meant by that?

The opening chords of Tom Cochrane's "Life Is a Highway" filled the car, and I seized the distraction to lighten the heavy mood. "Oh, do you remember this?" I spun the dial and cranked up the music, singing the lyrics at the top of my lungs.

"Stop," Ben shouted.

"You used to like this song."

"Yeah, before you murdered it with your wailing."

I lit into an impressive air harmonica solo. "See, still got it."

"Got what? Spasmodic tics?" By now he was laughing so hard that tears were leaking from his eyes. "Oh my god, stop it. I'm trying to drive here. You'll get us killed."

Without the summer influx of RVs and campers on the road, we were making good time, and we only got caught behind a logging truck for a few miles. We spent the next forty minutes or so singing along to the songs of our youth until we finally lost the station outside of Terrace. By then we'd been on the road for three hours, and I was starting to get restless. And hungry.

"I should have picked up some snacks before we left," I said. "Maybe we can grab something before we head to Cleary's."

The lines around Ben's eyes crinkled in amusement. "Still the same Alex. There's a cooler in back with some sandwiches."

I grinned at Ben. "PB and J?"

"It was stupid, I know . . ."

"I can't believe you thought of that." I unbuckled my seat belt and plucked the small cooler off the backseat.

"I figured you wouldn't. That was always you—eager to dash off somewhere without thinking of provisions."

"'Cause I knew you always had us covered."

He smiled back, and my heart did an odd flutter. *Us.* Funny how one word could mean so much.

I lifted the cooler lid and laughed out loud. "Twinkies too! You remembered." My throat was thick with emotions.

He spared me an amused glance. "What? It's only sandwiches."

It was so much more than sandwiches. "Hungry?" I asked.

"I could eat."

Ben had also thrown in a couple of bottles of water, so I pulled out one for each of us, then unwrapped the wax paper from a sandwich, and handed him half.

I grinned as the familiar flavors rolled over my tongue. I couldn't recall the last time I'd had peanut butter and jelly sandwiches—probably not since I was a kid. "This is so good." A blob of jelly landed on my thigh. "Shit."

"Can't take you anywhere. There's napkins in the glove box."

I grabbed a couple of napkins and cleaned myself up so I wouldn't have a big stain near my crotch when we met Cleary. As I reached to close the glove compartment, I let out a bark of surprise and drew out the old-fashioned lensatic compass. "Is this . . .? This is the same one?" I flipped the cover open. "The one I gave you?"

A flush swept across Ben's cheekbones. "Why wouldn't it be? It still works. No sense in getting another one."

He kept it. All these years, he kept it. I couldn't stop smiling. "You didn't replace it with a GPS."

"GPS's don't always work in the mountains when you're hiking. The signal's fine on the highway, but once you get up in the hills . . . Stop it, you freak. It's just a compass." He took it and tossed it back in the glove box.

After that, we munched in companionable silence as we approached the coastal logging community of Prince Rupert. The highway hugged the Skeena River, and the sweeping views were breathtaking. But I wasn't a tourist, and the rugged beauty only emphasized the loneliness and isolation of this country and swelled the knot of apprehension in my belly.

Once we entered the city limits, I gathered up our trash, put the cooler away, and pulled out the directions I'd jotted down earlier. Douglas Cleary lived in a nice neighborhood near the harbor and worked out of his home in a converted garage—I'd checked on Google Maps last night.

We parked on the street in front of Cleary's well-manicured house. Though modest by most standards, it perched on a hill overlooking the water. The real estate business must have been treating him well if he could afford a prime spot like that.

Benji's body had grown tense. His fingers clutched the steering wheel tight enough for the knuckles to turn white. A wave of guilt rolled over me. I'd been so focused on my own selfish needs when I asked him along, that I hadn't thought about how this must be for him.

"Do you want to stay in the car?" I asked.

He seemed to give himself a mental shake. "No, I'm good."

We walked up the flagstone path to the office entrance.

The door was unlocked, but a bell above our heads rang when we entered. Immediately a large-framed man with a fringe of white hair barreled out to meet us with a puzzled smile and outstretched hand. "Hi there," he said. "Doug Cleary. Nice to meet you." Despite the years, I recognized Cleary immediately as one of the cops who had interviewed us after Misty's disappearance. I hadn't realized that from my research.

He paused in the act of shaking Ben's hand, brow wrinkling. "Ah, I know you, don't I? Wait, it'll come to me . . . Morning, right? Benji?"

Ben blinked in surprise. "Yes. I can't believe you remembered."

"Saw your mother on television the other day. But it would have come to me eventually anyway. It's always the unsolved cases that stay with you. Good to see you again." He turned to me. "That must make you . . ."

I decided to go for honesty. "Alex Colville. I'm the one who contacted you. I'm a journalist. But I'm also a friend of the family's. You might remember me—"

"The kid across the street," he finished. I was impressed. Clearly the former cop was still on the ball if he recognized me when no one else seemed to. "Well, I'm guessing you're not in the market for a house, are you? What can I do for you, boys? As if I don't already know."

"We're here about my sister's case," Ben chirped.

"I wish you hadn't come all this way. I've been retired for seven years, so there's not much I can help you with. You should talk to the sergeant in charge."

"Actually, Mr. Cleary," I said, "we're not here about the current investigation. We're interested in your impressions from back then. Off the record, of course."

Cleary looked between us. I'd been hoping that having Ben with me would prod his conscience, and my strategy appeared to have paid off because he ushered us into the house proper. "Come on through," he said, and then "DeeDee, put the coffeepot on, we have guests."

He led us into a glass-walled sunroom with a view of the harbor. In summer, the view would have been stunning, but with winter approaching it was only gray and gloomy. A blanket of fog lay across the water.

Ben and I sat next to each other on a wicker love seat. Cleary took the chair.

"How's your mother handling things now?" he asked Ben.

"She's as single-minded as ever."

"I've never met a more determined woman. You could set your clock by Angela Morning—every year on the anniversary of Misty's disappearance, we'd get a phone call. Or sometimes a visit." He smiled fondly before turning to me. "So, you said you were a journalist—TV? Newspaper? Or—let me guess—you're writing a true crime book. That seems to be all the rage these days."

"Magazines," I admitted with an anxious glance at Ben. I handed Cleary one of my business cards.

"American," he said with surprise.

"But, as you know, I have a personal connection to Ben and his sister. I was hoping we could take a look at some of your private notes on the case. I know there's sometimes a lot that doesn't make it into the reports."

"No need." He tapped his forehead. "All up here. Every detective has at least one case that sticks with him. Misty's was mine." His eyes glazed, and I wondered what he was thinking. "Something never sat right with me. She never fit the pattern of the others."

"Others?" Ben asked.

"The other girls that have gone missing on Highway 16 over the years."

I leaned forward. "Is that why she was never added to the official list?"

"There are only eighteen cases on the so-called official Highway of Tears list. Those are the ones managed by the task force."

"And the others—like Misty—don't matter?"

"Don't put words in my mouth, young man," Cleary snapped. Whatever I thought about the investigation, it was clear Misty had mattered to him. *Still* mattered. "We're talking about a seven-hundred-kilometer stretch of highway through sheer wilderness—there's no way to police all that. They can put up all the cameras they like, but things are gonna happen. Misty, though, she wasn't a high-risk girl. She wasn't tricking, and she wasn't hitchhiking. She had her own vehicle."

"So did Madison Scott." I'd done my research. The twenty-year-old had disappeared in 2011 after camping with friends near Hogsback Lake.

"I wasn't around for the Scott case, but as far as I know that's still unsolved too. Only difference is there was a crime scene. Her truck and tent were there, abandoned. With Misty, we had nothing. Not then, anyway."

"The general consensus in town is that the police didn't try very hard," I pointed out.

Cleary's wife, carrying a tray of coffees and a plate of assorted biscuits, interrupted before he could reply. "You go on," she said. "Don't stop on my account. I've heard it all before." I wondered if she thought we were shopping for houses, or maybe as the wife of a cop, she was just used to people showing up unexpectedly.

"I take it you don't believe this could be the work of a serial killer?" I asked bluntly.

Cleary actually snorted. "You writer-types, always searching for more drama. Do I think *some* of these cases are the work of a serial murderer or murderers? Sure. But, trust me, most of these girls are a one-off—and they were attacked by people they knew."

I shivered, thinking back to the newscast we'd heard on the drive over.

"Look," Cleary said, with a flash of impatience on his face. "Misty was a seventeen-year-old girl who'd spoken many times about getting out of town to her friends. She'd been seen driving away by the neighbors, by you in fact. She had a contentious relationship with her mother. She'd been in a bit of trouble—"

"Whoa, what kind of trouble?" I demanded.

Cleary glanced at Ben before turning to me. "She'd been given a few warnings by the local force—minor stuff really. Underage drinking. Shoplifting."

Shoplifting? I knew Misty had been no angel, but had Janet been aware of this? Had she participated too?

"Misty had a record?" I asked.

"No, no. Just some warnings."

A dozen questions hovered on the tip of my tongue, but I didn't want to interrupt Cleary further and risk him shutting down.

"Then there was the matter of the missing Spring Formal funds."

Beside me, Benji tensed. My heart kicked into overdrive, but I wasn't quite sure why. "You knew about that?" I asked, pretending that I did.

"Not entirely incompetent." Cleary winked. "Someone—I don't remember who—tipped us off about a rumor going around the school that Misty, and your sister, I believe, had stolen money intended for the dance. It was a couple thousand dollars. But we could never get the school to confirm it. And the dance went off as planned, so there was nothing to look into."

I struggled to hide my surprise. Was this what Arlene Jerkovic had been alluding to? As a social outcast, I'd had no use for school dances, but I would have thought I would have known if my sister had stolen money in high school.

"Anyway," Cleary was saying, "there was nothing to suggest Misty wasn't a runaway. But, just in case, we did mount aerial and foot searches."

"What did your gut say?" I asked.

Cleary sipped his coffee. He was avoiding eye contact with either of us.

Ben had been strangely silent. Now, he spoke up. "You can be honest. I'm not my mother. I'm well aware of my sister's . . . shortcomings. There's not much that would surprise me."

Cleary sighed and set down his mug. "Once you scratched the surface, there were an awful lot of people who didn't care for Misty too much. Oh, it was all petty teenaged stuff for the most part, jealousy and broken hearts, but if there's one thing I've learned after so long on the job, it's to never underestimate what people can do to each other."

"What about Derek Gagnon?" I inquired, thinking of the conversation I'd had with him.

"The boyfriend? Of course we looked at him pretty close. Some of her friends said they'd had a few fights, and he was rough enough around the edges. But he had a solid alibi for the day she went missing."

"Isn't it possible she could have met up with him later?"

"Anything is possible. But he was working in his dad's shop until eight that night. And to be honest I didn't really get a guilty vibe from him. He told us they weren't dating seriously. That he thought she'd moved on. Apparently she'd even implied at one point that she could do better, that she *had* done better, and they were going to 'run away together.'"

I stiffened. This corroborated the story Derek had told me—that there had been someone else. The first person who leapt to mind was my dad, and unease stirred under my breastbone. I cleared my throat. "That's not in any of the official reports. Why didn't you ever mention this?"

"The other-lover theory? We never found any conclusive evidence. No one else could substantiate the story. Not even her friends. It's a small town—something like that would get around. Most likely it was just teenage boasting, and frankly, I didn't think a mother needed to hear those sorts of details about her daughter. Gagnon did have some sketchy acquaintances though," Cleary added. "Small-time drug dealers. We spent some time running down those leads."

"A drug angle?" Derek had implied he'd given marijuana to my sister and Misty. I turned to Ben. "Did Misty do drugs?"

His downcast eyes told me she had. "Nothing hard that I know of," he clarified. "But I found joints in her backpack now and then." He flushed, likely embarrassed to have been snooping.

If Misty had been involved with dealers, Janet would know about it. I'd have to ask her.

Cleary answered a few more routine questions, and not too long after that, I thanked him for his time and hospitality, and we prepared to leave. At the door, I turned back to him. "Off the record, do you think she's dead?"

Cleary looked at both of us. "Yes, but unless someone confesses, I doubt you'll know for sure. If there's ever a place to make someone disappear, it's up here. Forget finding a needle in a haystack—it's like searching for a needle in a *field* of haystacks. Back in ninety-seven, guy over near Prince George shot his wife, buried her body in the woods, and claimed she ran off. Eleven years later, he got caught confessing on a sting operation. Never did recover the body even though we tried to find the spot. If he'd kept his mouth shut, he'd probably be a free man right now. But guilt has a way of catching up with you. No matter how deep you bury it, the truth always works its way up to the surface in the end."

"You drive," Ben said as soon as we were outside. He tossed me the keys. Only then did I notice the strain on his face.

"Did you know about all of that?" I asked as I slid behind the wheel.

He nodded. "Most of it. I thought you knew about the shoplifting. Janet was involved too. Don't you remember the cops bringing them home one winter?"

So that was what had happened the night the cops came to our house. "Mom would only say it was between her and Janet."

"I only found out what really went down later. I guess they took some stuff from Murphy's Drugs. He never pressed charges though, since he got it all back."

"Jesus. I wonder why no one in my family ever said anything," I muttered. "It explains a lot actually. The fights Mom and Janet had. The tension in the house. What was that stuff about the Spring Formal?"

"Beats me. Dances were hardly my thing, remember? Why didn't you ask him?"

"I was afraid he'd clam up. But I know someone who might be able to fill in the blanks," I said, thinking of Arlene. "Hey, are you hungry?"

Before leaving, we stopped in town for a bite and to refuel, and then we were on our way back home. There were no street lamps on the highway, and as dusk fell, my view narrowed to the two beams of light from the headlamps. When I looked over to check on Ben, I could barely see his face. "Are you okay?" I asked.

"Yeah. It just sort of hit me today that all of this is real."

I put my hand on his thigh. Muscles bunched beneath my palm, but he didn't protest, so I left it there. A moment later, his cool fingers curled around mine and emotion tugged at my throat.

"You know, I spent last night going over your mom's clippings. You're not mentioned by name. Ever. There are no quotes, no interviews. It's all Angela."

The whites of his eyes glinted in the dark as he turned toward me. "What are you saying?"

"I'm not saying anything. It just struck me as odd."

"I like my privacy."

"Back at Cleary's, it seemed like you might know more than you let on. Why didn't you ever tell me about the weed?"

"There are a lot of things I never told you, Alex."

Was he talking about being gay? Because I'd known from Misty how he felt about me without him saying it. Or was it something else? I'd always thought we'd shared everything, but now I realized I was just as guilty of keeping secrets. There were things I'd kept from Ben too.

The sudden ring of my phone made us both jump. I fumbled one-handed in my coat pocket. "Shit. Can you . . .?"

Ben managed to tug the phone loose. "It's Janet," he said, checking the call display. My stomach knotted. I nodded, and Ben put her on speaker.

"Where the fuck *are* you?" she shrieked without preamble. "I've been trying to reach you for the last hour."

"You have? I must have lost my signal. I'm in the mountains. What's wrong? Is it . . .?"

"He's gone into a coma. They say it won't be long."

Ben's gaze was on my face, and although every instinct told me to run, I knew I couldn't. "Are you at the hospital now?"

"Yes."

"I'll be there as soon as I can." I checked the time on the dashboard clock. "I'm about an hour out."

"But, where—"

"I was running some errands. See you soon."

I felt rather than saw Ben's frown. "You didn't tell her what we were doing?"

"No."

"Why not?"

"She has enough on her plate right now."

I drove as fast as I could in the deepening twilight, keeping an eye out for moose or deer on the road—hit one of those and we might not make it home—but it was almost six by the time we made it to the outskirts of Smithers.

"Do you mind dropping me at the hospital?" I asked, heading automatically in that direction.

"How will you get back to your motel?"

"I'll catch a ride with Janet."

"Are you sure? I don't mind—"

I made a sharp turn into the hospital parking lot and came to a shuddering stop in front of the entrance. Needing to ground myself, I turned and touched the side of Ben's face. His beard tickled my fingers.

"Trust me, there is nothing I'd like more than to keep you with me, but I think this is something I need to do alone."

Ben nodded. "I understand."

Before I could change my mind, I climbed out of the truck, and Ben scrambled over the console into the driver's seat.

"I'll call you later?" I said.

"You'd better."

"Text me when you get home, kay?"

His lips twitched in amusement. "I've been driving these roads all my life."

"So? That doesn't keep me from worrying."

"It's been a long time since someone's been worried about me." He said the words lightly, but they still broke my heart. With a final good-bye, I closed the car door and strode into the hospital not the least bit ready to face what lay ahead.

Evening visiting hours were underway, so there were a number of people on the ward. Janet must have been listening for me, because she rushed out of Dad's room, and threw herself into my arms.

I staggered back. Janet had always been the older sister, little more than a stranger for most of my life. As far as I could recall, this was the first time we'd actually hugged.

"Is he . . .?"

"Not yet," she mumbled against my shoulder. "I didn't want to be alone when he goes. I was scared you wouldn't make it."

"I'm sorry, Jan. I should have been here."

She tensed in my arms, straightened. "Benji?"

I whirled around. Ben had followed me inside.

"Hi, Janet," he said quietly. He halted several feet from us. "I'm sorry to interrupt."

I let go of Janet and moved toward him. "I thought you'd left."

He held up my phone. "You forgot this in my truck, and I thought you might need it. Especially if I'm supposed to text you," he finished with a sad smile.

"Thanks."

Janet walked up to Ben with a dazed expression on her face. "I'd recognize you anywhere," she whispered. "You look so much like her."

Ben paled. "I'm sorry, Janet. Your dad . . . well, he was always good to me."

Something unspoken seemed to pass between them. Janet nodded, tears spilling silently from her eyes.

"I should go," Ben said. He gave my hand a meaningful squeeze and left. I watched his retreating figure through blurred vision, and when I turned around, Janet had gone. I found her in Dad's room, seated next to him and holding his hand. I took the chair near the window. My throat was tight with all the things I'd never said, that I would never get to say now.

Dad was still and quiet. He might have been gone already except for the steady blip on the monitor next to his bed.

"You and Benji, huh?" Janet's question broke the silence.

"How—"

"The way you looked at each other."

"It's . . . complicated."

"I didn't realize. I mean, I know we teased you, but I didn't know . . . I'm sorry."

"It was a long time ago, Jan. It's okay." And to my surprise, it was. At some point over the last few days, I'd let go of the jealousy, the resentment I'd carried toward her for so long. She was my sister, and she needed me.

"But you care about him," she said.

"I do," I admitted. "A lot."

"You should do something about that. Don't wait until it's too late."

"Jan." I shifted in my seat. "Let's not discuss this now."

Her soft sob drew me to her side. "I'm so sorry," she said again.

"Don't be. There's nothing to apologize for." I put my hand on her shoulder, shocked at the sharpness of her bones as she leaned into me. "I'm glad you brought me here—I really am. And maybe, after this, we can start over. Get to know each other."

Janet raised her tear-stained face. "Do you mean that?"

"Yeah, I do."

She wiped her cheeks and turned to look at Dad. "I haven't called Mom yet."

"Don't worry. I'll do it when it's time."

"Thank you." She gripped my hand tight.

"I wouldn't forgive him," I croaked, guilt tearing at my chest. My throat was thick with regret. "He asked me to, but I wouldn't."

"Oh, Sandy." Janet laid her head against my side and cried softly. My own eyes stayed dry.

We stayed like that, each of us deep in our own thoughts, until it was finally, mercifully, over.

CHAPTER THIRTEEN

My mother doesn't talk much about my father. I assume she loved him once. She eloped with him after all, over the protests of her parents, who were devastated by their twenty-year-old daughter's decision to leave college and chase after a Canadian tree planter she'd met while on a cross-border girls' weekend in 1978. At that time, Dad had left the east coast when the fisheries closed, to work in BC's booming lumber industry.

I would often sneak into her room and look at old photo albums, and I remember once seeing a photo of my parents on their wedding day and wondering who these young and happy people were.

—From "My Father's Son" by Alex Buchanan

"Alexander? Is it Jerry?" Mom asked, guessing the moment I'd called that something was wrong. Then again, it was nearly midnight.

"He's gone," I said, surprised when my voice threatened to crack.

I sat down on the edge of the bed, the phone clutched in my hand, a low-pitched whine in my ears.

"How is Janet?"

"Not good." Janet had just dropped me back at the motel. She'd barely said a word since Dad passed, and her silence was worrying me.

"Are you going to be all right?" I'd asked before climbing out of the car.

"I don't know, Sandy. I really don't know." Janet's words had raised the hair on the back of my neck. I'd told her to get some sleep and that I'd stop by tomorrow morning and we could figure out where to go from here.

CHRIS SCULLY

It still seemed unreal that he was gone. He was truly gone.

Truthfully, I was a little numb. I hadn't expected that—this hollow feeling inside.

"He's being cremated tomorrow," I told Mom.

She sighed. "I'm sorry."

"Why? What did he ever do to deserve your sympathy?"

"Ah, Alexander. Things didn't work out for us, that's true, but it doesn't mean I stopped caring about him. It doesn't mean you should either."

If Mom had been able to forgive him, should I have done the same?

"Why did you leave Dad if you still cared for him? I know that things weren't good, that you fought, but *why*?" I hadn't meant to bring this up now, but the question burst from my lips. While we spoke on the phone about once a month, we stayed away from anything too personal, and you couldn't get much more personal than this.

There was a low murmur of voices. "Hold on, let me go somewhere quieter." I waited while she left the room. Soon, I heard footsteps, a door closing. "I'm here. What's this about?" she asked when she came back on the line.

"Did Dad have an affair?"

Her pause said it all. The glimmer of hope I'd been nursing winked out. Finally, she gave a deep sigh. "I don't know for sure. I did ask him, and he told me he wasn't having one."

"But?"

"I could always see through him. Something was troubling him more than usual."

"Was it Misty? Did he have something to do with her disappearance? Is that why you left?"

"Oh, Alexander." She sniffled.

"Mom?" I asked in alarm. "Are you crying? What did he do?"

"It's the memories," she replied cryptically, as if that explained everything. "He didn't *do* anything. What happened with your father and I was inevitable. He was never the same after he lost that job. It changed him. Even then we might have got through if it wasn't for his drinking. I admit, there were times I thought he might be having

146

an affair. What woman wouldn't? Misty was a young, beautiful woman—"

"She was seventeen, Mom. A minor. The same age as your daughter."

"I know that, but she was mature for her age, and she was . . . sensual—I don't know how else to explain it. Maybe he did sleep with her. But if you're suggesting that he harmed Misty . . . Your father was a lot of things, Sandy, but I don't believe he would physically hurt anyone. I never saw him violent. He didn't have it in him."

After seeing Dad's outburst at the hospital, I wasn't so sure.

"I left because there was no other choice. He refused to see he had a problem and seek help. Just like you, he wouldn't open up or talk to me, so I told him we'd go if he didn't quit drinking, that it was no way to raise a family. He called my bluff, told me to go ahead and go back to Seattle. He said he didn't want to try anymore. That it was over and we were better off without him." She sighed shakily. "I guess you and I should have talked about this sooner. But you never seemed curious, and I didn't want to dwell on it."

I hadn't asked for details because I was afraid of hearing them. And now that I had, it was worse than I'd imagined. He hadn't wanted us around.

"Alexander? Are you still there?"

"I'm here."

"Why are you bringing this up now, after all this time?"

I wanted to tell her about the earrings I'd found, about the suspicions pounding through my brain, but I couldn't. She didn't deserve any more pain. "Being here—it's dredged up a lot of stuff. I needed to know, and there's no one left to ask."

We didn't stay on the line long after that. She wanted to call Janet. "Mom?" I said before I hung up, "Will you give Dan my love? And tell him thanks."

"Thanks for what?" she asked.

"For everything." And as I ended the call, I was more confused than ever. A hurricane of emotions buffeted me: resentment, anger, sorrow, guilt.

Damn you, Dad, I wanted to snarl as I jumped to my feet. It felt like he'd quit on us, *on me*, once again. And I still had no answers.

I saw that Ben had texted me earlier, telling me he'd arrived home safely. I seized those words, desperately seeking the peace Ben had always brought me. Then I knew; there was only one place I needed to be.

It was well after 1 a.m. by the time I pulled off the highway and onto North Star Lane. The Morning house was dark, but a dim light shone from the big window above the garage. Benji was still up.

I was halfway across the yard when second thoughts took root. What was I doing, bringing this to Ben's doorstep in the middle of the night? It wasn't fair—to him or us—if I wasn't going to stick around.

But I *needed* him. The need was an ache in my chest, a hole deep inside that only he could fill. He'd been the only one who ever could.

And it was too late to back out. I'd taken one step too far, and floodlights burst on, announcing my arrival, followed by muffled barking from inside.

I didn't have to knock. Ben opened the door as soon as I reached the landing, as if he'd been expecting me. Once again, I had that sense of inevitability. That the last twenty years had been building toward this moment.

Ben took one look at me and stepped out into the cold, wearing nothing but sweatpants and a knit shirt. "Alex? What is it?"

For a second, I could only stare at him and marvel at how stupid I'd been to try to hide from this, to pretend this wasn't the most significant relationship of my life. Then I grabbed his face in my hands and kissed him—kissed him hard. Smashing lips and knocking teeth. The soft hair of his beard tickled my cold palms as I plundered his mouth, driving my tongue in deep.

He didn't exactly kiss me back, but he didn't resist either, and when sanity caught up to me and I pulled away, he was breathing heavily. "You'd better come in," he said, his expression shuttered.

I let him go reluctantly, then followed him inside, where a fire crackled in the woodstove. Only then did I realize how cold I was.

It was a chill that went deep, to the bone; not even the warmth seeping from the fire could take it away. I shivered.

Luna stood at attention, clearly waiting to see if I was an intruder or not, but Ben waved her away. I noted the classical music playing softly and the book splayed open on the sofa.

"I'm sorry to disturb you. I didn't know where else to go. I needed . . . I needed to see you."

"It's okay. I couldn't sleep anyway."

He tugged the damp coat off my shoulders and hung it on the hooks near the door. I toed off my boots so I wouldn't track mud on his nice gleaming hardwood floors.

"He's . . . he's gone," I managed.

"Oh, I'm so sorry, Alex," he murmured with a gentle touch on my shoulder. Then he was pulling me into a hug, and I accepted it gratefully, eagerly, breathing in the warm wood-smoke scent of his skin. It eased something inside me.

All of the doubts and worries I'd kept to myself these past few days began to bubble up in my throat, demanding to be heard. Ben would know what to do—he always did. And yet, how could I tell him what I suspected about Dad and Misty?

He'd be shocked, horrified. I felt like a fraud, accepting comfort when these secrets were clamoring in my chest. The guilt made me pull away. Avoiding eye contact, I glanced around the cozy studio. "Do you have anything to drink?"

"I think there's an open bottle of wine in the fridge."

I helped myself, grabbing a tumbler from the cupboard and pouring a generous glass. I carried it back to the sofa and sat down, cradling the glass in my hands just for something to do.

As if sensing my turmoil, Luna leapt up on the seat beside me and laid her head in my lap with a soft whine. I dug my fingers into her thick fur and sighed. "Why does everything have to be so fucked up, Ben?"

"Because it's life. That's generally how it works."

Ben came to stand before me. His bare feet filled my line of sight. I felt his light touch on my shoulder and then on the back of my neck.

I squeezed my eyes shut and pressed my face into his stomach. The fabric soon grew damp against my cheek, and I realized I was crying.

But for who? For Dad? For myself? For the years wasted? "Maybe Janet's right. Maybe we are punished for our mistakes—Lord knows I've made enough of them."

Ben's fingers ruffled my short hair. "We all make mistakes, Alex. But they only destroy us if we don't fix them."

It was a comforting idea, but some things just couldn't be fixed.

Beneath my chin, Ben's cock was thickening. A slow heat began to fire through my veins, and I knew he felt it too, because his touch changed, became more sensual. I ducked my head and rubbed my cheek against the soft cotton bulge, drawing a swift inhale from Ben. His fingers paused on the back of my neck, but he didn't pull away. Encouraged, I turned my head and nuzzled his crotch; his erection swelled further. I breathed deeply, filling my lungs with his scent.

A gentle tug on my hair tipped my head back. Ben's eyes glittered as they stared down at me, full of . . . something. Something infinitely strong, yet fragile at the same time.

Not breaking the gaze, I raised his shirt an inch, then pressed an open-mouthed kiss to the skin above his waistband. My tongue dipped into the indent of his belly button, surrounded by a circle of red-gold fluff, and he immediately convulsed in a burst of giggles.

"Oops, sorry," I murmured. "I forgot how ticklish you are."

Ben gradually stilled, and I drew his bottoms down farther, following the tantalizing trail that led straight to a trimmed ginger bush. "This is nice," I mumbled before licking and nibbling my way from one hip to the other. When I was done, the tent in his sweats was even more pronounced.

The other night I hadn't gotten the chance to touch Ben much, and I wanted to make up for that. I wanted to explore every inch, learn every taste and texture, until my head was full of him. His nostrils flared as I massaged his stiff penis through the sweatpants. All the while he watched me watch him, those large, hooded eyes soft and warm, fluttering closed every few seconds.

Ben's hands caressed my neck, and then moved again. With gentle fingers, he traced the ridge of my brow, my temples, my ears. Almost as if he were memorizing my face. He brushed my earlobe, making me tremble, and then cupped my cheek, and urged me to my feet.

I swayed toward him, or maybe him to me. Either way, our bodies came together like two magnets. And, finally, our mouths met.

Our first kiss, twenty years ago, had been chaste and innocent. Our second, this evening, rough and desperate. This one . . . this one was perfect. It began soft and hesitant: a brush of lips, the whisper of whiskers against my chin. An unspoken question. Then his lips firmed, tugged at mine, demanding more.

I let Ben take charge. He kissed the corners of my mouth, nibbled my lower lip, before sucking on it. Bit by bit I fell under his spell. I'd never had anyone kiss me like this, with such intensity and deliberation, as if the kiss itself, this exploration, was the goal instead of simply a means to an end. *This* was what I'd unknowingly been trying to recapture all my life.

Ben cradled my head. His tongue flicked at my lips, and I let him inside. The slow and tender dance of our tongues set off fireworks under my skin. My arms stole around his back so there wasn't an inch of space between us. I felt his every breath, every heartbeat as if it were my own.

Then his lips moved, blazing across my cheek and to my neck.

"You're a much better kisser than you were twenty years ago," I gasped, the warm buzz in my head seeping throughout my body.

Ben nipped at my earlobe, and my cock jerked inside my jeans. "God, I should hope so," he said with a chuckle.

"Just sayin' for a guy who doesn't seem to get much practice, you're pretty good at it."

"To be fair, that first kiss wasn't great to begin with."

"You're wrong." That kiss had haunted me my entire life.

Ben gazed at me with moist eyes. His thumb rubbed my lips, and then he kissed me again, long and deep.

When we came up for air, it took me a moment to find my voice. "I take it you've rethought the whole abstinence thing."

"I blew that the other night. Can you handle it?"

Could I? "I don't know," I answered honestly. Sure I'd had plenty of sex, with both men and women, but this felt different. Tonight wasn't about thinking, though.

We shuffled toward the bed, lips still locked, arms tangled. My sweater. His shirt. Our clothes fell to the floor, creating a scattered path. Then Ben went crashing down on the mattress and took me with him.

Woof.

Luna crouched in attack-dog mode at the foot of the bed, low to the ground, a growl growing in her throat.

"Uh, Ben," I choked out.

He had the temerity to laugh and push me to one side. "Luna. Go." He waved, and off she went back to her spot in front of the woodstove, but still keeping a watchful eye on me. I couldn't blame her for protecting her man.

Ben reclined on his elbows, his lips reddened from our kisses. "Where were we?"

"I think we were about to get naked."

"Yeah?" He surprised me by shucking his sweatpants in one swift move and flinging them over his shoulder, revealing nothing but bare skin underneath. "Done."

His cock lay hard against his stomach. I curled my fingers around the shaft, and felt the beat of his pulse beneath my palm. I settled into a slow rhythm, watching his face, which I almost never did with a partner, noting the way his eyes softened, the way he sighed with each downward stroke.

I'd never wanted to please anyone more. "How did you picture it? When you imagined us together?"

"I don't know. I didn't have much experience at the time. Any, really. It was all a mysterious blur with a lot of kissing and grinding."

Ben's fingers tangled in my hair, drawing me back in for a slow kiss. I sucked on his tongue while I played with the head of his cock.

"You're overdressed," he murmured breathlessly after a while.

I had lowered the zipper on my jeans to give my erection more room but hadn't removed them. Now Benji suddenly jacked upright, pushed me over onto my back, and struggled to work them down my legs. I laughed at his impatience and helped him out.

My boxers soon followed.

And then our naked bodies were finally together. Benji gave a low moan and shifted until we lined up perfectly. I rolled him under me, then peppered his face, his lips, with little kisses.

"Was it like this?" I asked as I ground against him with my mouth pressed to his neck.

"Actually it was more like this." Once again, he flipped me over. This time he straddled my hips and planted a hand on my chest to hold me down.

My cock seemed to like that, because it flexed eagerly. "Oh? Did you seduce me?" I teased.

"I might have." Ben flicked my nipples, then soothed them with a swipe of his tongue. His palms skimmed down my chest and over my belly to grasp my erection. My breath caught as he brought our cocks together, flesh to flesh, and circled his fingers around them.

"Look," he said. "We fit."

Indeed, my downward curve and his upward seemed made for each other.

"And, uh, what was I doing in these fantasies of yours?" I barely got the question out because now he was rubbing his slippery cockhead over mine, painting me with his pre-come.

"Nothing. Mostly you were asleep."

I stroked the side of his neck, the indent of his collarbone. "That's horrible. Who could possibly sleep through this?"

"I told you, I didn't know anything at the time."

"So you never imagined I'd want to participate? That I might want to suck your cock? Or eat out your ass? Or better yet, have you fuck me?"

He moaned at my graphic words. "Never thought you'd want me." His fingers tightened, his strokes growing harder, faster. My orgasm was right *there*.

A shaky laugh burst from my throat, and I reached up to cup his face. "Who do you think I was fantasizing about when I jerked off that time?"

"Me?"

"You. Kiss me again," I begged. "Please."

With a faint smile, Ben bent down and did as I commanded, his hand busy between us as his breath filled my lungs and his touch ignited fires across my skin. And when I came, he did too, in perfect synchronicity. As I gazed up into his flushed face, every minute of the last twenty years was wiped away, forgotten. There was only now. Only Alex and Benji. Like we were always meant to be.

The squeal of metal woke me from my doze. I opened my eyes to see Ben squatting before the woodstove and feeding logs to the embers. Between the moonlight pouring in through the windows and the firelight, the hair on his chest and thighs shone like filaments of gold. As he walked back toward the bed, slim-hipped and glowing, something hitched in my chest.

"You turned out so good, Benji Morning," I mumbled.

Ben dove under the covers and threw himself on top of me. "'So good'? And you call yourself a writer?"

I shrieked. "Aiiyyyi, your feet are like ice."

"You'd better warm me up, then." Laughing, Ben trapped my shin between his icy feet. I wriggled beneath him, trying to settle him more fully against me, and sighed in contentment as we found the perfect fit. For the first time in a very long time, I felt like I was exactly where I should be.

"Comfy?" I asked.

"Mm-hmm. You're like a hot water bottle. Better than Luna."

I swatted his butt cheek playfully, then left my hand there. For a while, there was only the sound of the logs crackling in the fire. It wasn't long before my mind began turning. "What made you change your mind tonight? Not that I'm complaining."

Light from the woodstove danced across the room, but our little corner was mostly in shadow. I could see the outline of Benji's features as he raised his head but not enough to discern his expression.

He blew out a sigh. "I'm going to end up with a broken heart anyway. I figured I might as well get something out of it."

"It doesn't have—"

A finger on my lips cut me off. "Don't. Just don't." Ben replaced his finger with a quick kiss, and then rolled off me. He pulled the duvet up to our chests and tucked in against my side. "You know, I always wanted you to be my first," he said. "But now I'm glad you weren't."

"Was it that bad? I mean I know you had high expectations . . ."

He pinched my left nipple. "Not now. *Then*. I didn't lose my virginity until I was nineteen. And when it happened, it was awful. Embarrassingly awful. I was so nervous. Mostly I remember just wanting to get it over with."

He rubbed his bearded chin over the aggrieved nub, which sent a ripple of pleasure directly to my spent cock.

Now that he'd brought up the subject, I couldn't help but wonder what it would have been like if Ben had been my first. Technically I'd lost my virginity to some girl from math class when I was fifteen. It had been at a party—I knew that much. Other than that, the experience had been a blur. I couldn't even recall her name.

The distinction of my first time with a guy had gone to an anonymous freshman at UBC, and once I'd gotten that hurdle out of the way, there was no holding me back. I'd fucked anybody who'd have me until Tanya had come along and we'd gotten married.

Now I couldn't help feeling like I'd lost out on something. Something far more special than drunken one-night stands with nameless strangers. My fractured childhood memories of Benji were stronger than any of them. Which, I supposed, said it all.

With Ben it would have been different.

I aimlessly stroked the inside of Ben's arm, and paused when I felt those tell-tale marks. "Ready to tell me about these now?"

"I'd rather not."

"Tough. You always made me talk about stuff I didn't want to."

Ben remained stubbornly silent, but I knew to wait him out. Finally, he heaved a sigh. "There's not much to tell. After you left, I had some bad years and I didn't handle them very well."

"And cutting yourself helped?"

"It seemed to at the time. I felt so alone. And angry. You were gone, and Angela . . . well, she's never exactly been maternal, but in a way she was worse than before. All her energy went to finding Misty. I know it doesn't make sense, but this was something I could control when there was nothing else I could."

His words pummeled me like fists.

"Stop," he said.

"Stop?"

"This is why I didn't want to talk about it. You feel guilty, and there's no reason for you to."

How could I *not* feel guilty? He'd needed me, and I'd selfishly cut all ties. "I can't help it," I said.

Ben raised up on one elbow and looked at me. "I don't blame you for anything, Alex. I want you to know that. We were kids. And whatever happened with our families—whatever happens in the future—it has nothing to do with *us*."

I traced the lines on his arm, my breath caught in my throat. I couldn't recall ever hurting for another person before. If only my parents hadn't split up. If only we hadn't moved away. If only I hadn't been such an idiot. So many regrets. My thumb skated under the leather cuff he wore, and froze when it encountered another scar there. This one was thicker, the ridge more pronounced. My stomach plunged.

"Ben?" I choked.

This time he jerked his arm away and sat up, hugging his knees to his chest. "It was a long time ago," he mumbled.

My heart galloped with an off-kilter beat. *Not my Benji. He wouldn't do that.*

I touched his back. The muscles were tight, and he flinched at the contact. He gulped for air, panting as though he'd run a marathon.

"Ben?"

"It's not you," he managed. "Just give me a minute."

I sat quietly beside him, helpless, and waited until he was ready. After a few minutes, he seemed to get himself under control.

"Sorry, I wasn't ready for that. Panic attack."

"Does that happen a lot?"

"Not so much anymore."

This time, when I stroked his back, he relaxed into the touch. "I had a breakdown in my first semester at UVic. Everything caught up to me. One night I went into the residence showers with a penknife and tried to kill myself." He gave a hard laugh. "Made a mess of it. The jock down the hall found me. Called 911. After that, I spent some time in a hospital and then a treatment center learning how to deal. That's where I was introduced to art therapy."

He swung his head around to look at me. "I'm not unstable."

"I never thought you were." Folding him into my arms, I rubbed my cheek against the silk of his hair.

"I'm good now," he insisted. "Really. I was in therapy for a while, and the Xanax is only for emergencies—when the anxiety gets bad. You don't have to worry about me freaking out when you leave. I can handle it."

The thought of leaving made my chest hurt.

"Alex?"

I took hold of his wrists and pressed a kiss to the inside of each elbow. "Damn it, Alex." He yanked his arms from my grasp and folded them over his chest.

"Please?" I whispered. "Will you let me . . .?"

Ben bowed his head, silent. With trembling fingers, I stroked his hair, the nape of his neck, and then he leaned into me, burrowing into my shoulder. His arms fell limply into his lap.

Tentatively, I caressed his palm. I raised his hand to my lips and kissed it, ready to let go at the first sign he was uncomfortable. Then, unsnapping the leather cuff from his wrist, I lightly traced the thick scar tissue with my lips. Ben held his breath, his eyes glistening in the shadows.

I almost lost him. My heart thundered at the thought. Were it not for a chance intervention by a stranger, he might not be here with me now.

Overwhelmed, I pushed him back against the pillows and buried my face against his neck, where I could feel his pulse, strong and steady, and the reassuring rasp of his breath tickled my ear. He pulled my head up by my ears until our mouths were level. And then, once more, he kissed me. Devoured me as though he'd never get enough.

"I can't believe you're here. Why'd it take you so long?" he gasped when we parted.

You scared me. You still scare me. But "I don't know," was what I said. "I'm sorry."

Ben's cock was hard against my hip, and I moved out of the circle of his arms to slowly kiss my way down his chest, sucking his nipples into tight points, nuzzling the fluff of his happy trail, savoring every sigh that sprang from his lips. Finally, just as my mouth reached his cock, I sensed we had company. Luna was standing beside the bed, tail wagging and an oddly human tilt to her head.

"Your dog is watching me. She's giving me performance anxiety."

Ben groaned and pushed the hair out of his eyes. "She's used to sleeping in the bed. Want me to put her outside?"

I tightened my grip on the base of his shaft and licked him like a popsicle. "Mmm, no. Not if it means moving."

"Okay, good," he breathed, his voice rough and ragged. His fingers dug into my scalp as his head fell back on the pillow. "Don't stop."

"Didn't plan to," I said, sucking the head of his penis into my mouth as I drew the duvet up over my head for privacy. Instantly, I was cocooned in darkness and enveloped in the heady scents of sweat and sex and soap. With a wicked grin Ben couldn't see, I set about fulfilling a few fantasies of my own.

CHAPTER FOURTEEN

I woke for a second time with a warm body curled around my back and something cold and wet nudging my palm. My eyes flew open. Luna was once more beside the bed, snuffling my outstretched hand. Seeing me awake, she whined and then trotted over to the door expectantly. "I suppose you need out," I muttered. "Ben, your dog has to go."

No sign of movement from him.

Grumbling under my breath, I climbed out of the warm bed, shivering as I searched for my underwear on the floor. A misty gray dawn filled the windows and skylights, making it seem like we were suspended in clouds.

"Make sure to put her on the chain so she doesn't go too far," mumbled a sleepy voice from beneath the covers as I slid my bare feet into my unlaced boots.

"Oh, *now* you're awake." Suspecting that I'd been manipulated, I shuffled out the door with Luna, affixed the long chain to her collar, and then dashed back inside before my balls froze off.

"Fuck, it's cold out there."

Ben raised his head, his unruly hair sticking up in all directions, and burst out laughing. "You went out like that? No wonder."

"I didn't hear you volunteering," I returned, kicking off my boots.

He gave a bemused smile as he stretched on his back. "I'm a little messed up, not stupid."

I snorted. "Will Luna be okay out there?"

"She's a husky, Alex. She's made for this weather."

I snorted. And leapt beneath the covers. "I sure as hell am not. And you're not messed up."

Ben's shriek filled the loft. "You're like an ice cube."

"Not so funny now, is it?"

Later, after a leisurely shower together—to save hot water was the excuse I used, although by the time we were done it bordered on tepid—I sat at the table sipping coffee while Ben cooked breakfast on his little propane stove.

I'd never thought of myself as domestic. Since my divorce, I'd always lived alone and liked it. Even Will and I had maintained separate apartments while we were together, partly because of our unpredictable schedules, but mostly because I preferred it that way.

But there was something to be said for waking up next to someone you loved.

Loved? My brain sounded the alarm.

"Stop watching me. You're making me nervous." Ben's voice drew me out of my momentary panic.

"Can't help it," I replied. "I like watching you." That much was true. I loved watching him. No matter what he did, he moved with a languid grace that brought a goofy smile to my face. His hair was drying in wild curls that made him look like a kid again, and he was wearing a soft plaid flannel shirt and sweatpants that sagged in the ass. I laughed. "Do you own anything that's not plaid?"

"What's wrong with plaid?" he asked.

"Nothing. It's growing on me."

With the woodstove stoked, the loft was warm and cozy, despite frost-coated branches outside the large window. It was so quiet and peaceful, like we were the only two people in the world. New York seemed very far away right now. I poured myself another cup of coffee from the French press and topped up Ben's. "I really like your place."

"Thanks."

"You've come a long way from peanut butter and jelly," I joked as he expertly flipped the omelet in the pan.

"What's that saying about necessity? It was either learn to cook or starve."

I devoured the eggs and toast Ben set in front of me, and afterward I volunteered to wash up. Anything to delay the inevitable day ahead.

Coffee in hand, I wandered over to the big front windows. Like the rays of sun that were even now rising higher in the sky and punching through the clouds, reality was beginning to intrude.

A half-finished painting on the easel drew my attention, and I stopped to admire it. The colors in this one seemed brighter than the heavy palette I'd seen so far. It looked like a meadow with the mountains in the distance.

Ben came up behind me, wrapped his arms around my waist, and leaned his chin on my shoulder. "This piece is pretty," I said.

"It's not done. I only started the other day."

"Is it a real place?"

"Yes. You should see it in spring—it's carpeted with wildflowers."

I smiled, until I remembered I wouldn't be here in the spring.

"Did you notice that they tore down your dad's old shed across the street?" Ben asked, mercifully changing the topic.

"How could I notice? You can barely see the roof of the house through the trees," I pointed out. "Who lives there now?"

"It's an older couple. I don't see much of them. They keep to themselves."

"And the new house? At the end of the lane?"

"Some lawyer from Calgary. He comes up here to hunt."

"It's kind of lonely, then."

"It can be." He nuzzled my neck. "I guess you'll be leaving soon."

The lump in my throat prevented me from responding immediately. Instead I leaned back into his warmth and asked, "Did you ever think of me?"

Ben stiffened. I wished that I'd held my question until I could see his face, but maybe it was better that I hadn't. "All the time."

"But you never tried to look me up?"

"I wrote you a letter once. Actually, I wrote you a lot of letters, but this one I put in an envelope and everything. Your dad gave me your grandma's address. But I never sent it. I thought it was safer to keep you in my head. The way I remembered you."

I understood what he meant. I'd done something similar.

I set the mug down on his stool and folded my hands over his. His fingers were like ice.

"You weren't wrong when you accused me of hiding," Ben said softly. "It's not that I'm unhappy here or that I don't love what I do, but after what happened in Victoria, there's a part of me that's always been afraid I couldn't handle the world outside this place."

"Does that include me?"

"It most definitely includes you."

"I don't think you give yourself enough credit."

Ben kissed the side of my neck, and the tickle of his beard made my toes curl.

"Mmm, that's nice. Keep going." I reached back and tangled my fingers in his curls.

"Don't you have things to do today?"

I groaned. There was Dad's cremation to deal with, and I'd promised to check in with Janet. "Thanks for the reminder. Couldn't we just go back to bed?"

"Wish I could, but I've got a lot of work ahead of me." Ben gave me a squeeze.

My phone rang, and I laughed as I reluctantly pulled myself from his arms and hurried to grab it from my coat. "See, this is your fault."

The number was unfamiliar, but local, so I answered it anyway.

"He didn't come home last night," said the caller in a husky voice I'd recognize anywhere.

Angela? Why was Angela Morning calling me?

I swung around, putting my back to Ben, and lowered my voice. "Who?"

"Derek Gagnon."

"So? He's a grown man,"

"It's a weeknight. His wife and kids are here, but he stayed out all night. That's suspicious, isn't it?"

"What?" I went back over to the window and peered out. Angela's car wasn't in the driveway. "Where are you?" I held my breath, afraid I already knew the answer.

"I'm at Derek's house."

"Jesus," I exclaimed too loudly. I glanced at Ben, who was watching me with worried eyes. *Janet?* he mouthed. I nodded and hoped he couldn't see the panic on my face. The last thing I wanted was for him to know what Angela was up to. He'd freak. After everything he'd told me last night, I worried how he'd react.

"And what the hell are you doing there?" I whispered. If Derek found Angela stalking his family again, who knew what he'd do.

"I've been here all night. Watching."

I groaned.

"Don't worry. I parked down the street."

"Oh, that makes me feel so much better. You need to leave."

"I'm staying here until he gets home. And then I'm going to confront him."

Fuck, there was trouble. "You're only making the situation worse."

"Worse? How can things possibly be worse? For twenty years, I've been told to be patient, to have faith—well, I'm tired of waiting."

This conversation was going nowhere. "Look, don't do anything. I'll call you back in a few minutes."

"Problems?" Ben asked after I hung up.

"No, but I have to go," I said, already shrugging into my jacket.

His eyes narrowed, and for a heart-stopping moment I was certain he saw through me. Even more sure of it when he stiffened and forced a tight smile to his lips. "Oh, sure. I've got class this afternoon anyway, and I have to get things ready for the art show."

He thinks I'm running out on him. Inwardly, I wanted to scream. The secrets were piling up, but as my gaze strayed to his bare wrist, I knew it was time somebody started looking out for Ben. "That's tonight, right?"

He nodded. "Do you want to drop by? I mean, if you've got nothing better to do." He said it casually, but his downcast eyes, the chewed lip, told me that it was important and he wanted me there.

I closed the gap between us, cupped his face in my hands and planted a quick kiss on his lips. "I'll be there." If Angela didn't get herself arrested first.

He beamed, and I was glad I'd said I would. Another kiss, this one a bit longer, and then I finally tore myself away. I regretted leaving the second I closed the door, but someone had to straighten Angela out before she caused irreparable damage.

I called her back as soon as I reached my car.

"I followed him as far as Telkwa last night," she said. "He stopped at a hardware store. But then I lost him."

This kept getting worse. "Come home, Angela."

"He *owns* a hardware store. Why would he have to go to Telkwa?"

"Where does he live? I'm on my way."

"Oh, here he is now," Angela cried excitedly. "There's mud all over his truck. Do you think he was out there moving her body? Oh no, what if there are others?"

Through the phone's speaker, I heard an angry male voice growing louder.

"Angela, get out of there," I ordered, but she was past listening to me.

"I know you killed her," she shouted—to Derek I assumed. I could only listen in horror to muffled voices, then a couple of loud thumps, like someone banging on the car.

"Oh good, the police are here," Angela said. Sure enough the faint call of sirens was coming through the speaker.

More shouting. Then I was disconnected.

"I'm looking for someone," I told the woman behind the counter at the Alton RCMP detachment. When I hadn't heard back from Angela, I'd figured this would be the best place to start. And it was simpler to drop by rather than try to dig up a phone number. "Angela Morning? She was involved in an incident . . ."

"They just brought her in."

"Is she under arrest?"

"Not yet."

That was good news. "Can I see her?"

"Are you her lawyer?"

"Friend of the family."

She took my name and then disappeared through a doorway. She returned several minutes later. "You can come on through."

I followed her down a narrow hallway and into a small, windowless interview room where a large, ruddy-faced man in uniform greeted me. With a firm handshake, he introduced himself as Sergeant Steve Kirk.

Angela sat at a table. She seemed terribly small and fragile in the enclosed space, but definitely not ashamed or contrite. She sat up straighter when she saw me, a determined set to her jaw.

"I'm glad you're here," Kirk said. "Thought I was going to have to drag Ben into this again, and I hate doing that. I take it you're aware of what's happened?"

"I am. Are you charging her with something?"

"Gagnon is asking for a peace bond."

"What's that?" Angela asked.

"It's a restraining order," I explained, wondering how Ben would take the news. He'd likely be furious.

"I managed to talk him out of it," Kirk said, "but if it happens again . . . We all sympathize with Angela, but she can't keep doing this."

I had no idea what he expected me to do.

"But he's guilty," Angela insisted. "He might have been trying to move her remains. If you check his cell phone logs, you'll be able to see where he went."

The sergeant's lips almost twitched. He must have found it amusing to be instructed on investigative procedure by a sixty-year-old homemaker and mother. "Ma'am, we've been over this. Mr. Gagnon went fishing."

"On a weeknight? In November?"

"There's still late-season coho in the Bulkley and the Morice. Caught a nice steelhead myself the other week. Gagnon booked the week off. He only came back because he got a call from his wife about a strange car outside their house. That would be you. His wife confirms this story."

"Of course she'd confirm it," Angela murmured. "What about the hardware store in Telkwa?"

"Bait. And they had the fly he needed."

Angela huffed and crossed her arms over her chest, the same way I'd seen Ben do countless times before when he'd been frustrated.

"Have you spoken to Sergeant McNamara from Major Crime?" I asked Kirk. "He's handling the missing-persons investigation."

"I have. He reiterated that Derek Gagnon is not a person of interest in their case." Sergeant Kirk turned back to Angela. "Listen, as a friend, I'm giving you this warning. Stay away from Derek Gagnon and his family. If I'm forced to issue a peace bond and you break it, you could be charged. I don't want to arrest you."

I'd been watching Angela closely, and at Kirk's words she immediately sagged in defeat. Tears sprang to her eyes. The transformation to meek old lady was far too quick, not to mention uncharacteristic—was she playacting? For a second, I glimpsed a bit of Misty in her.

"Can she go now?" I asked.

Kirk sighed and threw up his hands. "She can go. Remember what I said, Angela. I don't want to see you here again."

I hurried her out of the station before they changed their mind. Once safely in the parking lot, I stopped. "Where's your car?"

"Still out by Derek's house. They brought me in in a squad car."

Like that news wouldn't be all around town by noon. Ben was bound to hear about this.

"Get in. I'll drive you," I ordered.

She gave me directions to Derek's as I pulled away from the station. "You didn't tell Ben about this, did you?"

My anger had been building as I drove. "Are you kidding? No way. Jesus, Angela. He's going to flip out."

Angela nodded. "He doesn't like it when I do things like this."

"He's worried about you."

"Ben? No, he's only worried that I'll embarrass him."

"You're wrong about that. He cares about you very much." Too much. More than he should, given how little attention she'd paid him over the years.

"So, what are we going to do now?" she asked.

"Do?"

"About Derek. I can't tail him anymore—he knows my car too well—but we could use yours."

I gaped at her. "Nobody is tailing anyone. Didn't you hear what Kirk said? This has to end."

What a mess. How much longer before Angela crossed the line? Before Ben was pushed to the end of his limits? I needed to fix this before Misty's disappearance tore Ben and Angela farther apart.

"Look, I talked to Derek, and I don't think he's involved. I usually have a good sense about stuff like that."

Angela regarded me suspiciously. If she wouldn't even believe the police, I doubted she'd take my word, but she surprised me. "What do you know?"

"Nothing. Yet," I conceded, reluctant to discuss my theory about Dad. What did I really have after all? A missing pair of earrings and a hunch. Everything else was coincidence. Conjecture. It wasn't even enough to take to the police at this point. "But I'm working on it. In the meantime, you have to promise me you'll stop this."

"I can't. Misty was so full of life, so beautiful, I can't bear to think of her out there."

I couldn't take it anymore. "Christ, Angela, this fantasy Misty you've created in your head; she's not real. She never was. Misty was a bitch. Not only to me and Ben, but to a lot of other people." I gentled my tone. "I'm sorry to be so blunt, but she was."

"She was my daughter," Angela cried, one fist pounding her chest. "Don't you dare talk about her that way."

My throat clutched. "You're right. I shouldn't have said that."

"What gives you the right to judge me? My family?"

"Because I was there! I'm the one who held Benji when he cried, who tried to cheer him up when he was hurting, who made sure he wasn't alone. You were working all the time. You didn't see the way Misty constantly put him down, how she mocked him for being different. Trust me, she was worse than any of the bullies at school." God, I really was an asshole to be guilt-tripping a grief-stricken mother.

"All siblings squabble."

It was useless. I gave up.

"Do you have children?" Angela asked abruptly.

"No."

"Then don't lecture me on parenting. You don't know what it's like."

"I know that you need to be there, that you don't let them grow up alone and—" *Whoa. Who was I talking about? Ben or myself?* My eyes widened; my palms turned slick on the steering wheel. The anger in my gut slipped away as quickly as it had arrived. "I'm sorry," I said again, once I was back in control of my emotions. "I think I have some of my own issues to sort out."

Angela sniffled quietly with her cheek pressed to the window. "Misty was troubled," she said reluctantly after a few minutes. "And yes, it's my fault for not giving her the attention she needed. When Sam died, a part of me died too. I was numb for a long time."

It wasn't easy for me to think of Misty as having been just as lost as Ben was, not when she'd always been the bad guy in my mind. Had she been acting out, seeking attention? I frowned at the thought. I'd still been thinking of Misty from the perspective of a thirteen-year-old boy, but wasn't bullying typical of insecurity?

We turned onto Derek's street, and I pulled up behind Angela's abandoned Jeep. There was a large dent in the driver's-side door, which I assumed Derek was responsible for.

I waited for Angela to get out, but she didn't. "I didn't know it was like that," she murmured. "Benji never complained. He's always been so quiet. So self-sufficient."

"He's self-sufficient because he had to be. Because no one was ever there for him. He's quiet because he thinks no one cares enough to listen. Do you know about his art program?" My voice crept up a notch. "Or how hard he's fighting for this town? He's a good man, Angela. You should be proud of him." In the back of my mind, I realized I was no longer simply talking to Angela, I was talking to my father.

I sucked in a breath. "I'm going to wait here until you get in the car, and then I'm going to follow you home."

"I don't need a babysitter," Angela snapped.

"Yeah, you do." I understood Ben and his conflicted relationship so much more now. I wanted to shake Angela for her blindness, while pitying her at the same time. In a way, she was as much of an addict as my dad had been; only her addiction was grief. She could no longer help herself.

Her eyes filled with tears as she gazed at me. "You want me to give up on my daughter? How can I do that?"

"What happens if you find her, Angela?" I asked.

"I don't understand."

"If you find her and finally get the answer you're looking for. If someone's brought to justice—will it be over for you? Will you have what you need?"

She blinked as though she'd never considered this question before.

"Think about it," I said. "I'm not asking you to choose between your children. You don't need to give up on Misty, but your son still needs you. You may have lost one child; you don't have to lose the other too."

CHAPTER
FIFTEEN

I was contemplative as I pulled up in front of Dad's trailer, after first making sure that Angela went straight home. I'd driven there without thinking, but it wasn't surprising. In trying to reason with Angela, something had become clear to me.

The truth is a funny thing. Everyone claims to want it, but most of us spend our lives hiding from it. We see what we want to see, *who* we want to see, because it's easier. We delude ourselves. Like Angela and Misty. Me and Dad. Ben was the only person I knew who seemed to face life head-on and accept it as it came. That he'd found the strength to do so was something I envied.

In many ways, I was as guilty as Angela was when it came to avoiding reality.

We'd both failed Benji. I'd pushed him out of my life as a teenager, out of my mind, because the thought of falling in love at thirteen—with a boy—had been too terrifying to contemplate. For two decades, I'd convinced myself those feelings meant nothing.

And I *had* shut Dad out just as much as he'd shut *me* out. Why? Because I hadn't been able to handle the possibility that *I* had been the reason he'd walked away. That I hadn't been good enough. That even if I reached out, he might not want me. But that had been the thinking of a hurt child, not a grown man.

So I tried to distance myself as I stepped inside Dad's crappy trailer and see it with fresh eyes. To see it less as a hoarder's hovel and more like the last refuge of a man consumed by secrets; a man who had only been able to deal with his guilt through alcohol. Would that make his withdrawal, his abandonment easier to accept? Or was I only applying my own wishful thinking to his actions? I honestly wasn't sure anymore. But when I removed my personal feelings from the equation, I saw a lonely, isolated life.

Thanks to my efforts over the last few days, the place looked worn, but no longer filthy. I'd cleaned out the junk and garbage, and now all that remained were a few personal effects.

I scanned the living room, not certain what I was looking for. Just *something*. Something that would tell me one way or the other if he'd been involved in Misty's disappearance. I needed to know.

Dad's words echoed in my head. *"Pictures . . . in my house."*

He was full of shit, I'd told myself on the way over here. I was stupid to give his words credence. As Janet had said, you couldn't believe anything he'd said.

Yet he hadn't wanted me to tell her. In my gut, I knew if proof of his guilt existed, it had to be here somewhere. Everything he possessed was within these four walls. I refused to accept the alternative: that I might never have an answer.

The warble of my phone startled me. *Please don't let it be Angela again*, I prayed, but it wasn't. It was someone from the mortuary telling me Dad's ashes were ready to be picked up.

I winced, my promise to meet up with Janet today forgotten. "Um, I thought my sister would do that," I said.

"We've left several messages for her, but she hasn't gotten back to us," the receptionist informed me.

Take that, Dad. Looks like neither of us wants you.

I sighed. "All right, thanks for letting me know. I'll stop by when I can."

As soon as I hung up, guilt crept in. Had we let Dad down? He'd died much the same way as he'd lived—quietly, without ceremony. He wouldn't even get an obituary unless one of us wrote it.

Brushing aside a sudden bout of melancholy, I got to work with the thoroughness of a forensic technician. There weren't that many possible hiding places in the trailer. I overturned furniture, scoured the cupboards, even combed between the cushions and patted the upholstery for anything suspicious. With the exception of some new garbage and dust bunnies, I came up empty in the living room and kitchen.

Moving on to the bedroom, I paused. Although it was equally bare now, this space felt way more personal. I'd already cleared out the small closet on a previous trip, but I went over it again, feeling my way to the very back of the top shelf. Nothing.

My heart skittered for a second when I lifted the stained mattress and spied a flattened black gym bag. But it was empty, and I tossed it into the corner in defeat.

Had Dad sent me on a wild-goose chase for something that existed only in his mind?

There was no place left to look. The bed itself was a wooden dais bolted to the floor, so he wasn't likely to hide anything under it. Unless . . . there were built-in storage drawers underneath—two on each side of the bed. I leapt on them, but to my dismay, each drawer was bare.

Fuck, I'd been so sure.

I kicked the base of the platform bed in frustration. It sounded hollow.

Of course, there would be void space behind the drawers.

I dropped to my knees, and this time, I pulled the drawers all the way out.

And that was how I found it.

Taped to the back of the second drawer was a business envelope: the kind that used to come stapled in the middle of magazines to encourage people to subscribe. This one was for *Hustler* of all things. The tape holding it in place was yellowed with age and the envelope well-handled and stained. It had been kicking around a long time.

With a surge of adrenaline, I tore the envelope off and cast the drawer to the side.

The adhesive had long ago dried up so the flap wouldn't close, and three Polaroids fell out into my hand. They were brittle, the colors faded and the images blurry, but I'd know the girl in them anywhere.

Prepared as I was to find damning evidence, the shock still made me gasp. Not so much seeing Misty in the photos, but what she was doing.

In the first, she had her bare back to the camera, head turned to smile coquettishly at the photographer. The next was more explicit— she was reclining on a bed, covers held to her chest but revealing one perfect, pink-tipped breast. In the third, she lay on her stomach, naked, skin glowing, strawberry hair falling over her shoulders, lips puckered as she blew a kiss to the camera.

I recognized the floral bedding and curtains immediately. My parents' bedroom.

The third one even had an inscription written in blue ballpoint pen along the plastic white border.

To J.C., So you won't forget. Love, MM.

She'd signed it with a heart.

My stomach heaved. The photos fell from my hand, and I ran to the bathroom just in time to vomit what was left of my breakfast into the sink.

When there was nothing left but dry heaves, I rinsed my mouth and splashed my face with water.

Having suspicions was one thing, but seeing the truth another. Dad had naked pictures of Misty. Taken in *his* room, in *his* bed. No wonder he had wanted me to wait until he was gone to find them. *You bastard. How could you?*

I wobbled back into the bedroom on unsteady legs and gathered up the photos, pausing as I stuffed them back in the envelope. Dad had owned an old Nikon SLR. Why would he have used Janet's camera? *Because he couldn't very well take pictures of his naked underage lover down to the photomat to have them developed, could he?* my inner voice jibed.

I swallowed hard. These photos weren't the confession I'd hoped for, but it wasn't much of a leap to think Dad had been involved in her disappearance.

"So you won't forget." Those seemed an odd choice of words. Forget what? Was I missing something here?

"You'll know what to do with them."

Had he wanted me to destroy them or turn them in to the police?

"You fucker," I yelled to the silence. "You goddamn fucker. How could you leave me with this?" I slammed my fist into the wall, wishing it was him instead. "Forgive you? How am I supposed to ever forgive you now?"

The circle of broken drywall provided no answers.

My knuckles throbbed, but the skin wasn't broken. I wished I could go to Janet. Would she believe me now? I doubted it. She wouldn't *want* to believe this. Or maybe she already knew.

Sergeant McNamara's number was in my call log, and I had my thumb on the button when a new thought made me hesitate.

What about Ben?

It was his art show fundraiser tonight. And he didn't deserve to have it overtaken by news like this. I couldn't do that to him.

My eyes burned with frustration as I glared at the incriminating envelope in my hand. It wasn't fair. I took a deep breath to steady myself.

Misty had already waited twenty years. Tomorrow would be soon enough to decide.

I must have changed my mind about going to Ben's art show a dozen times on the drive over. How could I possibly face him now? He'd said he could handle anything, but did that include your best friend's father sleeping with your sister? Or worse, potentially killing her?

But I'd made Ben a promise that I'd be there, and I couldn't break another one.

The Community Hall parking lot was already full when I arrived, so I parked on a side street and sat in the car awhile, struggling to bring my shaky limbs back under control.

This was Ben's night. He deserved to enjoy it.

Finally, with a deep breath for courage, I zipped up my coat, realizing as I did so that the Polaroids were still tucked in the inside pocket. In my haste, I'd forgotten to leave them at the motel. *Shit.*

I opened the glove compartment to stow them away, but my hand faltered on the envelope. Misty's face hovered in the back of my mind, and my gorge rose again. I was hit with an irrational fear that they might fall into the wrong hands, that I couldn't risk letting them out of my sight no matter how vile they were. With another curse, I left them in my pocket and hurried down the street toward the building. A blast of warm air hit my face as I entered the rotunda, and I blinked at the number of people milling about. Most of them were dressed up, which in Alton meant not wearing jeans, and I was glad I'd taken the time to go back to the motel and change after leaving Dad's place.

Although no one paid attention to me, I still felt conspicuous. The plastic corners of the Polaroids poked my chest with every movement, a constant reminder of the awful truth, and I began to regret my impulsive decision to not leave them in the car after all.

"Can I take your coat, sir?" a pimply-faced teenager asked me. "Coat check is only a dollar."

I was about to hand it over, but thought better of the idea and draped it over my arm. "No, thanks, I'll keep it with me."

He shrugged and gave me a dirty look, likely thinking I was too cheap to part with a dollar.

As I stepped farther into the rotunda, my awe of Ben moved up yet another notch. He had done it up like a real art opening, with servers passing hors d'oeuvres and a cash bar. Freestanding presentation panels broke up the space and displayed the mounted artwork. How had he managed to pull something like this off in Alton? The woman from the restaurant had been right: this was a big deal.

My eyes automatically sought out Ben, and found him talking with an older man in a suit on the far side of the room. He gave the man's arm an affectionate squeeze.

Who was that?

I bought a soda at the makeshift bar, grabbed a cold spring roll off a passing tray, and began to circulate, keeping my distance from Ben but aware of his every movement.

The image of him as he'd been last night filled my mind: his panic attack, the scars on his arms, his vulnerability. What if he couldn't handle the truth about Dad and Misty? What if it proved to be too much? From the very beginning, he'd told me not to get involved. Now I understood why.

The need to protect him clawed at my throat. It was almost enough to give me second thoughts. Dad was dead, Misty was . . . gone—what good would it do to expose their affair, Dad's possible involvement, now? Instead of providing the answers everyone wanted, all it did was raise more questions.

But deep inside, I knew it was the right thing to do. The secret had been kept long enough. I could only hope that Ben would understand.

There were about fifty paintings of various sizes and expertise in the exhibit. They'd all been professionally framed and hung with little placards below that listed the artist's name and a price. The prices were symbolic—ranging from five dollars to twenty-five—and while you could tell these were done by novices, several showed real promise to my uninitiated eye.

At the silent auction table, I perused the offerings—mostly free services from businesses in town—until my eyes landed on a photograph of a landscape painting that had clearly been done by Ben. I was beginning to recognize his unmistakable style—the bold strokes and brooding trees.

I wanted it as a reminder of us. Of him. I had no idea how I'd get it home, or even how I'd pay for it, but at that moment I would have done anything to possess it. Four people had already placed bids, and not low-ball amounts either.

Abandoning caution, I wrote down a bid I couldn't really afford. It would be worth it though to have something to hold on to.

"Why are you hiding over here?" Ben's voice at my ear made me start in surprise. Apparently I hadn't gone unnoticed after all. I sucked in a breath at his proximity, afraid to look at him, afraid that he might see the guilt on my face.

"I'm not hiding," I mumbled. "Just staying out of the way."

"Have you looked around?"

"I have." Finally, I faced him. Only someone looking very closely would notice the slackness in his face and the unfocused set to his eyes, but they worried me. If he'd had to medicate to get through an art show, how would he ever deal with what I had learned? "I was surprised you don't have a painting showing here."

"This show is for them, not for me. To help build their self-esteem. I don't want to detract from that." Ben's brow creased at my grin. "What?"

"Nothing. You're amazing is all."

He blushed and ducked his head. "Shut up. Anyway, as you can see I have a painting in the silent auction."

"I know. I bid on it."

"You did? I'll have to make sure you win, then." He leaned over and checked the bid sheet, and his eyes widened. "You didn't have to bid that much. I would have let you have it for free."

"Are you saying it's a bad investment?"

He wrinkled his nose. "No, but—"

"Or an undeserving cause?"

"No."

"Then let it go. You did a great job here. I mean it; this show of yours is impressive."

Ben raised an eyebrow. "I'm sure it must seem provincial compared to a real New York gallery show, but thank you. It's all done by volunteers or donations. There's a lady in town who does the framing for free, and the refreshments are all donated, as are the silent auction items. It's nice to see so many people get behind this program."

I frowned. This wasn't the first time I'd noticed Ben shrug off compliments. "Why can't you just take the credit?" I chided. "It's you. This wouldn't exist without you and you know it. Stop negating yourself."

Ben's face reddened. "I guess I'm not good at hogging the spotlight."

"Knowing your own worth is not hogging the spotlight."

A small smile tugged at his lips. "You sound like a therapist I once had."

"Except I'm not charging three hundred dollars an hour." I clasped him by the shoulders so that he was forced to look at me. "Now, repeat after me: I'm a good person."

"Alex . . ."

"Do it."

"You're a good person," he mimicked.

"Ha-ha. For real this time."

"I'm a good person."

"Better, but I'm still not convinced. Try: I'm a talented artist."

He rolled his eyes. "This is silly."

"I'm not letting you go until you say it."

"And that's supposed to be a deterrent?"

I suppressed a laugh and gave him a gentle shake.

"Fine. I'm-a-talented-artist," he repeated quickly.

Lowering my voice, I leaned in closer so only he would hear me. "Now: Alex gives killer blowjobs."

"Alex gives—" He sputtered, laughed, and then punched me in the arm. "There are children present."

"So? They're not paying any attention to us."

Ben leaned in to me, his hand coming to rest on the small of my back, a smile teasing his lips. He looked so happy, it almost made me forget about the photos in my coat pocket.

Then his face grew serious, his gaze probing. "Enough about me. How are you doing?"

Ah, the sixty-four-thousand-dollar question. I shrugged. "Coping."

"And Janet?"

"We haven't spoken much." I winced. "Oh shit. I was supposed to stop by and see her today." In the chaos of dealing with Angela and then my search of Dad's place, I'd completely forgotten about Janet.

"There's still time," Ben said. "You should go."

"I'll call her in a bit. This is more important."

"It is?"

Ben's startled expression made my heart twist. "Yeah, it is." I glanced around, searching for a familiar face, not entirely surprised when I didn't see it. "Angela's not here."

"No." The carelessness in Ben's voice made me sad. He was used to it. Used to being ignored. My heart twisted for all that she'd missed out on by focusing on the daughter she'd lost instead of the son she had. "I heard about your field trip today," he said.

"A town this small, I figured you would eventually. You're not mad?"

"I've given up. There's no point in getting angry anymore."

I couldn't stop myself from reaching out and tugging on a loose curl of hair. Then I remembered where we were and pulled my hand back reluctantly.

"What's wrong?" he asked, eyes narrowing.

"Nothing's wrong."

"Don't think I can't still read you like a book, Alexander Colville. You haven't changed *that* much. That vein in your temple is ticking like crazy. And then there's the fact you were hiding all the way over here and I had to come and find you."

"You were occupied. I didn't want to interrupt." I motioned to the guy in the suit that I'd seen Ben talking to earlier. "Is that your friend from Prince George?"

"You're kind of obsessed with him, aren't you? No. That's Jared Vandercamp. He's an art dealer from Banff who acts as our judge. We award prizes—although between you and me, they're all symbolic. He comes every year to participate and picks up some of the other pieces I have at home to take back to his gallery."

"An art dealer?" I narrowed my eyes. "How successful are you?"

"Success is relative. I sell a few paintings a year. I'm one step above starving artist."

"Somehow I doubt that."

A young girl, dressed in all black with bright magenta lips, crashed into us. She grabbed Ben by the arm, almost jumping up and down in her excitement. "Ben! Ben! Somebody bought it. And not my mom either."

"That's great, Shauna." Ben grinned, clearly caught up in her delight. "See, I told you it was good."

"Can you put one of those red dots on it?"

"Sure, I'll be right there." He gave me a questioning glance.

"Go," I said.

He searched my face. "Why do I keep thinking this is a dream and that tomorrow I'll wake up and you'll be gone?" He tugged on my shirt sleeve. "Promise you won't leave without saying good-bye."

I had the feeling he wasn't talking about tonight. It was like he knew what I was thinking. *After I tell you the truth, you won't want anything to do with me. You'll be overjoyed if I just disappear.* "I won't."

"I'll be busy for a bit. Why don't you check in with Janet? Then you can come over later. If you want, I mean." Ben's gaze dropped to my lips and my pulse spiked. "This ends at ten."

I opened my mouth to respond, to tell him it wasn't a good idea no matter how much I wanted to, but the words died on my tongue when I spied Angela in the entryway, face pale and hands clutched in front of her, as if she wasn't sure if she should be here or not. In fact, I'd never seen her look so uncertain.

"What's *she* doing here?" Ben exclaimed, after whirling around to locate the source of my distraction.

She'd listened to me after all. "Maybe she's suddenly into art," I said.

"What did you do, Alex?"

"Nothing." I shrugged.

"Liar." He shook his head. "I wish you hadn't done this."

"Now who's a liar? You haven't changed that much either, you know."

"What's that supposed to mean?"

"It means I know when you're pretending something's not important to you. You say you've accepted Angela the way she is, but that doesn't stop you from wishing things were different."

His eyes widened.

"I see you, Ben Morning," I whispered, resisting the urge to fold him in my arms right there in the rotunda of the Community Hall. "I've always seen you. All these years. I didn't know how much I missed you, how much a part of me you still were, until I was here again." The words were out before I knew they were there, ready to be said. "And I wish I could do everything over, but I can't. I just . . . I want you to know that."

Ben blinked, his large blue eyes glistening even as his brows knitted with confusion. "What are you—"

Clearing the gravel from my throat, I gave him a little push. "Go be a good host and greet her."

"This conversation isn't over," Ben warned. "You don't get off that easily." With a final frown at me, he moved forward on tentative feet. They met each other like strangers, but I knew Benji well, and I could see the carefully banked hope in his smile.

I had to get out of here. Get my thoughts in order and talk to Janet before I faced Ben again.

With Ben occupied, I snuck away out a side exit. It felt as though I was leaving for good, and with each step I put between us, the pain in my chest grew.

Outside, a light snow had begun to fall. I turned my face up to the dark sky and let the flakes fall on my face and melt until they ran down my cheeks like tears. I shrugged into my coat and hurried back to the Explorer, calling Janet on my way. Her phone rang through to voice mail, so I left a quick apology, asking her to call me back.

I'd only just managed to start the engine and adjust the heater when the dome light burst on as the passenger door opened and someone got in.

"Okay, what's going on?" Ben demanded, shaking snow out of his hair.

I gaped. "What are you doing out here? You should be in there. You've got a show to run."

"It's under control."

"But Angela—"

"Angela can wait. You, on the other hand, I'm not so sure about. I appreciate a romantic declaration as much as the next guy, but that sounded like a good-bye in there."

I couldn't deny it. There was a sudden burning behind my eyes, and I mutely shook my head.

"What is it, Alex?" Ben asked, grasping me by the back of the neck with a cold hand and forcing me to look at him. "You've been acting strangely all day. Is this because of what I told you last night?" His breath sucked in sharply when I didn't answer. "Damn it, I knew it. I knew it would change the way you saw me. That you'd think I was weak and unstable."

"I don't—"

"It always does. People look at me differently once they know."

"Jesus, Ben," I roared. "I don't want you to get hurt. I don't want you to go through that again. Is it so wrong to want to protect you?"

"Oh, Alex. I'm not a kid anymore. It's not your job to protect me. It's mine. You found out something, didn't you?"

"I can't . . ."

"Stop treating me like I'll break. Tell me."

He left me no choice. I had to show him.

With fumbling fingers, I turned on the overhead light and then handed him the envelope. "I found this at my dad's place today."

He studied the Polaroids in silence, and I studied him. His lips thinned, but that was it. Then he calmly slid the photos back into the envelope and closed his eyes for a second. I gaped. His reaction seemed strangely subdued for someone who'd just seen compromising pictures of his sister. Was he in shock?

"Do you know what this means?" I asked. "Read the inscription. Does that sound like a threat to you? Like maybe she was blackmailing him?"

Ben's sigh was loud in the confines of the car. "I think you need to talk to Janet."

"Janet? Why?"

Now he held up the Polaroid with the hand-written inscription. *To J.C., So you won't forget. Love, MM.*

"Alex, don't you realize Janet and your dad have the same initials?"

CHAPTER SIXTEEN

Janet still wasn't picking up when I tried her cell phone again, which only elevated my anxiety. I hadn't heard from her since yesterday. Maybe she just wanted to be left alone. Then I thought about how haggard and depressed she'd been lately, how she'd sounded last night. I'd assumed it was because of Dad, but could it be she had secrets of her own?

I had a bad feeling. "I need to find Janet."

"I'll come with you," Ben volunteered as he fastened the seat belt across his chest.

"But you have people in there."

"I have people in here too."

His words warmed my heart, made my eyes sting with tears of gratitude. A better man might have sent him back to his friends, but I wanted him with me. Okay, I needed him with me. I didn't know if I was strong enough to deal with this on my own.

"What are you waiting for?" he asked. "Go."

I began to drive in a daze through snowflakes that rippled across the windshield like a lace curtain. It would have been beautiful if I hadn't been in such a hurry.

Ben called someone on his cell phone and told them he'd needed to make an emergency exit.

"Tell me what Janet has to do with any of this," I demanded when he was done. "I found those photos at Dad's. I think he must have been having an affair with Misty because he even gave her Mom's earrings."

"You really should ask Janet," Ben insisted.

"I'm asking *you.*"

He heaved a deep sigh. "I saw them once, a long time ago."

"Who? Misty and my dad?"

He shook his head. "Misty and Janet."

"I don't understand." The rush of white noise in my head was beginning to drown out everything but the rhythmic *thunk, thunk* of the wiper blades.

"I saw them . . . kissing," Ben said softly. "I wasn't supposed to. Misty never knew."

The car skidded on the wet pavement, veering into the other lane before I thought to take my foot off the accelerator and turn the wheel. Fortunately for us, there was no oncoming traffic, and I quickly regained control of the car and let out the breath I'd been holding.

Ben said nothing, but he left one hand braced on the dash.

Janet and Misty? I tried to picture them as lovers. How clueless had I been back then to not have noticed something like that?

"When was this?" I croaked.

"It was fall, I think. A year or so before you left. I couldn't sleep one night. You and I had been talking on the radios, when I heard Misty's car out front. I got up to take a look so I could rat her out for breaking curfew. She stopped in the street, and when the passenger door opened and the light came on, I saw Janet was with her. That's when they kissed."

I didn't bother asking if it could have been a friendly kiss. Benji would have known the difference.

"I can't believe you never told me." I was a little hurt. I thought we'd shared almost everything.

"I wanted to. But then I realized it wasn't my secret to share. I mean, they weren't so different from me. If Misty *were* sleeping with your dad, and I'm not saying it's not a possibility, wouldn't we have noticed? Think about it—she spent more time with Janet than anyone."

"If the photos are Janet's, I don't understand why Dad would have had them. Why he'd explicitly wanted me to find them."

"I don't know. Maybe so they didn't fall into the wrong hands?"

"Then why keep them? Why not just destroy them?" I asked desperately, not wanting to dwell on the other reasons he might have hung on to them.

But Ben didn't have an answer. Or if he did, he wasn't sharing it.

Janet had a one-bedroom apartment in a low-rise building on the west side of town where the units all had their own exterior entrances. Her windows were dark, and there was no answer when I knocked. I tried the doorknob, and it swung open, which only compounded the unease in my gut. "Janet?"

Ben stayed in the entrance while I searched for a light switch and then took a quick look around.

The place was sparsely furnished, as though hardly lived in. I walked down the hallway to the bedroom, where the door stood ajar and light shone around the edges. "Janet?"

I rapped my knuckles on the door faintly in case she was sleeping, and as soon as I eased it open, I saw her. Janet was lying semireclined on her bed, fully dressed, shoulders propped up on the pillows. Her head hung at an odd angle, her face tilted away from me. "Hey, Jan, it's me," I called softly, not wanting to startle her. She didn't stir. Maybe it would be best to let her sleep.

It was only as I was closing the door that I saw the clear glass bottle wedged in the crook of her elbow.

"Janet?" I said, louder now. Moving swiftly to her side, I gave her shoulder a gentle shake. Her torso slid limply toward me, her head lolling unnaturally when I caught her. The bottle rolled off the bed and onto the carpet with a muted thud. "Shit! Ben, she's in here."

I slapped Janet's cool cheek, but she didn't make a sound. "Come on, Jan, wake up."

"Alex, I think she took something," Ben exclaimed, appearing in the doorway. He held up a pill bottle. "I found this on the bathroom vanity."

My gaze flew to the bottle on the floor—a fifth of vodka, almost empty. Fear thrust an icy blade into my heart. "Jesus. Call 911,"

I instructed Ben as I scrambled to find a pulse. It was weak but steady beneath my fingers. "Don't you do this, Janet," I barked, praying she could hear my voice. "Don't you leave too."

Behind me, I heard Ben on the phone.

"She's still breathing," I cried. "But she won't wake up. Help me, I need to make her vomit."

"No, don't," Ben said, at my shoulder. "She's unconscious—that could block her airway. Paramedics are on their way. Keep her upright." He read the prescription off to the dispatcher over the phone, but I struggled to focus on his words.

"What is it? What did she take?"

"Ativan," he said, his mouth drawn tight. "It's for anxiety. It doesn't look like that many are missing, which is good."

"What do I do?" I cradled Janet in my arms, my guts turned inside out. "I'm so sorry, Jan. I should have been here. I let you down."

Something poked out from beneath Janet's hip. With my free hand, I pulled out two Polaroid photographs, like the ones I'd found at Dad's. *Just* like the ones I'd found at Dad's.

The air burst from my lungs. The bedding, the curtains—all the same. Misty, too, head tilted coyly, long hair obscuring the tip of one naked breast. But in the second one: Janet and Misty, arms around each other, Misty grinning happily as Janet kissed the corner of her lips. Janet had one arm extended as she held the camera. An early selfie.

Janet. Janet had taken the pictures.

J.C. Janet Colville, not Jerry. Ben was right.

He must have noticed my silence. "What is it?" he asked. "What are those? Pictures?"

The sound of sirens in the distance pushed me into action, and I quickly thrust the damning Polaroids into my coat pocket along with the others.

Ben scowled. "Alex, you can't—"

"Later."

The wait for the paramedics was the longest of my life, but finally they burst into the apartment in a flurry of stomping boots, and then I was shoved to the side. My entire body was numb as I stood by and let them work. My mind struggled to piece everything together. I heard the word *suicide* thrown out once or twice.

"There's no note," Ben said quietly at my side.

"Huh?"

"I don't see a note anywhere. Sometimes when people—"

"What the hell are you suggesting?" I snapped, whirling on him. "She didn't do this on purpose."

Ben's eyes filled with pity. "Alex . . ."

"She wouldn't," I insisted, although a yawning pit was opening up in my stomach as doubt took root. *Those photos.*

They wouldn't let me see her at the hospital.

Time slowed to a crawl as I sat in the nearly empty emergency waiting room. In reality, it probably wasn't much more than an hour, but with no information—*"a doctor will be with you shortly"*— it seemed like an eternity. When two Mounties in uniform walked through the ER not long after Janet was admitted, and then spoke to the nurse at the desk before disappearing down a hallway, my heart jumped to my throat. What was happening? Were they here because of Janet?

"She'll be fine," Ben reassured me.

I nodded. "Of course she will."

Ben had stayed with me, but I could sense his conflict and his rising anxiety. He kept fidgeting: occasionally jumping up to his feet, taking a step, and then sitting back down in the chair like one of those carnival whack-a-mole games.

"You should go home," I finally told him. "There's no point in hanging around here. I'll call you as soon as I know more."

"Can't," he said with a sad smile. "I came in your car."

"Take these, then."

He frowned down at the keys I was offering. "I'm fine where I am for now. If I want to go, I'll call someone to pick me up."

"Thank you. I'm glad you're here." I scrubbed my hands down my face. "I should have seen it, Ben. She was depressed. I *knew* she was drinking . . ."

"Alex, there's something I never told you," he blurted out. "About Janet." He hugged his midsection tightly, and the old, familiar gesture sent a chill down my spine.

"Something *else* you never told me, you mean? What is it?"

"The police found a necklace in Misty's car."

"Yeah, I know. Angela mentioned it. The half-a-heart pendant. Janet had the matching piece. What does that have to do with this?"

"Alex!" Katy burst into the waiting room. "I just heard about Janet. I'm so sorry." She hugged me, and then pulled back to cradle my face. I couldn't help noticing the way Ben's eyebrows knitted together as he watched us.

"Is she . . .? Have you heard anything?" I demanded, afraid of the answer.

"Dr. Singer's with the police right now, but he should be out soon to give you the details. I can tell you she's out of danger. They've got her on flumazenil, but she'll need to be monitored overnight."

I nodded, surprised to find my eyes welling up. "Where is she?" I asked. "Can I see her?"

"I'll see what else I can find out for you." She gave my hand a firm squeeze before leaving the waiting room.

"Do all nurses throw themselves at you, or just this one?"

Heat crept up the back of my neck at Ben's question. "She was the nurse on Dad's floor. We . . . ah, we had drinks one night."

"She's pretty. Did you sleep with her?"

"What? No."

Ben grunted, leaving me wondering what the hell that meant. Did he believe me? Did he think I was lying? Was he jealous?

I moved my coat from the back of the plastic chair as I sat down to wait for Katy, and the Polaroids fell out of my pocket. Ben snatched them up off the floor.

He seemed to freeze at the picture of Janet and Misty together. "Is this what you took from Janet's place?"

"Yeah, she had those two new ones with her. It seems like you were right about them," I pointed out. "But none of this makes any sense. If these photos belong to Janet, does that mean Dad *wasn't* having an affair with Misty? Something must have set Janet off, and she had those beside her."

Ben appeared too occupied gnawing at his fingernails to answer at me. He was studying the photo intensely.

"Ben?" I prodded.

"The necklace in Misty's car . . ."

"Yes, you were saying?"

Now Ben faced me. He held up the photo of Janet kissing Misty's cheek. It was a close-up, and both wore their respective halves around their necks. "*This* isn't the half they found," he said, tapping Misty's face.

"I don't—"

His eyes pleaded with me to understand. With my gut churning, I took the Polaroid from him and studied it more closely, my eyes arrowing in on the two pendants. I didn't recall which of them had bought the necklaces—it had been one of those sentimental things girls always seemed to do, but I remembered Janet wearing hers all the time. Except maybe that fall.

"It was Janet's half in the car?" I breathed.

He put a hand on my thigh. "I'm sorry, Alex."

"For what?" A bark of nervous laughter escaped from my throat. I jumped to my feet. "Jesus, Ben, that's some kind of leap you're making. Maybe they *were* more than friends, but what you're suggesting . . . There's no telling how long that necklace had been there. A good defense lawyer would punch holes in that straightaway." *A defense lawyer*. I was already talking like Janet was guilty. "Janet was in that car all the time. She and Misty were joined at the hip."

"I know, and—"

"So what? You're assuming this overdose was a guilt-ridden cry for help? That it was intentional? She was upset over Dad, she mixed pills and alcohol—it happens."

"Who are you trying to convince, Alex? Me or yourself?"

I sucked in a desperate breath and let it out slowly. "Fuck. Do the cops know it's Janet's necklace?"

Ben shook his head. His eyes were huge, wounded pools in his pale face. "Not from me. And I don't think Angela ever paid close enough attention to notice the difference in pendants."

I squinted at him with new eyes. "But you did. You've known all along, haven't you?"

"Not for sure."

He was lying. "Bullshit. You weren't surprised by these pictures. All this time you let me run around chasing shadows when you suspected Janet was involved."

"No! I mean, yes, when they first showed us the necklace, I had some suspicions. I always remembered Misty's as the left half—'BE FR,' but that was twenty years ago. I could have easily been wrong."

"But you weren't, were you?" God, my head hurt. "You're assuming Janet was there. That doesn't mean she . . ." I stopped, unable to say the word *killed*. "No, I don't believe it. Misty was her best friend. It doesn't fit."

"*I know*. You're right, the necklace itself proves nothing. That's one reason I've kept quiet. Look at how Angela went off on Derek Gagnon with no evidence. I didn't want her to do the same to Janet." He perched on the edge of his seat.

"One? What's the other?"

Ben's face crumpled. "She's your sister, Alex. If she was involved, how could I have done that to you? Misty ruined enough lives while she was alive. She didn't need to ruin any more."

Here I'd worried about showing him the pictures and causing pain, and he'd been protecting me all along. At his own expense. "Is this why you wanted me to stay away from the case?" I sank back into the chair with a weary sigh.

"When you first showed up in town, I thought that's why you were here," he murmured. "That Janet must have said something to you, and that's why you were so interested in Misty."

"I don't get it. You're the one who told me to go ahead with the story, to see what I could learn."

"By then I knew it was too late. You would have done it regardless. I could only hope there might be another answer, or that you'd eventually get bored and leave."

The sound that tore from my throat was part sob, part hysterical laugh. I buried my face in my hands so Ben wouldn't see me come undone. "You should have told me."

"I know." He gripped the back of my neck and nuzzled my temple. "If I had, we might not be in this situation now. I'm so sorry.

But it's going to be okay, Alex," he said, his breath blowing warm and reassuring.

How could he say that? "It won't, not if Janet's involved."

"Alex? Oh." Katy stood a few feet away, a blush quickly rising in her cheeks as she saw our intimate position. Ben's hand dropped from my neck to his lap, and I missed the touch keenly.

"Sorry to interrupt," Katy said, unable to look me in the eye. "They're holding Janet for a psych eval, but I can sneak you in if you like."

I was on my feet and five steps from the door before I remembered Ben. He gave me a sad smile and a nod, and for a second, it felt like saying good-bye again.

The young Mountie leaving Janet's hospital room scrutinized me closely as we passed in the hallway. His face revealed nothing. *Why is he here?*

For a second, I faltered in the doorway, appreciating the irony. I couldn't seem to get away from this hospital.

They had settled Janet in a double room, but she had it to herself. Her face was turned toward the window when I entered, so I cleared my throat to draw her attention. When she saw me, she gave me a tired smile. In the hospital bed, even with her stomach recently pumped, she looked younger, more relaxed than I'd seen her since I got here. "Sandy. I didn't think you'd be here."

Was I that much of a dick that she thought I'd abandon her? Hell, why wouldn't she? I hadn't exactly been brother of the year. "Of course I'm here. I haven't called Mom yet. It's the middle of the night, and I wasn't sure what to tell her. I imagine she'll be on the first plane here once she knows."

"Don't bother. There's no point in her being here. I've already given my statement and confessed."

"Confessed? Confessed to what? And without a lawyer? Did you sign anything? Jesus, Janet. You've just overdosed."

She shook her head. "Sandy, stop. You don't understand. I'm ready."

"Ready for what?"

"Ready to pay for my mistakes."

I was struggling to process Janet's words. *What mistakes?* But my gut already had an inkling. All the things I hadn't seen. Or hadn't wanted to see. Grief alone hadn't caused the strain on her face, or driven her to wash down those pills with vodka. Guilt had done that. But guilt over what? I stood with my hands fisted inside my coat pockets. "I don't understand any of this."

"I know."

"Tell me what happened. I don't believe you're a murderer. I *can't* believe it."

Her laugh was weak and brittle, but it still made the hair on the back of my neck stand up. "Then you'd be wrong. It *was* me, Sandy. I killed Misty."

CHAPTER SEVENTEEN

I dropped into the nearest chair, mentally and physically exhausted. "How? Why?"

"It was an accident," Janet said dully. "I pushed her. She hit her head."

Twenty years of torture and suspense, of lives ruined, and that was it? *She hit her head*? I didn't believe that for a second.

"There's got to be more to it than that. What really happened?" I repeated.

"I just told you."

"Hey, I *saved* you."

"No one asked you to."

"You're my sister," I cried. "Is that what you really wanted?"

She closed her eyes. "I don't know. I thought so, but maybe it's better this way."

Those nude photos of Misty were stuck in the back of my mind. I pulled them from my pocket and tossed them in Janet's lap. "What about these?"

She blanched. Ignoring the ones I'd recovered at her place, she picked up the three from Dad's trailer. "Where did you get these ones?"

"At Dad's."

"Dad's?" Confusion shot across her face. "I thought I got rid of these. Why . . .? How . . .?"

"You tell me." I'd asked myself the same questions. Was it possible that in his own way he'd been protecting her? Dad must have known how incriminating they'd be if they were found in his possession. That he'd be blamed. Was that what he'd wanted? To take the fall, knowing that he wouldn't be around?

Had he thought that far ahead?

Or, as I was beginning to suspect, had he pulled them out every now and again to have a look at his long-lost fantasy girl?

I shuddered. "Dad knew the truth, didn't he?"

"Yes." Janet had yet to take her eyes from the Polaroids. She was holding them almost reverently. "Have you shown these to anyone?"

"No. Not yet. So. Were you . . .?"

"What?"

"Lovers?"

Janet sighed. "No, not really. Not like you think." But her face was soft and tender as she gazed at the photos, and her eyes glittered with tears.

"Ben says he saw you and Misty kissing. And she's naked here," I observed. "What else am I supposed to assume?"

She sighed and looked at them again. "It wasn't like that. It wasn't some dirty thing."

"I never said it was," I pointed out. Whatever they had been to each other, clearly there had been an emotional attachment on Janet's part, or else she wouldn't have kept the photos all these years. Wouldn't have had them beside her as she gobbled pills.

"I'm not a lesbian." Janet held the Polaroids out to me with her free hand. "These were practice modeling shots. Here. Take them."

"They're yours. Are you saying Ben was wrong?"

"No, he's not wrong." Her arm dropped back to the blanket. "It's difficult to explain. Yes, we kissed, but it never went beyond that."

"What didn't she want you to forget? Her?"

"As if I ever could," Janet muttered under her breath.

"You loved her," I insisted. "Didn't you?"

Once more Janet turned her head away from me, but not before I'd glimpsed the truth in her eyes.

Had she been scared by her feelings for Misty, like I'd been by my mine for Ben?

She began speaking. "Looking back now, it seems like I was another person. Like I lost myself for a while. She said she loved me, that we'd always be best friends. But that was a lie. She used me like she used everyone else."

"Was this because of the shoplifting incident at Murphy's? Because she got you into trouble?"

"Oh, Sandy." Her voice was thick with disdain. "You don't have a clue, do you? Never did. The only person who ever mattered in your universe was you. And maybe Benji. Did you think that was the only time? That wasn't even the first time we'd taken stuff from Murphy's. We'd been at it for much longer than that. It was always little things—makeup from the drugstore, a bag of chips from the market, some junior's bracelet from her purse. The riskier, the better. We did it for the rush. "Misty made me special. Out of all the girls, she chose *me*. I was happy to take the fall. I would have done anything for her." The wistfulness in her voice was alarming.

"Was it you who gave her Mom's earrings, or did she take them herself?"

Two bright spots of color flared in Janet's pale cheeks and told me all I needed to know. "I forgot about those."

"I found them in her jewelry box."

"Well, at least she didn't pawn them. That's something." Janet took a sip of water from the cup on her tray, and then lay back on the pillows as if the effort of talking had exhausted her. I probably should have left her alone and let her rest, but the truth was too close to stop now. I let her continue.

"We were supposed to go away together in the spring," Janet said. "That's what Misty promised. We'd go to Banff and work in one of the hotels for the season until the modeling jobs started coming through. But we needed money to get started. We had some from my tutoring work, but it wasn't enough."

"Oh, Janet." I sighed, picturing my gullible sister handing over the five dollars an hour she'd earned tutoring so Misty could spend it on whatever she wanted. It didn't take a genius to see where this was going.

"We took the money from the Spring Formal fund. Between the ticket sales and the fundraising we'd already done throughout the year, there was two thousand dollars."

I knew how Misty had got off on playing people: Ben, Angela, me. "Was it 'we' or 'you'?" I asked.

Her face revealed the truth. No doubt it had been Misty's brainchild, but Janet had done the dirty work. I struggled to recall what had happened that spring. Something didn't add up. "The dance went on though."

"Principal McGregor got an anonymous tip about me. He called Mom, but I wouldn't rat out Misty. Mom knew though. She told Mr. McGregor that Misty must be involved too, and they even brought her into the office. She lied to their faces, said it was all my idea and that she'd tried to stop me. He believed her. I gave back what money I had left, and Mom made up the rest out of her own pocket so the school wouldn't press charges."

That explained why Janet had to miss the Spring Formal.

"You know what the worst part is?" Janet asked, her voice breaking on a sob. "I still didn't see it. I took the money for us. So that we could be together. Misty said it was the only way. If she'd told me to, I would have done it again. Do you know how scary that is? To completely let another person take over? I knew it was wrong, but I couldn't stop myself because I wanted—needed—to be with her."

A part of me didn't want to hear the rest. Didn't want to acknowledge it. Somehow it was easier to believe Dad was responsible than Janet. But here was that truth again, coming to the surface. "So what happened that day?" I asked.

Janet grabbed a tissue off the nightstand. "You and Benji had gone off somewhere as usual. I was home, grounded. Dad had started drinking before lunch . . ." Ah yes, just another day at the Colville house with Dad seated in his canvas chair on the front porch, his feet propped up on the rotted railing and a can of Molson's in his hand as he surveyed the weed-strewn front yard.

"Misty came over. Flirted with Dad. Asked if he could take a look at her car and see why it was making a noise." Here she paused to blow her nose.

I could see the events as Janet described precisely, because it had happened before.

"Hey, Mr. C," she'd have cooed, and flashed that smile. She'd have been wearing something sexy enough to get his attention, maybe those

denim cut-offs with the artfully ripped pocket. And Dad, Dad would have got that dazed look in his eyes—the one that most men got around Misty. He'd have stood up straighter, preened a little, because someone valued his skills.

"Let me get my tools," he'd have said. "And I'll check it out."

Janet pulled me back to the present. "Dad went over to her house, but Misty stayed behind. She'd hardly spoken to me all summer, not since I got caught with the money. She said we had to keep our distance until we were ready to go, and fuck, I believed her, even though Jenny Lawrence had been telling me that Misty had been chummy with Sam Evers. I was so dumb. I still hadn't got it yet.

"'When are we leaving?' I asked, and I'll never forget the way she sneered.

"'Leaving?' She laughed. 'I'm not going anywhere with you. I'm only here to give this back.' Then she gave me her necklace, her half of the pendant, the one she'd had for years. She said 'I don't need this anymore.' As if it was nothing. As if *I* was nothing.

"That's when I saw it. It was like I'd been under a spell and it finally broke. She got off on controlling people, on getting them to do what she wanted, and I'd been her greatest patsy of all. Only now she was done."

Janet sobbed quietly, her breath hitching. "It hurt, Sandy. It hurt so much. It was like she'd ripped my heart out and tossed it aside. I called her a bitch, shoved her—hard. You know that step? The one Mom was always complaining about?"

Oh God.

"Her foot went through, and then she was falling, and I couldn't reach her in time, and . . . she hit her head on that stupid cast iron planter of Mom's."

Jesus. I ran a hand over my suddenly dry mouth.

"It was an accident," Janet insisted, but with a slight inflection at the end that made it sound almost like a question. "That's when Dad came back home."

There was a loud buzzing in my ears. Janet had killed someone, and Dad, *our dad*, had gone along with it? "Why didn't you call for help? She might have been—"

"She was dead, Sandy. Her eyes were open." Janet's throat clicked drily as she swallowed. She shuddered, remembering something only she could see. "She was dead."

"You still should have called the police. It was an accident."

"Don't you think I've told myself that a thousand times?" she cried. "I was a mess. I couldn't think . . . I was already in trouble for the shoplifting, and then there was the business with the tickets. What if no one believed me?"

Unable to sit still any longer, I began to pace. There were too many emotions swirling through me to sit still. But Janet wasn't done.

"It was Dad's idea to bury the body. We wrapped her in a tarp and put her in the back of the truck. Then we washed the blood off the planter in case you came home early. But then I thought people would be suspicious if she just disappeared; they'd know something bad had happened to her, like those other girls. It was my idea to make it look like she ran away for real. So I grabbed some of her clothes and her purse—their house was never locked, remember?—and Dad drove her car out to MacFarlane Lake. I followed later in the truck and together we pushed it in."

My mind seized on the fact that it *hadn't* been Misty behind the wheel that day. Never had I imagined then that it had been my own father. Once again, my stomach gurgled in rebellion. "Your pendant," I said.

"What?"

"The Mounties found your half of the pendant in Misty's car."

Janet's hand flew to her throat as if she still wore the necklace. "I always wondered. I reached in to put the car in neutral." Her voice cracked. "It's ironic, isn't it? Misty gave me back her half and then I lost mine."

"And all that time she was where, in the truck?"

"Dad had that cap on the back, remember?"

"Holy fuck, Janet," I breathed. Unable to look at her another second, I turned my back and stared out the window, gripping the sill.

"There's nothing you can say to me that I haven't said to myself. Why do you think I wanted to die?" She dissolved into loud, guttural sobs and turned her face into the pillow to muffle them. I watched her reflection shimmer in the glass of the windowpane.

"Finish the story," I ordered in a voice I hardly recognized. "Where is Misty now?"

It took a few moments for Janet to quieten enough so that she could speak. "It took longer than we thought to get rid of the car, so we came straight home. Dad went out later that night and took her up near the radio tower. That's all I know. He said he buried her."

I shuddered at the thought that we'd all eaten dinner while Misty's body had sat in Dad's truck in the driveway. That they'd been able to act as though nothing had happened.

Good God, what if Ben and I hadn't gone to the lake that afternoon? If we'd gone home as originally planned? I would have found Dad and Janet gone, and that surely would have come up at some point in the questioning.

"Jesus," I said again, at a complete loss for words. My sister had killed someone. How had I not seen any of this? "Does Mom know?"

"I don't think so. I've never told her at least. It was my and Dad's secret."

But she'd likely sensed something wasn't right. Mom had known that Misty was bad news. Was that why she'd been so eager to leave?

"You almost got away with it. I thought it was Dad. All you had to do was stay quiet."

"Look at me, Sandy. I'm a mess. I can't eat, I can't sleep. I couldn't do it anymore. I couldn't live with that secret, with that guilt."

I snorted. "You could have come clean at any point. Why wait twenty fucking years?"

"It wasn't only me. Dad was involved too."

And so they protected each other.

"My whole life it's been hanging over me," Janet said. "This is the only way I know to finally be free."

I didn't know what to feel. There was a mix of sympathy and hatred for Janet, disgust at what she and Dad had done, and fear for her future. And mine. Buried beneath it was a healthy dose of self-pity. She'd never know what she had cost me. What she had cost Ben. If it weren't for her and Dad, things might have been so different. We might have had something good. How could I face him now with this hanging between us?

"I can't— I need some time . . ." I turned to go, but Janet stopped me.

"Hey, Sandy. Will you take these?" She held out the Polaroids to me. "I've asked to see Mrs. Morning. I want to tell her everything in person, to explain, before it gets out. I owe her that much. But she might not understand about these."

I took them reluctantly.

"Do you think she'll come?" Janet asked.

I was sure of it. "Probably."

"Will she forgive me?"

I thought of all the lives ruined in the last twenty years. "I don't know, Janet. I really don't know."

When I walked into the waiting room a few minutes later, Ben had already gone.

CHAPTER EIGHTEEN

I n a sense, this journey back has become a journey forward. It's only now that I'm realizing the full effect of my dad's legacy, that by focusing on what I never had, I've overlooked what I do have, what's been there in front of me all along. I've grown up to be so much like him, even though he's been out of my life longer than he'd been part of it.

I resented the man Dad became and let myself be overcome by that resentment. It took someone special to show me that anger is fruitless, so I will use my father's failures to push ahead, to forgive not only him, but myself. I won't end up alone and closed off from the people I love.

I still don't truly know my father and probably never will. That's something I accept now. Dad gave what he was capable of giving, and my greatest regret is that understanding came too late for me to tell him that I loved him. I hope he went knowing that.

—From "My Father's Son" by Alex Buchanan

"Seriously Alex, this is great stuff," Brad said excitedly in my ear.

"Really? You think so?" I wasn't half as pleased by his enthusiasm as I would have been a couple of weeks ago.

"I *know* so. It's some of your best work. I haven't seen so much emotion from you in a long time. Hell, I had to go phone my dad right after I read it, and if it got to a cold-hearted bastard like me, I can only imagine the effect it will have on others. I'm giving it the feature spot in next month's edition."

"The feature?" Top spot. I should be thrilled, except I felt strangely empty.

"You deserve it. When will you be back in the office?"

"Next week," I replied as I zipped up my suitcase and cast a glance around Dad's bedroom to make sure I hadn't forgotten anything. I'd paid up Dad's back rent and had been staying at the trailer for the last two weeks instead of living out of the motel. In my exile, I'd finished up my article for the *Journal* as well as some other home-improvement projects.

"Great," Brad said. "How's that other article coming along? I can't wait to read it. Small town, missing girls, secrets—it's got Pulitzer written all over it."

"About that . . ." Brad could wait a bit longer. In fact, I wasn't sure there was going to be something for him to look at. I'd broken a cardinal rule and pitched a story without knowing who all the characters were. I'd had no idea it would be my own story I was chasing. Now, every time I sat down with my notes, I became paralyzed. It was all still so raw and—

A familiar voice on the television made me whirl around. "Sorry, Brad. Gotta go." I bolted into the living room in time to see Angela Morning on Dad's small, snowy TV.

"People ask me how I can forgive Janet Colville for what she did," she was telling a small audience outside the courthouse in Prince George. There was no sign of Ben among the attendees. "But we all make mistakes. There is no place for hate. Hate won't bring Misty back. All I ever wanted was justice and to find my daughter, to know what happened. Now I have answers, but no daughter to bring home."

The local news jumped to a prerecorded scene of Angela, ankle-deep in snow, placing a wreath on a wooden cross in the spot Janet had led them to, but where no remains had been found.

Whether Janet had identified the correct spot was still being hotly debated. Even to an expert hunter, the woods could all look the same; after twenty years, and with only Dad's word to go on, what were the chances she would be able to pinpoint the exact location? Not to mention that any organic evidence would have long since succumbed to time and scavengers. But miraculously, a women's sneaker had been uncovered in the area—which Angela had identified as Misty's. It had survived the elements since it wasn't leather.

I'd heard they had tried cadaver dogs, and taken some soil samples to test for signs of decomposition, but the arrival of the first major snowfall a few days ago had dampened any further searches until spring.

Misty, it seemed, would stay missing a little while longer.

I switched off the TV, lowered the thermostat, and turned off the water so the pipes wouldn't burst. One final check of the trailer that had been my temporary home, and then I hauled my suitcase to the car. The blinds rattled next door, and I gave my nosy neighbor a wave for good measure.

When Janet confessed, I hadn't known what I should prepare for. Would I be dragged into the spotlight? Would there be reporters camped out on my doorstep or chasing after Ben and Angela? Would I be run out of town by hostile neighbors? But this wasn't New York, or even Vancouver. While the case was sensational for Alton, it never made headlines beyond a couple of sixty-second spots on the local evening news, and short articles in the *Prince George Citizen* and Smithers' *Interior News* had been all it had merited.

Although it certainly had stirred up some gossip, it seemed to blow over quickly. Folks up here tended to let sleeping dogs lie, and I was glad, for my own sake, but mostly for Ben's.

The wind bit through my coat as I slammed the tailgate closed, and I shivered. It was a good thing I was leaving—I hadn't brought much of a wardrobe with me; certainly not enough to make it through a winter here.

I'd put an ad online but hadn't found a taker for the mobile home yet. Darnell had promised to keep an eye on it, and I'd paid him three months' rent on the pad in advance; if I couldn't unload it in that time, Darnell was welcome to it. It would be his problem, not mine. After dropping the keys at the office, there was only one more stop to make.

I made my final drive back to North Star Lane.

Snow dusted the treetops and crunched beneath my tires as I pulled into the driveway. Instead of getting out, I sat in the car for the longest time with the engine running, trying to work out what to say. A part of me wanted to slink away. To hide from everything that had happened on this street. I couldn't look at our old house without feeling sick to my stomach.

I had no idea if he'd even see me. The weeks since Janet's suicide attempt had been a storm of police interviews and lawyer visits, and getting Mom settled in Prince George, so I'd had no time for anything other than a few texts back and forth—mostly to make sure he was okay.

And, of course, I'd been avoiding him.

But I'd promised Ben I wouldn't leave without saying good-bye, and I intended to keep my promise. I'd let him down twenty years ago, and I wouldn't do it again. In the end, however, it was Ben who came out to see *me*.

Bundled up in a ski jacket and wool hat, Ben approached. Luna barreled along in front of him, jumping through the snow with joyous abandon. An almost visceral pain knifed through me at the sight of him.

I won't cry.

His expression was neutral, his eyes a turbulent blue-gray that matched the sky. "Why are you sitting out here?" he asked as I stepped out to meet him.

"I, ah, was working up the courage to knock on your door. I saw Angela on TV. I didn't know if you'd be here."

He gave a small smile. "She doesn't know how to stop. If she did, I think she'd just fall apart, so maybe this is the way it has to be."

"After everything, it seems unfair that she still can't get closure. Not completely."

"'A needle in a field of haystacks,'" Ben quoted. "She's organizing a memorial service, so that's a start."

Luna started running circles around us as the silence lengthened. My toes were beginning to freeze in my hiking boots, but now that I was here, I wasn't about to complain.

"I'm glad you came," he finally said.

I blinked. "You are?"

"I wanted to call you so many times, but I was afraid . . . afraid you'd hate me."

"You?" I exclaimed in astonishment.

"For keeping secrets. For not telling you what I knew. That night at your hotel room—I went there to tell you about the necklace, but then I chickened out. I know it was wrong, but I wanted to keep you a little longer, and I couldn't bear hurting you. Mistakenly, I thought that if you discovered it for yourself, it wouldn't be so bad."

"Forget about that, Ben, how can you even look at me knowing what they did? I can barely face myself in the mirror." At times my guilt consumed me.

"It wasn't you, Alex. You've lost just as much as I have."

Was that how he saw it? How could he be so forgiving? "I keep thinking 'What if.'"

"I know. But you can't torture yourself like that." Ben toed little trenches in the snow, his head down. "Are you leaving?"

I nodded, unable to speak.

"When?"

"Now. I'm driving to Prince George to spend time with my mom for a few days before I fly back. She's got a temporary apartment there so she can be close to Janet."

"Will you see Janet?"

"Maybe." If I could see Janet in her prison-issued jumpsuit without that twist in my chest again. I was doing my best to forge a new relationship with what was left of my family, but it wasn't easy.

Janet had waived her right to a trial and pled guilty to manslaughter, despite caution from her lawyer. Sentencing wouldn't happen for another month or so. Because she'd only been seventeen at the time of the event, both parties were still arguing over the severity of the sentence. I think Janet would have happily served the maximum, but Mom was making sure her interests were represented.

Ben nodded. "How is she?"

"She seems . . . free." And that was what had bothered me so much about my sole visit to the correction center. For Janet, her troubles were over. For me, for Ben and Angela, the journey to acceptance was just beginning. I turned to Ben. "There's one more thing I have to do before I go. Will you come with me?"

"Where?"

"Where else? Our place?"

"Now?"

"Please?"

Ben looked me up and down doubtfully. "You're going to need warmer clothes."

A little while later, clad in a borrowed pair of waterproof boots, a sweater under my jacket, and a hat and gloves, I set out with Ben. We drove along the service road in his Jimmy until we were about halfway to the summit of Mount Roddick, and then parked in a gravel lot, locked the truck, and hiked the rest of the way on foot. Staying on the road would have taken us to the radio tower, and I tried not to think about how close we were to Misty's final resting place.

We didn't speak. The only sounds were the wind whispering through the trees and the crack of dry spruce and balsam needles beneath the snow as we walked. Instinctively I reached for Ben's hand, and my throat clutched when he let me hold it.

A fine mist glittered like diamonds on the branches, and although we were mostly protected by the trees, I was glad Ben had talked me into changing clothes.

"This has changed," I commented as we marched past a clearing with a picnic table.

"They turned this into an official mountain bike trail about ten years ago. It's quite popular. I suppose we were ahead of our time."

I frowned, not liking the thought of so many other people tramping through what had once belonged to only us and nature. Soon we left the trail and headed east into the brush.

Once or twice Ben stopped to take a reading on the compass. I was content to let him lead me where we wanted to go. After about an hour, he stopped.

"What is it?" I asked.

"We're here."

"We are?" I glanced around. The place we were standing in looked no different than the miles of forest we'd already hiked through. "Are you sure this is it?"

"I'm sure. See that rock over there?" He pointed to a mammoth flat-topped boulder that jutted out of the ground. It was speckled in moss and pale green lichen. He took another few steps toward a subtle drop-off. "And there's the waterfall."

I joined him, frowning doubtfully at the trickle running through the underbrush. "Not much of a waterfall now, is it?"

"It's winter. We were always here in spring and summer during runoff." Ben turned to me. "You're disappointed."

"It always seemed so much more . . . remote." I struggled to put my feelings into words. When I was a kid, this place had been magical. Now the magic was gone. "It's changed. I guess nothing stays the same."

"No. It doesn't." Ben eased his backpack from his shoulders and braced himself against our rock.

I whirled and paced out thirty steps from the boulder until I stood beneath a tall spruce. "I wish we'd brought a shovel. Then we could see if our time capsule is still here."

"They're just *things*, Alex. They belong in the past. I don't need them to remember the good times."

I frowned. "No, I suppose I don't either."

"Then why did you want to come here?"

"I wanted to go back for a minute." I took a deep breath of the crisp, wet air. "This is the last place I remember being happy." No, that wasn't quite true. At thirteen, I'd been carefree and clueless. Happy was a new bike, a day in the woods. But this time I'd spent with Ben—sleeping next to him, making love, simply being together—had been a different sort of happy: deeper, because now I understood how precious it truly was.

"But there is no going back, is there?" I wondered aloud as I walked to the edge of the dry streambed where the trees fell away. "I've been thinking about this a lot the last couple of weeks. About whether Dad withdrew from our lives to protect us. Out of guilt. But I don't think I'll ever know the answer for sure. And I'll have to live with that. Whatever his reasons, we both let each other down in a way. Either of us could have picked up a phone, reached out, but I was as stubborn as he was. He said I was like him, and he was right.

I close myself off the minute things get complicated. From Mom and Jan, and even you. I don't want to be that guy.

"I *wanted* to believe he was guilty, you know. The same way Angela was fixated on Derek. What does that make me?"

"Human?" Ben answered from behind me.

"I'm just so tired of being angry and blaming myself for him walking away. I have to let that go."

"Remember that camping trip we took to Sunset Lake?"

An image of Benji's face as he tried to bait his hook flashed through my mind. I laughed. "Yeah."

"Your dad was the closest thing I had to a father figure, and I'll always be grateful for that."

"Sometimes it feels like he's been out of my life so long, it's hard to remember he was actually there once. Did he talk to you when you visited the hospital?"

"No. But he did squeeze my hand."

"Knowing what he did, what *they* did, is that enough for you?"

"Alex, none of that has anything to do with us. It never did."

His patient acceptance made my blood boil. "Jesus. You can't possibly be okay with this."

"No, I'm not *okay*. I'm angry, and I'm sad—and I'm so fucking pissed that one mistake ruined so many lives. That it ruined *my* life—" Ben's voice broke, and he turned away from me. He was practically vibrating with suppressed emotion.

"You deserve to be angry. Let it out."

He shook his head. "If I only focus on that, then I'll be back in that dark place, and all of this will have been pointless."

"I won't let you go there." Grabbing his coat sleeve, I dragged him to the edge of the stream, tipped my face up to the sky, and screamed, "Fuuuck!" The sound bounced off the rocks, and a banditry of chickadees burst from the trees.

Ben snickered. "Feel better?"

"I do, actually. Your turn."

"I'm not doing that."

I shouted again, pouring out all my pain and anger until my lungs burned. I jumped when Ben's voice rose over mine, and grinned when he was done.

"Shut up," he grumbled. "So you were right for once."

We screamed until we were hoarse and Ben's cheeks were wet with tears. Then I pulled him into my arms.

"Stop," he choked, trying to push me away. "I don't need to be coddled. I'm not going to break."

"I know you're not. God, you're stronger than I am. I just want to hold you. Please, let me hold you."

Ben sighed and stopped fighting. I clutched him tightly, taking comfort in the thought that after this, he might finally be at peace.

"We should start heading back if you want to make it to Prince George before dark," he murmured after a while.

"Will you wait here a minute? There's something I have to do."

I picked my way along the stream until I was out of Ben's sight and I'd reached a spot where the water still flowed quickly. Then I drew out the small plastic bag I'd carried up the mountain from my borrowed coat pocket. I couldn't open it with the gloves on, so I removed them and then crouched down to sprinkle the contents in the fast-moving water.

Benji and I had never found the source or the end of the stream. Maybe Dad would. Or maybe he'd keep going forever, wandering through the place he'd never been able to leave.

"I'm sorry I never really knew you," I whispered. "I'm sorry you never knew me."

"I'm sure you'll be glad to get back to New York," Ben said as he walked me out to my car after we'd returned to his place and I'd changed into my own clothes.

No, not really. Back there on Mount Roddick, I'd had an epiphany of sorts, and now it seemed like Ben couldn't get rid of me fast enough.

"How is your writing going?"

"The piece on my dad is getting a feature in next month's issue."

"That's great. I can't wait to read it. Maybe you'll wind up with that Pulitzer after all."

"I left a lot out." *Like how he was an accessory to murder.* I bowed my head. "I can't write the rest of it, Ben. I've tried, but I can't."

"Not now, but maybe one day you will. When you know how the story ends."

"I know how it ends. And it's not good."

"Sometimes there are no happy endings, Alex. Life just goes on."

"That sucks."

"Not always. Good things can come out of bad places."

I forced a chuckle, but it was halfhearted at best. "You're such a philosopher." Finally, I looked at him—the man who, without knowing it, had been the center of my life for so long. "I'm still not sure what I'm going to do, but I'll let you know. If that's okay?"

"I'd like that."

Encouraged, I grasped for whatever olive branch I could reach. "And we can stay in touch. There's Skype. And email. And you could visit. New York has amazing art galleries. I'd love to show you around." What was I thinking? That we could have a long-distance relationship?

"Don't," he warned. "Don't make promises."

In our brief time together, we'd never discussed what might happen in the future, as if we'd both known that this was a temporary, fleeting thing, and now I stared at Ben with the tears pushing at my eyes, memorizing the lines of his face because it seemed as though I had been transported back twenty years, and we were saying good-bye all over again.

"Oh, I've got something for you. Wait here." Ben turned and ran up the stairs and into the studio. A few minutes later, he returned, carrying a small canvas. "You were outbid at the silent auction."

Right. I'd completely forgotten. "That's too bad, but it's great for your program."

"Anyway, I thought you might prefer this instead."

I sucked in a breath as he turned the canvas over. The painting wasn't the same as the one at the auction. This one was our place—the spot we'd just come from—with the flat boulder and rushing waterfall.

"I hope you don't mind that I made a last-minute substitution. And this one should fit in your suitcase better."

"It's beautiful." With his colors, he'd managed to capture the magic I remembered, the magic I hadn't felt there in person. "But how did you—"

"It was a special place to me too."

I took it with cold fingers. "Can I send you a check?"

He waved away my offer. "No. I don't want money. This one is for you."

Tears were clogging the back of my throat now, and I didn't know how much longer I would last before I broke down entirely. It was time to go. I carefully stowed the painting in the backseat before turning around to face him.

"I'm so sorry, Benji." What more was there to say?

He smiled. "I'm not. I got to see you again."

"Ben—"

Ben's beard tickled my cheek as he leaned forward and kissed me, then squeezed me tight before stepping back. "I'm a big boy now, Alex. I can say good-bye this time. I promise. Go get that Pulitzer. Go," he repeated, with a little shove in the direction of my Explorer. "Don't make this harder than it has to be." He whistled, and Luna trotted after him as he walked away.

He didn't look back once. *What the fuck?*

I managed to make it into the car and fumbled with the key, missing the lock cylinder twice because I couldn't see through the tears welling in my eyes. My heart pushed into my throat.

Fuck. What was I doing?

I jumped out of the car. "Wait," I shouted, striding toward him through the snow. "What if I can't?"

Ben froze, and then spun around on the bottom step, one hand gripping the stair railing for support. As I grew closer, I saw that he wasn't as together as I'd thought, and the vice gripping my chest relaxed its crushing jaws. Ben's eyelashes were clumped together, his cheeks wet, the way they had been that day so many years ago. "Can't what?"

"What if *I* can't say good-bye?" I asked. "What if I don't want to?"

"You don't want to?"

"If I stayed . . .? If I stayed, could we . . .?" Fuck, asking a grown man to be my boyfriend sounded so immature, like something a thirteen-year-old would do.

His eyes narrowed. "If this is because you think I can't handle it, because you're worried I'll do something—"

"Haven't you been listening? *I* can't handle it." Ben's impassive expression was enough to give me second thoughts. I inhaled sharply. *What if he didn't want me around after all?* "Do you really want me to go? Tell me our night together meant nothing to you, and I will."

"Of course it meant something. I loved you then, and I'm halfway to loving you now. But I can't ask you to—"

"That's just it, Ben, you don't *have* to ask." Giddy bubbles filled my chest. *He loves me.* "I want to be here. I want to be wherever you are. Without knowing it, I've spent two decades trying to recapture something I lost when I was a kid. I see that now, and I don't want to lose it again."

Benji walked off the bottom step and into my arms, and I staggered back in surprise, almost falling down in the snow. His breath was hot against my neck, and his whiskers tickled my face. I gripped him as tight as possible with all the layers between us. "It won't be easy, I know," I said. "People will gossip. They won't understand. And your mom—"

"Alex! Don't you get it? I've waited twenty years for this. I mean it when I say that stuff doesn't matter to me. If there is one thing I've learned, it's that all we really have is right now. I don't want to waste it."

"Does that mean if I come back, you won't be making any more visits to Prince George to see your 'friend'?"

In answer, he kissed me, slow and deep, and it went on for an eternity before we finally drew back.

"I can't feel my toes," I murmured.

"That good, huh?" Ben cupped the back of my head to bring our foreheads together.

I chuckled. "You do know how to make a good-bye memorable. How are you at hellos?"

"We'll have to see, won't we?"

A puff of reality shadowed my happiness, like a cloud passing in front of the sun. "I'll still have to go back to New York and tie up some loose ends," I said, picturing Brad's face as I handed in my resignation. "I need time . . ."

"I know." He pulled back slightly, his gaze boring into mine as if peering into my soul. "Are you sure, Alex? What about your career?

You said it yourself—this town is dying. There's not even a town paper anymore that you can write for. There's nothing here for you."

"You are."

"Is that enough?"

Enough? It was more than I thought possible. More than I thought I deserved. Someday soon I would tell him how unbelievably perfect this all felt.

"I was a freelancer before, I can do it again. I always did like the flexibility." I took his face in my numb hands and filled my voice with the same certainty thundering through my veins. My feet were frozen solid, but I would have stood there the whole day if he wanted me to. "I'll come back to you. I promise."

And this time we both believed it.

EPILOGUE

"Well? Is that how you remember it?" I ask as soon as Ben puts the tablet aside. He's seen bits and pieces as I wrote, but this is the first time he read the completed draft. Waiting for him to finish has been nerve-racking.

He doesn't speak. Doesn't even look at me in fact.

"Oh God, is it that bad?" I'm new to long prose and clearly worse than I imagined.

Ben prods me in the stomach with his foot, which until now, has been resting in my lap. "It's not bad, I promise. I just need a minute to compose my thoughts."

Unable to sit there while he thinks of nice ways to tell me how shitty my writing is, I get up and march over to the windows. The trees are in bud, about to burst any day now, and Luna is chasing squirrels in her pen below. Since I'm essentially unemployed, Angela and I have been working on cleaning up the yard and cutting back some of the encroaching trees since the good weather is here. We don't talk about Misty or Janet. Mostly we work in silence, although she likes to hear stories of Ben and me as kids. I'm hoping it means she wants to get to know her son better. We're making good progress, but there is still a lot to be done.

It's been almost five months since I returned from New York with my scant belongings. Technically I live in Dad's mobile home, but I'm spending more and more of my time at Ben's. It's been an adjustment. This is a small space for two grown men who are both used to living alone, so when we need a break from each other, I'll work out of the trailer for a while, although it's never for long. I miss our leisurely mornings in bed too much.

Ben has talked me into setting up a creative writing class this spring, which will run at the same time as his art one. I joke about competing over who gets more students, but in reality, I'm terrified no one will show up.

I've gotten a bit of work, primarily for online zines no one reads, but much of my time has been taken up with writing this story. What I do with it will be up to Ben.

"Okay, you don't need to sugarcoat it. Just tell me the truth," I burst out, tired of waiting.

His lips curve into a smile as he tilts his head back. "You're always so impatient."

Ben has me there. I'm not normally one to stress over what people think, but this feels like the most critical thing I've ever written, and Ben the most important reader.

"It's not what I expected," he says.

"Oh."

"I didn't know you were writing it as a love story."

"A love story?" I frown, grabbing the tablet from his hands to see if he read something else by mistake. "It's not a love story. If anything it's a memoir."

"Uh, no, it's definitely a love story, Alex."

Ben's grin makes my stomach flutter, the way it does pretty much every time I see it. There are moments when I still can't believe this is real, that I'm this happy, that he loves me and I him. If this is karma, then I must be doing something right for once.

"You think?" I ask. Maybe there is more of *us* in there than I intended, but in my mind it's all intertwined: past and present, love and pain, blame and forgiveness, and the mistakes we all make. The moments that stay with you forever and define who you are. "You're okay with it, then?"

Ben rises to his feet and comes toward me. "It's good, Alex. Very good. Although I don't think I'm nearly as selfless as you portray me."

"How do you think Angela will take it?"

"There's only one way to find out."

"I'll have to cut out the sex," I joke.

He laughs. "What are your plans for it? Have you thought about that?"

It's too long for an article, which means a book, but something is holding me back from taking the next step and approaching a publisher. Maybe I'm not ready to share this yet. Maybe I've written it just for me. For us. So that we can put it behind us and move forward. "I might hang on to it a bit longer."

"I'm with you no matter what." Ben loops his arms around my neck and leans in to nip at my lips. "See, didn't I tell you?"

"Tell me what?"

"Good things *can* come from bad places."

And then the boy I've loved forever kisses me, and I know he's right.

Dear Reader,

Thank you for reading Chris Scully's *Back to You*!

We know your time is precious and you have many, many entertainment options, so it means a lot that you've chosen to spend your time reading. We really hope you enjoyed it.

We'd be honored if you'd consider posting a review—good or bad—on sites like **Amazon, Barnes & Noble, Kobo, Goodreads, Twitter, Facebook, Tumblr,** and your blog or website. We'd also be honored if you told your friends and family about this book. Word of mouth is a book's lifeblood!

For more information on upcoming releases, author interviews, blog tours, contests, giveaways, and more, please sign up for our weekly, spam-free newsletter and visit us around the web:

Newsletter: tinyurl.com/RiptideSignup
Twitter: twitter.com/RiptideBooks
Facebook: facebook.com/RiptidePublishing
Goodreads: tinyurl.com/RiptideOnGoodreads
Tumblr: riptidepublishing.tumblr.com

Thank you so much for Reading the Rainbow!

RiptidePublishing.com

ACKNOWLEDGMENTS

Thank you once again to my Riptide family for their support and encouragement of stories that fall outside the realms of traditional romance, and for letting me write what I want to write. I owe a special debt of gratitude to my editors Sarah and Caz, who always push me to be a better writer, challenge my reliance on filters, and generally make my words shine brighter. Then there are all the other individuals who have touched this manuscript over the course of its journey and deserve major credit for catching errors and polishing the final product.

Many thanks to my fellow author Rob Damon for pointing out the faults and weak spots in my plot when *Back to You* was only a synopsis. I owe you one.

As always, thank you to the readers, old and new, for your support. You are what keeps me going.

ALSO BY

CHRIS
SCULLY

ABOUT THE AUTHOR

Chris Scully lives in Toronto, Canada. She grew up spinning romantic stories in her head and always dreamed of one day being a writer even though life had other plans. Her characters have accompanied her through career turns as a librarian and an IT professional, until finally, to escape the tedium of her corporate day job, she took a chance and started writing part-time several years ago.

Tired of the same old boy-meets-girl stories, she found a home writing gay romance and strives to give her characters the happy endings they deserve. She divides her time between a mundane nine-to-five cubicle job and a much more interesting fantasy life. When she's not working or writing (which doesn't leave for much time these days) she loves puttering in the garden and traveling. She is an avid reader and tries to bring pieces of other genres and styles to her stories. While her head is crammed full of all the things she'd like to try writing, her focus is always on the characters first. She describes her characters as authentic, ordinary people—the kind of guy you might meet on the street, or the one who might be your best friend.

Although keeping up with social media is sometimes a struggle given her schedule, she does love to hear from readers.

Find Chris at:

Email: cscully@bell.net

Facebook: facebook.com/chris.scully.author

Goodreads: goodreads.com/author/show/6152322.Chris_Scully

Blog: chrisscullyblog.wordpress.com

Enjoy more stories like
Back to You
at RiptidePublishing.com!

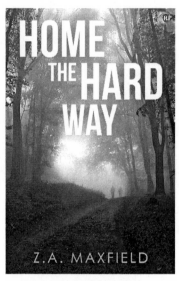

The Secret of Hunter's Bog
ISBN: 978-1-62649-374-2

Home the Hard Way
ISBN: 978-1-62649-146-5

Earn Bonus Bucks!

Earn 1 Bonus Buck for each dollar you spend. Find out how at
RiptidePublishing.com/news/bonus-bucks.

Win Free Ebooks for a Year!

Pre-order coming soon titles directly through our site and you'll
receive one entry into a drawing for a chance to win free books for
a year! Get the details at RiptidePublishing.com/contests.

CPSIA information can be obtained
at www.ICGtesting.com
Printed in the USA
FSOW01n2309260517
34719FS

9 781626 495753